DOCTOR WHO

THE RUBY'S CURSE

BBC
DOCTOR WHO

ALEX KINGSTON
THE RUBY'S CURSE

with Jacqueline Rayner

A RIVER SONG | MELODY MALONE MYSTERY

BBC
BOOKS

BBC Books, an imprint of Ebury Publishing
20 Vauxhall Bridge Road,
London SW1V 2SA

BBC Books is part of the Penguin Random House group of companies
whose addresses can be found at global.penguinrandomhouse.com

Storyline by Alex Kingston with Jacqueline Rayner

Doctor Who is a BBC Wales production for BBC One.
Executive producers: Chris Chibnall and Matt Strevens

First published by BBC Books in 2021
Paperback edition published in 2022

www.penguin.co.uk

A CIP catalogue record for this book is available from the British Library

ISBN 9781785947148

Publishing Director: Albert DePetrillo
Project Editor: Steve Cole
Cover design: Two Associates
Production: Sian Pratley

Typeset in 10.4/13.5 pt Avenir Next LT Pro
by Integra Software Services Pvt. Ltd, Pondicherry

Printed and bound in Great Britain by Clays Ltd, Elcograf S.p.A.

The authorised representative in the EEA is Penguin Random House Ireland,
Morrison Chambers, 32 Nassau Street, Dublin D02 YH68

Penguin Random House is committed to a sustainable future for
our business, our readers and our planet. This book is made
from Forest Stewardship Council® certified paper.

TABLE OF CONTENTS

For Salomé

HERE BE SPOILERS …

Doctor Who

Nebi / Oba / Djal / Seti: *Egyptian boat owners*

Shenti: *Another Egyptian boat owner*
    Imi: *his daughter*

Amy and Rory Pond: *newly immigrant parents*

Captain Jack Harkness: *flirtatious time-traveller*

The Doctor: *long-distance spouse*

Plus assorted goons, delivery persons, Egyptians and Romans

Melodramatis Personae

Melody Malone: *private detective in old New York Town*

Horace P. Wallace: *millionaire collector*

Harry Durkin: *hunk employed by Wallace*

Phil the Kid: *loyal assistant to Melody Malone*

Calvin Cuttling: *rival collector*

Susan Peterson-Lee: *eccentric reincarnationist*

Dolores Jones: *employee of Cuttling's*

The Badgers: *a cursed family*
    George Senior (father)
    Mrs Badger (mother)

George Junior (son)
Ruby (daughter)

Edwin Wivenhoe: *archaeologist, deceased*

Marvin Motson: *Wallace's courier*

Floyd: *Wallace's agent in England*

Jerry / Spats: *plug-uglies employed by Wallace*

Lenny: *Pink Tiger Club barman*

Masuda: *an Egyptian worker*
Dalilah: *his wife*

Plus assorted Pink Tiger employees, boat / flying boat personnel and hotel staff

CHAPTER ONE

STORMCAGE, AD 5147

One minute

I run along the ceiling. Upside down, back to front. Suddenly back where I started. But I keep running.

Their aim is to disorientate me, I know that. Mustn't let them. Must keep going.

Close my eyes. Feel my way. Feet on floor, no turning, no spinning, no falling. Just running. Ignore all other signals. Just feet on floor, running. Running. Running. Don't stop. Onwards. Onwards.

Split-second timing. Must be near the end. Can't stop until I'm there. Can't carry on or I'll die.

Should I pray to a god right now?

All I can do is run. All I can do is hope. All I can do is trust myself.

Nearly there.

Don't stop.

Must stop.

One second, two seconds. Step, step, step – *freeze.*

40 seconds

I opened my eyes again, and tried not to feel too smug at my perfect landing – feet poised on the very edge of the next zone. But the danger wasn't over. This was the Stormcage Containment Facility, the most secure prison this side of the universe, not Blackpool pleasure beach. I reached into my backpack, trying not to wobble as my brain started to take in all that contradictory sensory input again, tried to tell me I was on the ceiling, or going backwards, or falling endlessly. Whoever designed these defences had done a very good job, and they must have been pretty cold-blooded and cunning.

Hmm. Wonder if they have any job vacancies?

35 seconds

If I'd gone too far – if even a toe landed on the floor beyond – the bots would have swarmed. I'd seen it happen before. Nanobots so tiny, so copious, that it looks like you're being smothered in treacle. Once they're in your nose and mouth you're quickly suffocated, which at least stops you feeling it when they dismantle you cell by cell. I'd had to rely on my memory and sense of time to make that perfect landing with my eyes shut. But guess what. I'm half human, on my mother and father's side. The rest of me is a child of the Time Vortex. Time is in my blood. Time *is* my blood.

I'd come prepared for the next stage. I fumbled in my bag – damn! There went my lipstick. For a split second I considered trying to retrieve it, but it was already buried in bots. No time to reproach myself, I had to keep going. I went back into my bag and brought out a self-inflating crocodile. This might well tarnish my reputation as a sophisticated psychopath, but I'd needed something that packed down small and they were on sale.

Open. Inflate. Throw. Jump.

30 seconds
The crocodile gave a loud, unexpected squeak as I landed awkwardly on its back. The half a second I took to stabilise almost cost me my life; the treacle-wave of bots was fast consuming my blow-up stepping stone as I reached for a second inflatable.

29 seconds
Open. Inflate. Throw. Jump. Repeat.

I made it to the end. On turning back, all I could see was the sharp-toothed, air-filled mouth of the final crocodile as the bots overwhelmed it. All the others were already consumed.

20 seconds
The next obstacle was my favourite. I've never quite understood why a laser maze is considered a top-tier deterrent when a laser wall would be much more effective. But I'm not complaining. I've never felt more like a superhero than when I danced across the floor, deflecting each incoming beam with a hand mirror. *Up above! Down low! Never too slow!*

… and rest.

10 seconds
Two directions. The first leading straight to the staff area. Everything's run from there. I've considered making a detour before – turn off the defences, make a few discreet alterations to my file, maybe schedule myself a mani-pedi – but it's difficult, even for me, to get in without loss of life, and that could make a gal unpopular around here. I'd have to take the other direction.

There's a children's game in which you need to drop marbles through holes. The aim is to line up different holes to create an unobstructed path downwards, and bye-bye marble. Stormcage has something similar. The doors all need to align to enable you to get to your chosen location. Each corridor is accessible once

3

a day only. Trouble is, you can only see the first door. If you mistime, if one of the others is out of place … well, absolute best outcome is you arrive on the wrong floor. You really don't want to hear what happens if you're not lucky. But did I mention? Child of Time here. I could tell the second everything fell into place.

5 seconds
Deep breath.

4 seconds
On your mark.

3 seconds
Get set.

2 seconds
Go!

1 second
I ran. I dived. I flew through the first door …

… and I landed on the other side. Both feet together, don't stumble, arms up! I'd make any gymnastics teacher proud.

0 seconds
I still had the labyrinth to go, but I'd been through that so many times I could find my way even without a handy ball of string.

Achievement unlocked!

I let myself into Cell 426, and pulled the door closed behind me. How lovely, someone changed my sheets while I was gone. I must be sure to thank the guards.

I sat down on my bunk and pulled the typewriter out of my backpack.

What bliss. I'd finally found somewhere with the peace and quiet I needed to write my book.

I started to type:

Come through the doors of the Angel Detective Agency Inc., Floor 33, RCA Building, Manhattan, and maybe you're expecting just another private eye ...

Chapter Two

New York, ad 1939

Come through the doors of the Angel Detective Agency Inc., Floor 33, RCA Building, Manhattan, and maybe you're expecting just another private eye. I've got the trench coat. I've got the fedora. I've got the hip flask. I've got a .357 Magnum in my drawer and a .380 ACP in my boot. But I've got a couple more things you might not be expecting, if you know what I mean. (I'm talking a slash of ruby-red lipstick and a splash of Chanel No.5, what did you think I was talking about?)

Horace P. Wallace's goons weren't expecting them, that's for sure. In they come, not even bothering to knock, and demand to speak to 'my boss'. Oh joy. I was going to have some fun here.

'There's only one boss here, and you're looking at her,' I tell them.

They guffaw. I thought 'guffaw' was just one of those book words, not something people did, but there's no other way of describing it. 'Haw haw haw,' that's what it sounds like. Like they've read a description of how to laugh and are trying to follow the instructions.

'Stop kidding around, sweetheart,' says one of them.

He was about five two and as wide as he was tall, and I later learned he went by the name of Jerry. His partner – revelling in the moniker 'Spats' – was the worst-dressed man I've ever seen, and I've seen a man in yellow pinstriped trousers, patchwork coat and turquoise polka-dot cravat. Spats here went one up with his pink waistcoat and wide orange tie – not that I'm knocking the tie. It came in pretty handy for me a few minutes later.

'Who's kidding?' I say. 'If you want the best PI in the city, you've come to the right place. If, on the other hand, you want a PI with a Y chromosome, get the hell out of my office.'

Sad to report, Jerry and Spats think I'm joking, and if I'm not gonna fetch my boss they'll have to go through me to reach him. For some reason they assume Mr Imaginary Bossman is located through one of the doors on the other side of the room. One leads to my bedroom and the other's actually a storage closet, but hey, it's not surprising that neither of them had the nickname 'Brains'. I'm still trying to figure out why they decided that a secretary would want to keep potential paying clients away from her PI boss anyway; it wouldn't exactly be the best way to run a business. I guess they just enjoy shoving their weight around.

I sure enjoyed shoving their weight around too. As they advance on me, guns out, trying to get at those oh-so-tempting inner doors, I grab Spats's handy orange tie and swing on it, launching myself up so my feet whip into Jerry's face and his nose goes splat. I land as delicately as a butterfly and stand over them while Spats chokes and tries to loosen his noose and Jerry's trying to stop the blood streaming from his broken hooter with a hankie the size of a pillowcase. Somehow during all of this my Magnum has managed to make its way out of the drawer and into my hand, and now I'm pointing it at both of them, back and forth from one to the other like the ticking of a clock.

I take a few steps backwards, not taking my eyes off them, and use my free hand to open first the closet door, then the bedroom. Wouldn't normally let a coupla boobs like them see inside my boudoir, but I need to get my point across. I can see their eyes widening as they realise that there's no big boy boss on the other side of those doors and the only person in this office is me, just like I've been telling them this whole time.

'Listen, fellas,' I say. 'You can either tell me your business or you can stop messing up my office, and the way I'm feeling right now the latter's probably the safest course of action for you. Now do you want to take yourselves out like the trash you are, or do I have to clean up after you?' And I grabbed a mop out of the closet to make my point, smiling to see them give a little jump like I was going to whack them with it. Which, to be fair, was another option I'd been considering.

Anyway, it doesn't take them more than a second to decide, and there they go, scuttling out the door like a pair of cowardly crabs. Yeah, I might be turning work away, and god knows I need it, but a girl's got her dignity to consider.

Shame you can't eat dignity.

I sat around for the rest of the day until it became clear that no paying work was gonna materialise, then made my way down to the Cotton Club on Broadway and 48th. A gal in the right outfit there can get free drinks all night long. So I'm wearing a scarlet dress that could have been sprayed on – we're talking *The Bride Wore Red* territory, and I'm out-Crawfording Joan herself – and I'm on my fourth Manhattan of the night (red's my colour in drinks as well as frocks), when in walks Mr Horace P. Wallace.

He comes straight up to my table. 'Miss Malone?' he says.

'Depends on who's asking,' I say, even though I know exactly who he is. Everyone does. Horace P. Wallace made his millions during Prohibition, with bootlegging being one of the lesser charges on his rap sheet. He's legit now, though – well, as far as anyone knows. He's gone in for collecting in a big way, jewels and art and historical artefacts, and you can get pretty close to crossing the line in that kind of business.

'You'd know already if you'd listened to my associates earlier today,' he says.

I raise an eyebrow. I'm real good at raising an eyebrow just the right amount, and I add a little twist to my smile too. You can get away with just about anything with a flick of an eyebrow and a crooked smile if he's a guy and you're a doll. 'No idea what you're talking about,' I say. 'Can't be those two goons that bust into my office this afternoon. You're a classy man, you wouldn't have dimwits like that on your payroll.'

He sits down without even a by-your-leave and calls for an Old Fashioned for himself and another Manhattan for me. 'Tell me what happened,' he says, and I oblige. I'm betting my story's a bit different to the one his goons reported back, and the way he's frowning makes me pretty sure I'd win my bet. 'I'm after a good private dick,' he says, 'and I don't care if you are a chick. In fact, that could be a good thing.'

'I'm so glad it meets with your approval,' I say sweetly.

'Don't get uptight, girlie. I'm offering good money for an easy job.'

He tells me how much. Any thought of dignity goes straight out the window. Heck, for 50 bucks an hour I'd let people call me 'chick' and 'girlie' and not hit them even a tiny little bit.

We shake on the deal and have a couple more drinks to seal it properly. But this new job starts in the morning, so I decide an early night's needed and make my excuses by just gone two; I'm tucked up in my own little bed by half past.

Eight the next morning sees me in a hash house with coffee and frozen orange juice alongside a mushroom omelette, slices of ham and a pile of toast higher than the Empire State Building, all courtesy of Horace P. Wallace's advance on payment.

Once all that's inside of me, I wander on down to the docks. There's already a crowd, although the boat that we're all waiting for won't be in for another hour. I can see young men in their Sunday best suits clinging to posies of carnations and roses, waiting no doubt for sweethearts to return and rush into their arms. Anxious moms and pops praying their wanderlusting offspring will be safely back in Liberty's arms soon. Kids in shiny shoes being reminded by their mother what their father looks like so they'll recognise him coming down the gangplank.

And then there's Horace P. himself, bookended by a wary-looking Spats, Jerry (whose nose is the size and colour of a beefsteak tomato), and a couple of other muscle-a-likes. Useless as I know them to be, I wouldn't want to be walking into their outstretched arms, and there's a little circle clear around them, as the sweethearts and parents and little kids decide not to stand so close. I keep my distance too. After the first glance, I don't even look at them. It's all part of the deal.

Wallace was quite right when he said my gender could be an advantage. I'd left the trench coat and fedora at home and was done up as a good little homegirl: pinched-in waist and pleated skirt with white cartwheel hat and gloves and matching low-heeled sandals. I'd even put a ring on the appropriate finger – not a real rock, but it added to the picture of a lovesick Juliet waiting for her returning Romeo, which was the role I'd decided to play.

My job? Well, Wallace's agent over the pond had picked up some geegaw or other for him, and a courier had been entrusted with bringing it across the Atlantic and placing it straight into Horace's grubby little paws. Trouble was, Horace wasn't the only one who'd been after this trinket, whatever it might be, and he'd got it into his head that someone might try to intercept the delivery. So, soon as the gangway's down, I'll make my way on board (so desperate to see my honey-bunch I just couldn't wait!), take possession of the parcel and slip off again. Then down'll come the courier with all fanfare, meet with his boss and attendant heavies and be borne away with the spotlight shining down on all of them. Meantime, I put a lace-trimmed hankie to my eye, bewailing the faithless suitor who's skipped off somewhere without me, and hurry back to my office, dropping the goods off and picking up a nice packet of folded green on the way.

Easiest way I've ever earned a hundred bucks.

Or it should have been.

First bit, no problem. The RMS *Tithonia* comes sailing in, its rails crowded with homecomers waving in excitement as they get a glimpse of old New York again and new visitors gazing in wonder at the glories ahead of them. Everyone surges impatiently forwards as the gangway's lowered, and I'm able to mingle with the throng, easily bypassing the stewards who are supposedly keeping order as they usher people from ship to shore.

I have the deck and cabin number of the courier (one Marvin Motson), and a description too: white, five ten, skinny. There's a cute red-haired steward at the end of the corridor I want, ostensibly there to help the passengers if needed, really there with a white-gloved hand sticking out for tips. I could have slipped past him easily, but Marvin's fiancée wouldn't have done that, because she couldn't conceive that anyone would be mean enough to stand in the way of young love. So when the cute steward challenges me I just flutter my eyelashes and tell him my Marvy hasn't come out yet so I've come in to get him, like it's the most obvious thing in the world, and I just sweep right through with him gaping after me.

I find the right cabin and turn the handle, calling out, 'Marv, honey? It's me!' as I do.

The handle turns but the door doesn't open. Locked.

I call out again. 'Marvin! Open the door, sweetheart!'

Still nothing.

Luckily I have my little clutch bag with me, containing lipstick, compact, a couple of dollars, and a set of lock picks. Passers-by are concerned only with reaching dry land again and pay no attention as I fumble at the keyhole, waiting for the tumblers to click. A bare minute later and I'm inside.

Uh-oh.

There's a guy lying on the bunk. White, five ten, skinny. And dead.

I drop the lock picks back in my bag and snap it shut; I need to keep calm here, no point in advertising what could be construed as criminal intent. Then I cross to the bunk and examine the body.

We're not talking subtle here. There's a knife sticking out of his chest and the poor guy's shirt is stiff with blood. But I've got a job to do, even if the circumstances aren't ideal. Even though the logical conclusion is that Mr Motson's been done away with for the sake of the goods he was carrying, it's not cut and dried. So I start to search the place – under the bunk, in his suitcase (even the lining), jacket and trouser pockets, between the bed and mattress. And yeah, it's not a completely clean job. So perhaps it's understandable that when the steward comes in and sees me literally red handed, he yells the place down, but it's also understandable that at that point I cease to find him cute.

Few minutes later, there I am with the steward and the purser, and another steward's gone off to grab the almighty captain himself. I'm wondering whether to stick with the 'fiancé' angle and pretend I'd lost my head while overcome with grief, but much as I love playing a role, the truth might be best here. Or as much of it as I care to tell, anyway.

So, as the steward's gabbling away that he's caught a murderer in the act, I pull a card out of my purse and let them know I'm here on business.

They take a bit of convincing – it's not just Wallace's goons that think you can't be both a girl and a gumshoe – and the steward's still inclined to think he caught me in the act, until I patiently explain that he's actually my alibi: he'd seen me arrive and Marvin here had been dead for maybe 30 minutes, maybe 60 judging by the stiffened shirt and the sticky blood pools, not to mention I had no way of concealing a knife on me – it's too big for my purse, and would have shown under my clothes (and he'd known that from the start too, for sure). By the time the captain arrives, I'm the one doing the questioning. I want to know about anyone who's been in this section in the last hour, and luckily for me, the steward had been paying close attention in the hopes of getting those sweet, sweet gratuities. By the time I left I'd got a list and I planned to do a Santa – checking each and every name to find out if they were naughty or nice. That is, if I could persuade Horace P. Wallace to keep me on the payroll.

I decline their kind offer of hospitality until the cops get there, and demonstrate in a few moves just why they don't want to try and force me. They've got my card, anyways, and I ain't got no plans to skip town. Then instead of sneaking unnoticed off the boat, I walk boldly down the gangway, cool as a cucumber. Wallace is still at the bottom, waiting for the man who's never gonna come, and he looks furious as I approach him, yelling that I'm not sticking to the plan.

I explain, and it don't calm him down any. Guy gets so red in the face I'm wondering if he'll suddenly burst and spray the place with angry blood. 'Where is it?' he shouts. 'Tell me you got it!'

I shrug. 'I didn't find anything. I got some names, though ...'

But he's stopped listening, and his gaze is set firmly in the middle distance, his mind somewhere with the waves far out at sea. Jerry and Spats take an arm each and begin to lead him off, but I'm not going to let my meal ticket get away that easily.

'Hey!' I yell, grabbing at his jacket. 'What's the deal? What was in the package?'

Wallace turns back to me. 'The Eye,' he says.

I'm not squeamish – heck, in my line of work feelings get turned in at the door and you don't always bother to collect them on the way out – but I'm hoping he doesn't mean a real eyeball. Whatever, it sure weren't in the cabin back there. Two eyes only, both staring sightlessly at the ceiling. I must have looked a bit curious, though, because he keeps going.

'The Eye of Horus,' he says. 'It's a ruby. Size of a pigeon's egg.'

I've never measured a pigeon's egg. Heck, I've never *seen* a pigeon's egg. But I'm guessing the idea he's trying to get across is that this stone is a big deal.

'I'm sorry,' I say. 'You splash a lot of cash on it?'

'Cash? What does that matter? That gem is priceless.'

'Oh damn,' I say, trying to sound concerned that the millionaire guy has lost his pretty bauble, as I'm still hoping some of those millions will trickle down to me.

'Yeah,' he says. 'Priceless – and irreplaceable. That ruby? It belonged to Queen Cleopatra herself.'

CHAPTER THREE

STORMCAGE, AD 5147

I didn't read a lot of books, growing up. I was raised by Madame Kovarian and the Silence to become a fearsome weapon, and fearsome weapons don't tend to get bedtime stories. But I soon learned that words had power, that words could be arranged in more combinations than there were stars in the sky, made into patterns that created whole worlds inside the minds of those who consumed them.

But even knowing this, I had no all-consuming desire to commit words to paper. I'm an action gal, not a pen-pusher. I wrote my first book just so all of time and space wouldn't get ripped apart – the book already existed, you see, so not to write it would be a paradox. *Melody Malone: Private Detective in Old New York Town* was me telling the story of events I'd lived through – the time when the Doctor lost my mother and father for ever. The decision to give myself a hardboiled alter ego was therefore dreamed up somewhere within the paradox, both made by me and not made by me simultaneously. I liked it, though. I liked Melody Malone. She had her flaws, of course, but then don't we all?

The book got published, because it had to be. Strange to tell, people liked it. I'd not even considered that people other than the Doctor would read it – it had been written for him alone. My publishers wanted more. I gave them *The Angel's Kiss*, set before the previous book. I thought that would round it off. Melody's story already had an end, so here was the beginning.

Alas no! It seemed the people of the late 1930s were rather taken with the idea of a female PI. Little housewives in Scarsdale and Larchmont, dreaming of being the kind of dame with ice in her heart, a kiss on her lips, and a .45 pointing right at ya, couldn't get enough of her.

Money. It's not something I've had to worry about very much. But my parents, stuck in the 1930s, needed some. Yes, I could have popped across to the Tower of London and grabbed the Crown Jewels for them, or I could have zapped over to Voga and picked up a ton or two of gold (don't tell anyone, but that's how I paid for my own pad in NY; spots in 30 Rockefeller Plaza – formerly the RCA Building – don't come cheap), but they were set on it being 'legitimate'. It was part of fitting in, accepting that this was their life now. The royalties from my first two books had been enough to set them up in a sweet garden flat, near enough for us to visit, not so near that we'd trip over each other, but they still needed to put food on the table.

My mother, my lovely Amy, said that she rather liked the idea of writing books herself. She'd experienced so many worlds, she said, maybe that was a way she could share them with others who weren't so lucky. It pleased me, hearing her say that word – 'lucky'. She lost a lot, travelling with the Doctor, and at the end there she was, trapped in old New York for ever. That she could use that word, think of the things she'd gained rather than the things she'd lost, made me think she and Dad would be OK. But she wasn't in a place yet where she could carve out a new identity as an author. So when I was offered a considerable sum – a pile of cabbage, as Melody might put it – for another Melody Malone book, I decided to suck it up to help out Mum and Dad. I could pass the baton on to my mother later, all being well, but, for now, Melody was in my hands.

But goodness, writing is *hard*. No, that's not quite it – *being allowed* to write is hard. No one lets you alone! You're always there, typing away, easily get-at-able. People popping in for a cuppa, because 'you're not doing anything, are you?' People thinking *you're* the detective, and wanting you to find their lost dogs or lost diamonds. Invitations to appear on radio programmes, or give speeches to the women's movement about women having careers. It all adds up, and by the end of a week somehow you've only written six words and two of them are 'Chapter One'.

The weeks went on, and so did the interruptions. I was close to tearing my hair out. I'd started to think longingly of my cell back in Stormcage, where you could go days without seeing another human being apart from the guard who delivered your nutrition pill. Certainly no one knocked on your cell door with a dish of oatmeal cookies and invited themselves in for coffee. And the idea slowly formed. I *needed* that peace and quiet. I must have it!

There was no real obstacle. I had no cat who had to be fed while I was away and, while I spoke to my parents fairly often, I didn't plan to be gone for long – as long as my Vortex Manipulator didn't go kaput, I could return to somewhen quite close to the time I left, give or take a few hours. (The timelines around New York are extremely tangled; you can only sneak in using something small like a Vortex Manipulator and it has to squeeze you through the gaps like toothpaste. You might arrive a bit late, but at least you're minty fresh.)

I did, however, need to make sure I arrived in Stormcage at a time when I wasn't already in residence in my cell – two of me is a little too much of a good thing. Although I can think of a few ways in which it could be fun ...

And that is how I came to break in to the crème de la crème of maximum-security prisons in my desperate quest for peace and quiet.

Spoiler: the peace and quiet didn't last …

CHAPTER FOUR

NEW YORK, AD 1939

Cleopatra? Egyptian dame, died a long time ago. Yeah, I guess I can see why this jewel would be hot stuff. Straight-away I get stuck in to 'tec mode. Gotta make myself indispensable here. I wanted to learn more about this ruby, wanted even more to not have to give back the 50 dollars, especially as I'd eaten my way through the first 50 cents already, and had earmarked a fair chunk of the rest under the heading 'rent'.

I lay a hand on his arm. 'Look, the cops'll be here any minute, and they'll want to run the show. But if the cops get your stone back? They'll call it evidence and keep hold of it for months. Plus you know who has the most criminal connections? Cops! You'll still be sitting waiting nicely to get it back while some fence is already gloating over it in his basement and Mr Dirty Cop's set off on a round-the-world cruise with Mrs Dirty Cop. I say dealing with this in private is the way to go, and I've got one thing that the rest of your goons ain't got. Well, on top of the *other* things I've got.'

'And what's that?' he says, sneering a bit, but I think he's getting hooked all the same.

'Subtlety. I got on that ship all right and I'd have got off it all right if I'd wanted to. I can talk my way into places that the cops can't get near – let alone your four stooges here – and sometimes I don't even need to talk.' I don't elaborate. He knows what I'm saying; he's seen me in that red dress.

He nods. Yeah, this is speaking to him. I can see the cogs turning; he's beginning to see the advantages of having a broad on the payroll.

'OK,' he says at last. 'Do what you gotta do, then you're coming back to my place.' By which he means a joint he owns. I ain't *that* desperate for work.

So I sashay back up the gangplank. The purser's at the top with a couple of brawny sailor men, no one's allowed on the ship until the police arrive. But he knows who I am, and I flutter my eyelashes a bit and make it clear I'd be *real* grateful for his help, and he don't even have to let me on board – just get me a list of passengers.

He makes it clear this is a big favour he's doing me, then calls out for someone. Whoever it is, name of George, they don't come running, so he asks one of the bruiser brothers with him to go fetch the list for me instead. It takes a while, but the purser don't seem too unhappy to have me hanging around. I don't put him off – hey, you never know when a connection could come in handy. My eyes get busy making promises that I'm never gonna keep.

Just when I'm getting pretty fed up of the winsome act, Sailor One returns with a piece of paper. I fold it and tuck it in my cleavage, and tell everyone how grateful I am. Then I'm outta there.

*

History lesson. Cleopatra: last Egyptian pharaoh. Had a lot going on with her siblings (married some, murdered some, occasionally did both to the same person). Rumour has it she sneaked in to see Julius Caesar, Rome's head honcho, rolled up in a carpet (rumour don't state if anyone had bothered vacuuming it first). Had a fling with Caesar, had a son with Caesar. Caesar got a knife or six in the gut, so she moves on to another Roman swell, name of Mark Antony. Formed a drinking club with Mark Antony (that's my kinda girl). Big sea battle: Cleo and Mark versus Octavian Caesar. Octavian won. Mark Antony tops himself. Cleopatra does the same – legend has it she had a snake smuggled in and bares her breast until it bites her. Gotta give her marks for style.

I had to look up all this stuff at the public library, almost made me wish I hadn't demonstrated my pocket pistol to that encyclopaedia salesman who wanted me to take a volume a month at 'such a good price he was practically giving it away'. If I'd just ponied up for volume 1 (AAR-CYC) I'd have got not only Cleopatra but all of 'Antony, Mark', 'Caesar, Julius' and even 'asp' and 'carpet', just in case.

Do I need to know all this to solve the case? Smart money says not. But that library detour means I'm not going to look ignorant in front of Wallace. I'm the gal who has all the facts at my fingertips, no matter the subject. I reckon that's the kind of 'tec he's gonna keep hiring.

I head off to the joint Wallace owns, name of the Pink Tiger. It ain't much gone midday yet, and there's already a crowd of neanderthals knocking back the hooch as a crooner does his best Bob Hope and *Thanks* the audience *For The Memory*, though no one's stepping up to play Shirley Ross. One of the waitresses plonks a Manhattan down in front of me, while someone else scurries off to tell Wallace I'm here. Finally I'm shown to a little room at the back wherein sits the boss. He gestures me to sit down and pours himself a Cutty Sark, though he don't bother offering me one. I don't care about the drink, but didn't his mamma teach him any manners?

I get out my list and begin to read it through. Sad to say, no one had registered as James T. Burglar, or Mr Dennis Ruby-Thief. Not a single name meant anything to Wallace. Oh well, that would have been too easy. I might even have felt guilty for taking his money. I'd have still taken it, no question, I just would've felt guilty afterwards.

'OK, let's start from the other end. Who'd know your guy Motson had this ruby?' I ask. 'And who'd know he was on this boat? Any names on both lists?'

'My London agent, Floyd, he's the one that hired Motson. He's tight as a clam. Wouldn't have told a soul.'

'Was this Floyd the one who picked up the stone? Could someone discover *he* had it, maybe follow it through till they got to Motson?'

Wallace stays silent, but his eyes tighten. I could see what was going on behind those piggy little peepers. I'd just put my finger on a major and pretty obvious weakness in his system, and he wasn't going to thank me for making him feel stupid.

He picks up a copy of the London *Times* – guess that came by sea too – and flicks through the pages, landing on one that's headed 'DOES CLEOPATRA'S RUBY CARRY A CURSE?' Can't work out what else it says – I can read upside down as well as the next gumshoe, but Wallace's fat fingers are all over the print as he goes through it line by line. '"The winning bidder remained anonymous"' – he

pronounced it like it was Mickey's little sister Anonny –
'"but is rumoured to be American. The transaction was
completed by Mr A. Floyd, originally of New York State.
Mr Floyd declined to speak to our reporter."'

'There you go,' I say, pointlessly. His face is getting
redder than my Manhattan. I figure I'd better get out of his
way. 'Why not get on the long distance to your guy Floyd,
ask him if he saw anything suspicious, any strangers? It's,
what, late afternoon over there? He should be around.'
Wallace's face makes it clear he could not care less about
disturbing this Floyd's sleep. 'Meantime, I'm gonna go
chat to a few people,' I go on. 'See if any fences have been
put on standby, that sort of thing.' I stand up ready to go,
then turn back and pick up the newspaper. 'Mind if I take
this? Get me up to speed, then I'll do a bit of research of
my own.'

He nods, and I leave.

So I head back to the public library again. Libraries
aren't really my bag (creepy places full of silence and
shadows), but I've been here a heck of a lot lately; I'm
guessing pretty soon they're gonna put my name on the
back of a chair, like movie directors get. Reason is, I been
reading through the whole 'hardboiled' section, Sam
Spade and the like – being a classy British dame don't go
down too well in certain company, so as you may have
noticed I've adopted a much more 'pulp' vibe. It mainly
involves being extremely grammatically incorrect, for
example saying 'ain't' a lot and remembering to put
'wasn't' when you mean 'weren't' and 'weren't' when you
mean 'wasn't'. I've made myself a little lexicon full of
words like 'flimflam' and 'yeggman' and sprinkle them
into conversation here and there. The trouble is, it's
absolutely exhausting to keep thinking in that style;

sometimes I do slip up and halfway through saying something like, 'Who you say you was, you goddam fink?' I'll add, 'I hope you don't mind my mentioning it, but that zoot suit is simply stunning on you.' Still, if they find that funny I let my Magnum do the talking and they stop laughing real quick.

But back to the library. No 'tec fiction for me this time, I'm here to see what I can dig up. 'Dig up' being a pretty appropriate phrase.

You know Tutankhamun, right? The boy king with the fancy gold mask? You remember they dug him up a few years ago, poor kid? Trouble is, it wasn't just the gold and the goodies that they found. See, there was supposed to be a curse on anyone disturbing the boy king's last resting place. Lord Carnarvon, the guy who funded the dig, died six weeks later. A few others popped their clogs here and there. Howard Carter, the one who broke the seals? He died just last month. And OK, that's, what, 17 years later, which is a pretty good margin for a curse, but still. Dead is dead.

For a while, the world went crazy for all things Egypt. The lure of gold and maybe getting your name in the history books made every Tom, Dick and Ptolemy want to head out there with a spade, curse or no curse. But the frenzy faded, like frenzies always do, and Egyptology was eventually overtaken by exciting new crazes like jazz music, yo-yos and Stalinism.

But some people didn't move on. For some people, Egyptology remained not only their job, but in a lot of ways, their life.

Now, when I was reading all that stuff about Cleo earlier, what it didn't tell me was the location of her tomb. The reason for that? No one knows where it is!

And that's where my guy Wallace comes in. Have a look at what the paper says.

DOES CLEOPATRA'S RUBY CARRY A CURSE?

Over the last few decades all the world has thrilled to tales of exotic Egypt, with its incredible pyramids and mysterious mummies. The sad death in March of Mr Howard Carter, the distinguished archaeologist who discovered the tomb of pharaoh Tut-Ankh-Amun, has brought the subject back into the public's eye.

But what the world has not known until now is that another discovery may have been made that would put even the boy king's tomb to shame. It has been revealed that some years ago an expedition led by Mr Geo. Badger of Oxford may have come across the tomb of the most famous lady pharaoh of all, Queen Cleopatra.

Many tales have been told of the curse that smote down all those who disturbed the boy king's grave. Sadly, it seems that a similar curse may have struck the finders of Cleopatra's last resting place.

This is the story, as told to our reporter:

In the Year of Our Lord 1934, Mr Geo. Badger led an excavation in Egypt, assisted by Mr Edwin Wivenhoe of the Royal Society, alongside other helpers and native workers. At one point it is believed that Mr Badger went missing, returning to his colleagues some time later to their great relief, claiming he had made a most amazing discovery. He led a party back through the desert and they helped him uncover the entrance to a tomb in which lay an undisturbed sarcophagus. Hieroglyphs indicated that this held the remains of a most important person, and what is more, it was a woman of royal blood. Among the grave goods was found a ruby of great size, which Mr Badger referred to as 'the Eye of Horus'. He plucked this jewel from its setting, and no sooner had he done so than there came a cry from the entrance. The excavation had caused a rock fall. All made it out with no more than minor injuries, but the entrance to the tomb had been rendered impassable.

The party returned to camp to treat wounds and fetch tools that would enable them to enter the tomb once more. But the rock fall was not the only misfortune to befall the expedition. That very night, men began to sicken. The native workers got restless, believing in their primitive way that a curse had been brought upon them, and blamed Badger for removing the Queen's jewel. They wished to return the ruby to the tomb to obviate further harm. Mr Badger laughed at their superstition, describing himself as a man of science.

Unhappily, the curse, if such there was, fell then on Badger himself, and his science could not save him. He began to sicken and, believing he had little time left in this world, entrusted the ruby – together with a letter of farewell to his wife – to his friend Mr Wivenhoe.

All this we know from the letter itself. A little more is known from what Wivenhoe confessed to fellow passengers on his difficult journey back to England, although it is notable that he did not mention to any of these fellows that he had in his possession the priceless ruby. He said merely that he had had to flee Egypt, and was devastated that he was unable to repatriate the body of his colleague and friend, who had *died in his arms. He had given some coins to a native he believed trustworthy, hoping that a burial could be arranged, but he was warned to flee as bad feelings increased. This turned into a full uprising among the native workers that saw the rest of the party slain. Wivenhoe himself barely escaped with his life.*

Sad to relate, the curse of the ruby followed the archaeologist across the sea. On his return to England, Mr Wivenhoe went immediately to deliver the terrible news, along with the parcel, to Mrs Badger. He had almost reached his destination when he was hit by a car and killed instantly. However the package, being addressed, found its way to the unhappy widow, and enquiries made by the police unearthed the information above regarding her husband's death in Egypt. What was not unearthed at this time was information relating to the full contents of Wivenhoe's parcel, which did not come to light until the death of the widow in January of this year.

Following the death of Badger, his family found itself in somewhat straitened circumstances. It seems the son of the family wished to sell the ruby, but his mother jealously guarded the jewel, and who can blame her? For it was bequeathed to her with her husband's dying breath. Those who know the family speak of gambling debts that could not be repaid, which led to an estrangement between mother and son. Upon Mrs Badger's death, all she possessed, including the ruby, was bequeathed to the child that had stood by her through the last few years of poverty, her daughter – who by some strange quirk of fate Mr and Mrs Badger had, some 21 years earlier, named Ruby.

Young Miss Badger had no such sentimental attachment to the jewel; indeed, while not going so far as to acknowledge the curse, she nevertheless wished rid of the gem with all haste. She approached the world-famous auctioneers Bothesy's of London and, with Badger's final letter establishing its provenance, it was at this point that the existence of the ruby and its tragic history became known to the world.

The Egyptian government was approached, and finally agreed that the ruby could be sold, on condition that half the proceeds went to itself. This was a great relief to Miss Badger, who had endured a great deal of worry and grief, and in one of her rare interviews spoke of her desire to get away from the family home and all its associations as soon as the sale had been made.

Three days ago, the auction took place at Bothesy's. Many well-known names were there, including noted collector Mr Calvin Cuttling, and Mrs Peterson-Lee of Esher, who will be familiar to many from the pages of society magazines. The winning bidder remained anonymous, but is rumoured to be American. The transaction was completed by Mr A. Floyd, originally of New York State. Mr Floyd declined to speak to our reporter; however, it may be the case that the ruby is even now carrying its curse away from our shores. Our transatlantic cousins may need to take care.

So it's pretty darn clear that out of everyone who went into Cleopatra's tomb that day, not a one of them made it home again. Then Wivenhoe gets wiped out on his way back – the son gets chucked out – the widow dies – the daughter suffers. Now Marvin Motson, courier – dead.

Coincidence - or curse?

And so now I'm wondering, do I really want to find this ruby? Sure, I've got bills to pay. But dead men don't need to pay no rent - and dead women don't either.

And you're going to rot in hell for what you did—

CHAPTER FIVE

STORMCAGE, AD 5147

I stopped typing and ripped myself out of Melody's world, realising my fingers had automatically added words that had come via my ears, rather than my brain. Someone, somewhere, was shouting, and I could hear them in my isolated cell. Echoey ... distant, but also strangely close ... coming from my bed?

Well, I've come across a lot of things in my time, but a haunted pillow is not one of them. I pulled the mattress away from the wall, and there it was. Air vent. Floor level. I'd noticed it before – of course I had, I'd examined every inch of my bijou home-away-from-home during my various incarcerations – but as it's too small to function as an escape route it'd not been of any great interest, and I'd forgotten about it. Now it was channelling voices to me: there were people at the other end, perhaps some previously empty cell with its own hidden air vent had a new tenant. Lucky, lucky them.

OK, so I'd broken into Stormcage for a bit of peace and quiet – but a girl still gets a bit lonely sometimes, you know? And lacking a holotelly, a library, or a way of teleporting in an entire male voice choir (chorister robes optional), I wasn't averse to a bit of free entertainment. I pushed aside the typewriter and lay down on my bunk, arms crossed behind my head, listening in to see if the latest arrival might turn out to be a new BFF, or just a momentary diversion.

A male voice. Not one I recognised. Hoarse, gruff – despairing. 'Why can't you just let me die?'

'Because my job is to be out here, making sure you stay in there – safely – until you go to trial. That's it.' That voice I did recognise. Tomas. On my personal gaoler scale, which goes from 1 (monstrous sadist) to 10 (cute, willing to look the other way, cake on my birthday), Tomas is about a 5.5. Not nasty, just fairly indifferent.

'I didn't want any of this to happen.'

'No one plans to end up in Stormcage.' (Well, some of us do. But I admit we're a rare and precious breed.)

'But—'

Cutting across: 'Get used to it. Make sure you digest the rules before lights-out.'

'Don't leave me alone! Please!'

I waited for a few minutes, but there was nothing but the occasional groan or sob. Not great entertainment value. Oh well. I leaned closer to the vent and called out, 'Hello neighbour!'

A slight shriek. My new neighbour may be just a teensy bit on edge. Now I was wishing I'd pretended to be a ghost. My wailing is second to none.

'My name's River. Cell 426.'

'Oh.' A pause. 'You're a prisoner?'

'I prefer "involuntary inhabitant",' I said. Let's not confuse him straight off by telling him I'm in here voluntarily. It sounded like he was a prison virgin; I didn't think he'd understand.

'Oh,' again. Then, 'My name's Ventrian. I'm here because—'

Sadly, although I'd have been extremely happy to *overhear* the juicy details, thanks to having developed a conscience at some point (I was quite happy being a sociopath, but the universe had other ideas), I felt I had to abide by the prisoners' code. I jumped in and *shhh*ed him. 'You don't have to tell me. You're in the highest-security prison in the Seven Galaxies; you must have done something fairly noteworthy. To make things tolerable over the breakfast table, we don't generally divulge our ... shall we say, *felonious faux pas* to each other. Hard to enjoy your eggs when you know you're sitting next to someone who tortures kittens for fun.'

'But I didn't—'

'I'm afraid there are three types of people in here. People who are proud of what they've done; people who are full of excuses or justifications; and people who claim to be innocent. The first lot are insufferable, the second are pathetic, and the third ...'

'The innocent people?'

'The people who *say* they're innocent – well, they're the ones who're going to have the worst time. Because once you're in here, you're here for good.' I mean, that is true for most people. I'm not most people. But no point telling him that. I stay on reasonable terms with most of the warders here because they know I do solo breakouts only, and I come back.

'That wasn't what I was going to say,' he said. 'I'm not innocent. It was my fault. It was all my fault. I deserve to suffer.'

Ooh, who had 'martyr' on their prison bingo cards?

'Well, that's lucky,' I said. 'Because this place isn't exactly the Navarino Super Happy Time Fun Palace.'

He went quiet then, and I felt ashamed of myself. Just because I've come to terms with imprisonment over the years didn't mean I couldn't be sympathetic to someone just starting out on that journey.

There was silence for a few minutes before he said, as if he'd just been replaying our conversation in his head, 'What do you mean about breakfast table? I was told I'd never leave my cell.'

I shrugged, then realised he couldn't see me. 'Figure of speech. No breakfast table. No breakfast, actually – it's nutrition pills only, apart from Christmas. But we wave at each other on our way to the governor's office, or the meteor-shower block.'

'Why won't they just let me die …?'

'None of that,' I replied in my best teacher voice (seriously, I could practically feel the mortarboard on my head – not to mention the cane in my hand). 'Make your bed, learn the rules, keep your head down – for a while, at least. You'll find it easier than you think.'

'That guard, he said something about the rules, but no one's told me …'

Typical Tomas. Couldn't be bothered to explain properly. Apathy, rather than malice – some guards (the sub-4-pointers) would deliberately withhold the rules then punish you for not knowing them. 'He gave you the clue. "Digest the rules." Open your New Prisoner pack. See a yellow pill?'

I heard some movement, then he said, 'Yes.'

'You should have some sachets too. Dehydrated water, daily ration. Open one, it should liquefy. Yes?'

'Yes.'

'Now you can swallow the pill. The rules will get into your system, make it through the blood-brain barrier in a few hours. Rather more efficient than forcing you to read a 500-page manual. Done it?'

'Yes,' he said again.

'Good. Well, I'll let you digest in peace …'

'No!' he yelped. 'Please. Don't leave me alone.'

I was already feeling that I'd done my good deed for the day; Ventrian hadn't turned out to be a particularly interesting correspondent, and I wanted to finish my chapter before bedtime. But I'm a pussycat at heart (must be why I'm so sensitive to kitten torture). 'All right,' I said. 'But we'll have to stop speaking if any guards are around. I'm fairly sure no one would approve of prisoners having a tête-a-tête. So ... ' Inspiration failed. I fell back on the inane. 'Tell me about yourself, Ventrian.'

'I'm – I *was* – an archaeologist.'

Hot diggity! We have lift off! 'Me too!' I said, temporarily failing to be cool, calm and collected. Maybe he wasn't such a wash-out after all!

'Did you say your name was River? Not ... not Professor Song?'

Oh, I do like being famous. 'Well, as a matter of fact ... yes.' I wondered if it would be polite to pretend I'd heard of him in return but, while lying can be fun, I didn't really want to put in the work right now.

'I've read some of your papers. *Concomitant Development on the Ood-Sphere and the Sense-Sphere,* that was you, wasn't it? Fascinating! And the one about the earliest manifestations of Kroll. That was so insightful.'

I relaxed back on my mattress (non-prison issue, I had it smuggled in on one of the laundry trucks – maximum security is one thing but I'm not compromising my spinal health for anyone) and prepared to spend some time hearing about how wonderful I am. It would be my good deed for the day – taking Ventrian's mind off being in prison for ever. And if I happened to enjoy being feted, well, that was just a happy coincidence.

Chapter Six

Stormcage, AD 5147

For most prisoners – and even guards – time is hard to track in Stormcage. Clue's in the name: a permanent storm rages outside, violent, tumultuous, uncontrollable (rather like me, in fact). Day and night are differentiated only by the presence or absence of artificial sunlight. Our evening food pills contain a sedative that ensures the nights are quiet, but I never take them. I'd rather go to bed hungry than be subdued. In my line of business, if you don't sleep with one eye open, you risk never waking up again. Even in maximum security.

You start to hear signs of people stirring a few minutes before the artificial dawn breaks. I time myself to wake up then too – that whole 'child of the Time Vortex' business, you know? I don't want to raise anyone's suspicions by demonstrating I'm on a different sleep schedule to everyone else. Plus I like to maximise my working day.

Awake. Stretch. I salute the fake dawn. Choose an outfit out of my extensive prison wardrobe. A touch of powder, a spritz of 'Gallifreyan Goddess' ('The Scent that Regenerates to Suit Your Mood!') – I mean, you never know who might pop in. I'd filled in the application for conjugal visits just in case my old man found himself in the general galactic area. No luck as yet, but hope springs eternal.

I wondered if Ventrian had slept. New prisoners tend to take a while to get used to the regime, and the dope in the pills. I debated whether to call out a greeting, but thought it would be kinder to let him sleep. Having said that, I had no intention of creeping around my cell. I had a deadline to keep, and those words wouldn't write themselves. (Yes, deadlines are technically irrelevant to a time traveller. But you try telling that to my agent.)

I got out my typewriter. I was rather keen on the whole 'authentic hard-boiled author circa 1930s' vibe, not least because my publishers didn't understand any form of manuscript other than a big pile of paper with words indented inkily on it, and the click-clacking of fingers hammering on keys was very satisfying, if noisy. However, I've heard too many horror stories – my papers blew away / the Garm ate my work / I accidentally dropped my manuscript in the Black Hole of Tartarus – to be comfortable without a back-up, so I had connected up my Vortex Manipulator. A Vortex Manipulator is a fairly crude form of time and space travel – it's certainly no TARDIS, there aren't even onboard snacks – but I've given mine a few upgrades. A fast return switch (one-touch travel back to your last destination) makes sense for the user who needs to make a quick getaway, and verbal controls were another obvious mod. Access to a good library for the boring bits between adventures. Pairing it with my typewriter was slightly trickier, but I got there in the end after a bit of trial and error. So everything I type is automatically saved on my VM.

I'd been tapping away for about an hour – Melody was just investigating a seedy hotel and I was trying to think of a name for it – when a whisper came from the air vent. 'River? River, are you there?'

I stopped typing. 'I'm here,' I said.

'Oh! It's stopped. There was strange sound . . .'

'A sort of tapping?' I asked. He agreed that it could be described that way, so I explained. 'I have a sort of double life. No, strike that, a triple life. Archaeologist, convicted felon, writer. Currently I'm working on the third.' He didn't seem to get it, so I added, 'I'm writing. That's what you can hear, my typewriter.'

'A typewriter? One of those machines that you hit to make words?'

I agreed that it was indeed such a machine.

'Is it a replica or a real antique?'

The answer was 'neither'; it was real but not an antique, but I wasn't about to tell him I bought it for the princely sum of 53 dollars in 1938, especially as I'd have to explain that for me, 1938 was both four months *and* over three thousand years ago simultaneously. 'Oh, I always prefer the real thing,' I told him ambiguously. I also had to skate over the whys and wherefores of how I had a typewriter with me in prison when the induction cavity search is a thing that exists. Thankfully he went on to the rather more straightforward question of what I was writing.

'Is it a new paper?' he asked.

'No, this is fiction,' I told him. 'An old-fashioned crime novel – but with a few bits of archaeology thrown in. Well, when you're a criminal archaeologist, why not combine the two?'

He gave an uncomfortable laugh. I admit, it does take a while before you can look at the funny side of being locked up for all eternity, and a silence stretched out between us.

'Is . . . is this it?' Ventrian asked at last. 'Endless nothing? Sleep, wake, sleep, wake, nothing else for ever?' His gruff voice rose slightly at the end. I'd have to tread carefully, I didn't want him to descend into panic.

'You'll find ways to get through,' I said gently.

'But how? How do you stop the *thoughts* . . .?'

The thoughts. Something that's plagued mankind since day one. 'Ugh, me not stop thinking about caveman friend eaten by big tooth cat yesterday, me should have done something different oh no.' Luckily I have my psychopath training which helps me live in the moment without regret – most of the time, anyway. Sometimes that darn conscience kicks in.

The trouble is, even as a time traveller, what's done is done. Ventrian and I hadn't exactly become BFFs yesterday, but we had tentatively bonded due to our shared profession. Perhaps I should try to help him get through this. Admittedly I didn't know what crime he'd committed, but the prisoners' code is there for a reason.

'You said you deserve to suffer,' I reminded him. 'So I'm going to read you my book.'

He gave a weak chuckle, and I began to read to him through the vent. I expect it looked rather comical. We did *The Ruby's Curse* Chapter One, all the way to the 'Queen Cleopatra herself!'

And thus a proper friendship was born.

Although if I'd known where that friendship would take me …

Oh, who am I kidding? I'd have done exactly the same. I'd just have made sure my life insurance was up to date first …

CHAPTER SEVEN

NEW YORK, AD 1939

Oh, who am I kidding? Of course I want to find the ruby.

I put down the London *Times* and reflect on curses.

You know, I really should have taken those encyclopaedias. 'Curses' would've come under AAR-CYC too. Maybe I've still got that salesman's business card somewhere – it'd save on trips to the library. Heck, if this works out and I get enough of Wallace's dough, I might splash out on Volume 2 (DAL-LEK) as well.

But I don't need a book to tell me it wasn't old Queen Cleo that stuck a knife in Marvin Motson's chest, however sore she might be that some joe had run off with her rocks.

No, it was a regular, non-dead human who'd done that. And thanks to the paper I got me two suspects to start with: Mr Calvin Cuttling, collector, and Mrs Peterson-Lee (of Esher).

So I get stuck in, trying to find what I can about these guys.

Cuttling comes from Chicago. Can't find too much dirt on him – which is not to say there ain't none. He's got an eye for the main chance, that's for sure, and I wouldn't say he'd be averse to a bit of sharp practice, but nothing screamed 'murderer' at me.

Then there's Mrs Rudolph Peterson-Lee, a widow who I guess must have enough cash to stop anyone putting her in a lunatic asylum, because – get this – she insists she is the actual reincarnation of Cleopatra herself. (A British newspaper did ask her: 'If you're Cleopatra reborn, can't you tell us where you were buried?' to which the dame replied, 'But darling, I was already dead by then.' I liked her.) A few screws loose, maybe, but again – knifing a man? I couldn't see it.

I leave the library and speak to a few fences I know; make sure they're aware that it'd be real good for their health, not to mention their bank balance, to call me if a large ruby crosses their path. Because who's to say that it's the Cleopatra connection that's led to this? It's not unknown for thieves and conmen to work the big liners, maybe someone's passing by Motson's cabin, spots the sparkle and can't resist. I pass out the word on the streets, too, anyone sees anything, get in touch. Then I head back to the Pink Tiger.

Wallace had got that overseas connection to speak to his agent, Floyd – but there was a complication. Turns out the poor sap was rubbed out a couple days ago. The ruby's curse strikes again. Mind you, it's a pretty resourceful curse that puts a rod in someone's hand.

Wallace found out a few things, though. One thing the newspaper man failed to report was a bit of a scuffle at the beginning of the auction. Guy storms in, saying the ruby's his by rights, being as he's George Badger's son. But Bothesy's got the law on their side and the auction continues, getting into the hundreds, then the thousands, then the hundred thousands, and it goes on to get real near the millions, which is something else. Finally the hammer comes down and Horace P. Wallace has a ruby of his very own. The son comes and does a bit of a begging act to Floyd, but Floyd sends him off with a flea in his ear. Once the stone's been handed over to Floyd, he hands it over to trusted courier, Marvin Motson – not, at that point, dead – who hops on board the RMS *Tithonia* and sails off to the Land of the Free, unfortunately to arrive as a stiff. Which is, of course, where I come in.

Badger's son's gonna be a Badger too. I check down that list of passengers again. No Badger, no young single men at all. Disguise? Could be.

'Any description of the son?' I ask.

Floyd had taken note. Six one, slim, carrot top.

And that's where my investigator brain put two and two and two together and came up with one giant ruby. Sometimes I leap the wrong way, not gonna deny it, but four times out of five the connection's the right one, and I had a real feeling this time.

I knew who'd taken the ruby.

Maybe you got there before me. Maybe you worked it out like I did.

Because the thing was, I'd been given the list of passengers on the ship – but passengers weren't the only ones aboard the *Tithonia*.

It's pretty common for sons to be named after their fathers, and I'd heard the purser call out for someone called 'George' – and said George was nowhere to be found.

That cute steward could sure as heck have been called a carrot top. Plus he'd been wearing gloves. White ones, sure, and they hadn't been bloodstained, but what I'm thinking is he wore one pair to avoid leaving fingerprints,

45

chucked them out the porthole, wiped his hands – bloody hankie joining the gloves over the side – and he puts on a clean pair of gloves, which would kill two birds with one stone in hiding any smears he missed on his hands.

Now, I could explain my suspicions to the police. I'm not anti-cop, all that stuff I fed Wallace about keeping evidence and dirty cops was just moonshine so he'd hire me. And that's what I currently care about most – getting my hands on the goods first so I get a paycheck. Trouble is, if I tell Wallace what I've figured out, and *don't* tell the cops, there could be another dead guy by morning. Wallace don't like being taken for a fool and he'll be after the guy's head – like, you don't mess with Wallace, is the message he wants to get out there.

I think I can track down this Badger guy, I tell Wallace, and I can do it clean. He'll get his stuff back and no one'll be any the worse off. Yeah, he could have the guy rubbed out, but why get his hands dirty? He sniffs and scowls for a minute, and then he agrees. He also agrees to a pretty damn generous finder's fee on top of what's already in my name, so back I go to the *Tithonia*.

'Hey, remember me?' I say to the purser, and it turns out he does. 'I got a question. The name "George Badger" mean anything to you?'

'Sure,' he says, sounding a bit confused. 'You met him.'

'The steward? Redhead?'

'Uh-huh.' Oh yeah. Bullseye.

'Right. Just checking. I was hoping to verify a couple things with him,' I say.

So I'm invited on to the ship, and we set off on a Badger hunt. The guy ain't nowhere to be seen.

'I don't understand,' says the purser. 'He's supposed to be clearing up the cabins.'

'He's not clearing up – he's cleared off,' I tell him. 'Guess you'll have to put up a "Help Wanted" sign for the journey back. Talking of which – this guy, Badger, he was new, I'm guessing?'

'He signed on just before we left England,' the purser says. 'But he picked up the job straight away. He seemed a good kid. Hey – you don't reckon he knows anything about the murder, do you?'

Whoa. Get this guy an NYPD application stat. 'He's probably just weirded out by all this,' I say. After all, I don't have any proof. And I still have my eyes on the prize. That ruby and that finder's fee? They're going to be mine, no question. Don't want anyone jumping my claim.

I leave the ship and get to work. I know the right people to ask and the right questions to ask them, and I can find just about anyone in NYC. Which means that by the time the morning rolls around, I got a pretty good idea where George Junior is at.

So early the next morning, I'm knocking on the door of room number eight on the second floor of a seedy little hotel called the Liberty Crown.

Don't get no answer, so I knock again. Still no answer, but the door's suddenly flung open and a wild-eyed joe's staring at me. It's the steward from the ship, all right, but he's barely recognisable, and he don't recognise me neither – not straight away, any case. But finally it clicks, and when I say, 'Gonna let me in?' he lets me past.

Ain't no question this is the man I'm after. There's a cheap little wooden dresser next to the bed and on it's a wash bowl and jug, a Gideons Bible, a couple of pieces of paper, and, biggest clue of all, a giant ruby. There was red inside the wash bowl too: a hankie and a pair of gloves were floating on the surface and swirls of red made

47

patterns in the water as they soaked clean. Guess he hadn't had the wherewithal to dump them after all. But even though he's acting pretty crazy, even though I know he's a murderer, I don't feel frightened of the guy.

'You wanna tell me about it?' I ask him, all quiet-like.

'I didn't mean to kill him!' the kid cries – heck, he might be over 21, but he's sure acting like a kid right now, and a panicking kid at that.

'I know you didn't,' I say, calm as calm. 'You just got mad, I get it. Because that ruby took your father and split you from your mother, and you didn't even get one single penny piece from it. Anyone'd be sore.'

'It wasn't the money,' he says. 'The papers said that, said I had gambling debts, it wasn't true.'

'So what was it, then?' I ask. 'You saying you killed a guy and took the ruby, but you didn't want it?'

'I just wanted people to know about my father,' he says. 'He should've been in the history books.'

I don't get it. Murdering the courier and stealing the stone wouldn't help with any of that.

'If I could find the tomb myself ... That's what I wanted to do. My mother wouldn't show me anything. She thought people would try to steal it. So she threw me out – and then my sister did that stupid auction, all she cared about was the money ... '

'So you found out who bought the stone, and tracked Motson to the ship?' I'm still piecing it together.

'He caught me in his cabin. And when I explained ... '

'Let me guess,' I say, because I'm reckoning anyone employed by Horace P. Wallace would not be a master of tact and diplomacy – myself excepted. 'You explained, and he laughed at you? Told you to take a running jump?'

He nods. He's calmed down a bit now.

'And you saw red?' I look over at the gem as I say that. *Red*. There's an old English detective story called *A Warning in Red*, where the peculiar sensation of seeing red leads a man to discover a murder. And let's not forget the master 'tec, Sherlock himself, and his *A Study In Scarlet* – the scarlet in question being the thread of murder that he had to unravel. Here's this ruby, red as blood, bringing death with it, from Africa, to Europe, to North America. Here's this redheaded kid, probably never done anything worse than put on a scarlet coat and chase down a fox, and suddenly he's a murderer. And here's me in a crimson frock, with his life in my hands.

No. Not my business. I was hired to get the ruby, no more, no less.

'Look, I ain't going to turn you over to the cops,' I say. 'What you've done – that's between your conscience and your god, if you got one. But I need that ruby, mister. I'm telling you, you don't wanna get on the wrong side of the guy who bought it.'

He picks it up, looks at it hard.

'Take your punishment, or go on the run,' I say. 'Up to you. Not my decision.'

But he's not looking at me any longer. Suddenly, I realise he's not listening to me any more either. He's somewhere else, and it's not anyplace nice.

He lifts the ruby to his eyes and stares into its crimson depths. 'It's the ruby's curse,' he says. 'No man can rest easy once the ruby's got a hold of them.' He reaches into the dresser drawer. No wonder he'd had to take out the Bible – the revolver took up all the space. 'Got it for protection,' he says.

Now I'm really annoyed. My sources should've told me he'd picked up a piece. Still, I reckon I can disarm him before he can get off a shot at me – he's handling the gun like it's something gross he found at the bottom of a trashcan.

Which is why I'm not entirely sure if he meant to shoot himself or if he just didn't realise what he was doing, the poor sap.

Whatever, the result's the same. And turns out it's a good thing I'm wearing red today.

It's a clear case – self-inflicted gunshot wound, no question. No one saw me come up, no one saw me go in. If anyone had wanted to investigate the shot, well, they'd have been here already.

I check the room quickly, make sure I've left no trace. Then I take the ruby and skedaddle.

Back in the safety of my office, I examine the rock. I stare right into the blood-red heart of the ruby, and something shifts inside me. Curses don't seem so far-fetched any more.

Suddenly I do believe this ruby can kill.

Chapter Eight

Stormcage, ad 5147

Ventrian and I soon got into a daily routine. First thing each morning I'd read him the developing adventures of Melody Malone, facing murder and intrigue in Old New York, and then we'd discuss what my fictional detective should do next. I'm solitary by nature, but I rather liked the intimacy of the discussions. Having that one person to whom you could open up – not exactly a sounding board, more a passive collaborator – I found strangely helpful.

'Life's better with an accomplice,' I said to him once after I'd solved a particularly perplexing plot problem by utilising his listening skills.

After our fictional diversion we'd do a bit of history – I explained everything I could remember about Cleopatra, which entailed explaining everything I could remember about Mark Antony, which entailed explaining everything I could remember about Julius Caesar, which entailed explaining everything I could remember about the Roman Republic – back and back we went, turning down any interesting alleyway that presented itself. And if I occasionally implied in the language I used that I'd been an eyewitness to some events, he naturally assumed it was just the writer in me.

We did touch upon time travel, though, after a while. Just in general. Ventrian had heard of some of the people who'd worked in the field – Kartz and Reimer, Magnus Greel, Megelen of Karfel and so on – but he spoke of time travel as a kind of strange theoretical notion rather than something that had any impact on our existence. So I too talked of it as an intellectual curiosity, instead of telling him about, for example, the double date the other half and I went on with Napoleon and Josephine, where the emperor insisted on keeping his hat on throughout the whole meal because I was taller than him, even without heels.

A time-travelling archaeologist. It's a very strange thing to be. You might think it pointless – couldn't one always cheat? Take Cleopatra's tomb. It's true that, currently, no one knows where it is. Oh, there have been theories over the years, there have been almost-discoveries, but it has simply evaded detection right up to the present day. And there lie the issues. *Currently. Present day.* Meaningless phrases to a time traveller. I could go back to 30 BCE and watch what happens after Cleopatra's death. I could *scoot* forward to AD 20,000 and pick up the latest issue of 'What Sarcophagus?' magazine and see if later, more advanced technology has enabled someone to solve the riddle. But … where's the fun in that?

Spoilers! – as I often have to say to a certain Special Someone.

The discovery is wonderful, but only as the climax of the journey. Yes, it can be tempting to 'check your answers', and I confess to having done that once or twice – just a tiny peek, mainly so I can say 'I was right!' to said certain Special Someones who may have alternative theories. But looking up whodunnit before you've read the book – no, that's not for me. We study the past to learn about ourselves. And I happen to think I'm worth the effort.

Ventrian and I managed a few interesting arguments – after all, life without argument would be *dreadfully* boring – but it was pleasing to find out that essentially, he was figuratively and literally very much on the same page as me. After a while he relaxed enough to tell me something about his own work, although every now and then he would abruptly clam up. Those sudden silences tended to last a while; whatever it was he wasn't telling me was upsetting to him. Was his crime connected to his archaeological work? Had he stabbed someone with a trowel, or hit them over the head with an especially heavy soil sifter?

The first time I got close to the truth was after I'd read him the latest chapter of Melody Malone's adventures. He'd been impressed by Melody's detective abilities in identifying George Badger Junior, which had made me smile – it's easy to solve a mystery when the clues are presented to you by your creator; in real life, nine times out of ten leaps like that would smack straight into dead ends.

But it was after I'd read the last couple of lines that he put a tentative toe in the water.

'Do you believe there are really such things as cursed objects?' he said.

Luckily he wasn't able to see just how high I raised my eyebrows. I almost laughed out loud – but stopped myself just in time. I'm a good judge of character and I just couldn't believe that Ventrian was superstitious or that he believed in black magic or anything of that kind. We've both held enough mortal remains in our hands to know that if we were going to be struck down by divine forces, it would have happened by now. So for him to ask a question like that, ridiculous on the surface – well, there had to be something behind it. Something big.

I thought for a moment, then decided to treat it as a genuine question that deserved a genuine answer. 'I don't believe Ancient Egyptians could put a curse on a gemstone; superstition, coincidence, fatalism – they're the factors involved in those circumstances. But outside of that … it's not so straightforward as belief or disbelief. There's still so much in the universe that's beyond my understanding. The idea of a curse is to scare people away. Some unknown technology might be roped in to fulfil the same function, and "curse" might be the only way someone has to describe the consequences.'

'Yes,' he said, his voice sounding far away, dreamlike. 'I found something, and death has followed me ever since. If I call that a curse – it doesn't seem so bad, somehow. Like it's the fault of whoever cursed it. It wasn't on me – I was just the unlucky one who dug up my own Eye of Horus.'

How do you stop the thoughts?

That's what Ventrian had said. Was I going to learn at last what had brought him to Stormcage? I'd mentioned the rules enough times. If he'd decided to tell me anyway, I was going to listen.

But the silence continued. So I did something that went very much against the grain. I told him some of my own history. I told him why I'd ended up in Stormcage. How I'd been brought up by Madame Kovarian and the Silence to be the perfect assassin. 'So you see, death has followed me too,' I ended. 'Perhaps I carry my own curse. A living Eye of Horus.'

Finally he spoke. 'A … Device,' he said at last. 'I was leading an expedition on – no, I mustn't say.'

'I'm hardly going to tell anyone,' I said (not necessarily true. But I was slightly affronted, considering how much I'd just shared with him).

He wasn't moved, though. 'It's too dangerous,' he said. 'No one must ever know.'

Oh well, be like that, then.

'I shouldn't have gone there. There was a plague beacon warning everyone to stay away from – the planet. But I wanted to make my name.'

That was a theme running through my book. Everyone wanted their name in the history books.

'I wanted to find out what had happened down there,' he continued. 'I sent down a probe and it said the surface was habitable, that there was no plague. And I started to have dreams ...

'My wife was worried, but I pooh-poohed her concerns. I was determined. Stubborn, she called it. Stupid, is what it really was. But I waved her goodbye as I had done a thousand times before and set off.'

He'd never mentioned a wife before. A tiny smile sounded in his voice as he spoke of her – trailing off into despair.

'You know sometimes on a dig, when you look at a completely featureless plain, but something inside you goes: dig there. Instinct. Although that's just another way of describing how you're really deciphering a million tiny clues that your experience shows you. I looked in front of me, and I said, "Dig there." And I thought it was my experience talking, my instinct. I didn't realise something else was drowning them out.' An intake of breath, an audible shudder. 'It was calling to me, and I never realised how I was being manipulated. I just congratulated myself on my genius, how great an archaeologist I must be to make such a discovery.'

Now Ventrian was talking, the words tumbled out of him. How his dreams had led him to a site. How his dreams had told him where to dig, and he had done so, and he had found ... it. And how his dreams continued, wanting him to do ... things. He would wake up with ideas, and somehow the ideas would become reality. He stopped knowing if he was awake or asleep, all he knew was that the Device was part of him.

'It doesn't just get into your head,' he told me. 'It gets inside you, all of you. But for all that, I don't know what it *wanted*. What did it get from me using it? Or from *it* using *me*, more like.'

I looked around me at my small cell. 'Solitary confinement can cause irreparable damage to a person's psyche in just a couple of weeks. The longer it goes on, the greater the danger of break-down, psychosis, self-harm … Who's to say it's only people who feel that way? Maybe machines can get like that too. Perhaps your Device just wanted some company. Someone to talk to.'

'Perhaps …' It was clearly a new idea to Ventrian – which is unsurprising as I'd just pulled it out of thin air. Although it's not an entirely novel concept; I've had plenty of encounters with robots who were quite clearly *desperate* for my company. 'And it had been buried on that moon for centuries,' he continued, going further along the train of thought. 'It must have gone completely mad.'

'What did it do, Ventrian?' I asked softly, kindly, supportively, waiting for the big reveal.

'It wasn't my fault,' he said. 'Not if it was cursed. It wasn't my fault that I killed them all.'

CHAPTER NINE

NEW YORK, AD 1939

The main door of the Pink Tiger club is shut but not locked, and I let myself in.

'Hey,' I call across to the barman, who says, 'Hey,' unenthusiastically in return.

It's always odd to see things carrying on as normal when you've just seen someone painting a room in delicate shades of red and brain. But for everyone else, life goes on. This guy, polishing glasses behind the bar. The canary, all teeth and curls, who seems not to have realised you're supposed to put something on over your underwear when you're out in public. Looks like she's auditioning for a spot here and thinks flashing her gams will swing it for her. Mind you, she's probably right.

The barman waves me through and I head to the back. Ain't no one standing guard outside Wallace's door so I give a quick knock and head straight on in.

Wallace is poring over some paper, and thrusts it in a drawer when the door opens. Hey, I'm a big girl, I don't care what you're looking at in the privacy of your own nightclub office. Ain't nothing gonna shock me – I've seen just about everything in my time.

I note his safe is sitting open – ready for the ruby, I'm guessing. I march up to his desk, and I toss the stone onto it. I like making an entrance.

Wallace is pretty darn happy too. His eyes seem almost to glow red as he snatches it up, gloating and grinning away. I feel almost uncomfortable, like I've walked in on him doing something best done in private.

I need my fee, then I just wanna get out of there. So I break into Wallace's rubescent reverie, give him a quick overview of how I got it (to say he couldn't care less about the sad demise of George Junior is an understatement; I guess you don't get to be a millionaire by splashing out on too many wreaths) and remind him of his obligation to my bank account.

He counts out a wad of notes and hands them over, and I bid him a farewell that's as fond as I can manage. Don't like the guy, but I won't say no to him throwing a few more jobs my way. If I only worked for people I liked, I'd have a helluva lot of free time on my hands.

The barman's talking to some joe at the bar. I call out 'Ciao' and head towards the door. Then the joe shoots a glance my way, meaning I can take him in properly. Or maybe improperly. And would you look at that? Seems I'm not heading to the door after all – it turns out I really need to talk to the barman about something. Hopefully I'll work out what that something is by the time I reach him.

But the joe makes any ruse unnecessary. He sticks out a hand soon as I get within range. 'Harry Durkin,' he says.

'Malone,' I say. 'Melody Malone.'

'I like it,' he says. And heck, I can see something I like too. Harry is what you'd get if Cary Grant and Gary Cooper had a baby together – and the baby grew up to do a hell of a lot of weight-training.

'Hey, Durkin, you son of a gun! When you get back?' That's Wallace, shouting all the way from the door of his little office.

'Gotta go see the boss,' Harry says to me. 'You sticking around?'

'Oh, places to go, things to see,' I say casually. But we're having a conversation that's got nothing to do with the words coming out of our mouths. I'm guessing I'm going to see Harry again, but in the meantime just remembering this meeting's gonna keep me warm at night.

Harry goes on back to Wallace's office, and I resume my original course out of the club. The pile of cabbage is burning a hole in my purse and it's lunchtime. I head into the first place I find that's offering free coffee refills. But I'm only on my second cup when Harry Durkin slides into the seat opposite me.

'Good job I spotted you. Saves me a trip to your office.' My eyebrows scoot up high. The enthusiasm is flattering, but a little excessive at our level of acquaintance. But turns out it ain't just my charms that've brought him hurrying after me. 'I've persuaded the boss to bring you in,' he says.

'Into what?'

Harry shrugs. 'Come on back to the club. He'll explain.'

I guess I ain't doing anything better right now. I drain my coffee and take the rest of my steak sandwich to go.

Wallace gives me a bit of an eyeballing when I re-enter his sanctum, so I'm thinking that maybe he wasn't a hundred per cent sold on my participation in whatever this turns out to be. Guess Harry's desire to get to know

59

me a bit better was the major factor in bringing me back here after all.

'If you says a word out of turn … ' is what Wallace tells me the moment I walk in. I indicate my understanding. In my line of work, if you don't keep your mouth shut you end up either unemployed or at the bottom of the Hudson wearing concrete shoes, and I'm guessing Wallace would be going for the second option.

Wallace gestures for me to take one chair and Harry takes the other. He puts the piece of paper on the desk and smooths it out. Then he holds up the ruby, like he's about to chink glasses with it. Moves it this way and that way, staring at the paper the whole time, then shakes his head. I am careful not to show on my face what I'm thinking, namely that I'm in the presence of a lunatic. Because I am aware he is a rich and influential lunatic.

Now he looks at me. 'Harry here, he's my top agent,' he says. 'Got a roaming brief. Few years ago he was out in North Africa. There he is, passing through Egypt, when he hears some rumours. Now, rumours – most of the time they're not worth a red cent. But Harry, he can sniff out an opportunity like a pig can sniff out truffles. You tell her, Harry.'

I turn my attention to Harry, which is not a problem. 'Here's the deal. I'm in Egypt, and I come across this woman, Dalilah. Her husband, Masuda, had got caught up in some native uprising to do with finding a tomb. He made it out alive cos he was out of the way, dealing with a corpse at the time – not the occupant of the tomb; some British guy gave him cash to arrange burial of some other British guy, the one who'd been in charge. This Masuda finds a piece of paper on the body, takes it home to Dalilah, then he gets sick too. Real sick. I've heard of that

60

sort of deal happening before – it's maybe old-timey germs and stuff that got let out of the tomb when they opened it. Anyways, this Masuda's sick and there ain't no money for doctors. But I get her to show me this paper, and whatdya know?'

'Tell me,' I say.

'It was a map.'

It's not hard to connect this story to George Badger Senior. 'To Cleopatra's tomb?' I ask.

'Yes, ma'am.'

I'm not so keen on the ma'am. I casually push back my hair, making sure to angle my hand so as to demonstrate my complete lack of a ring. 'That newspaper story didn't say anything about a map?'

'I like things hush hush,' puts in Wallace. 'But there's more to the story, right. Harry, here, he does his thing. Tells the wife her man could be put in the big house for stealing, but as he's such a nice guy and he's sorry for her, he'll take the paper off her hands for a few piastres. Enough to get a doctor, anyways.'

'Oh, he sure is a nice guy,' I say. Damn. I'm not saying double-dealing's a deal-breaker, but it takes the gilt off the gingerbread, you know?

'The map don't make a lot of sense to Harry here,' Wallace continues. 'So he comes back to me. "Let's get in an expert," he says. "Get an expedition together." Trouble is, the map don't make any sense to the expert, either. Says there must be stuff missing. Details, you know. And in the end we figure Harry bought a pig in a poke. Lucky for him, he's a useful guy.'

Yeah, and lucky for me.

'Can I see it?' I say. 'The map? That's what you've got there, right?'

'You sure are a sharp cookie,' he says. Yeah, I sure am. If anyone tries to take a bite, they get scratched.

He hands over the paper and I look at it. Map? I guess so. Lines going here and there, I can see how you'd get 'map' from this. I can see how you get 'Egyptian' from this too, it's got all these little symbols, hieroglyphs. They look odd, but a bit familiar – I guess from all the stuff I was reading at the public library. 'You get this translated?' I ask, indicating the picture writing as I handed it back.

'Got a goddamn college professor on to it. He says it don't mean a thing. They ain't even proper Egyptian.'

'OK,' I say. 'So what am I missing?'

It got a bit funny, then. Wallace looked kinda sheepish. Embarrassed, even.

'Tell her, boss, she ain't gonna laugh,' Harry says, shooting me a look that says, 'Your life won't be worth living if you do.'

'Of course I won't,' I say. 'Hey, maybe I can help with whatever it is.'

So Wallace hums and he haws, and finally it comes out. 'It was a book I read,' he says, and he's looking straight into my eyes so I don't dare react apart from going 'Uh-huh?' 'A spy story, you know? There was a letter in it, looked all ordinary. But the spook, he figures out that you look through a stone, get the light shining right, this secret writing shows up.'

'Right,' I say. I guess I've heard stranger things. 'No luck yet?' I ask with a straight face, and he confirms he ain't had any luck yet. Wow. Can you imagine being so rich you can throw away a huge pile of cabbage on a lump of see-through red rock because you think it might be the key to reading something that you think might be a map? Because I cannot imagine that at all. Like the story even makes sense! Archaeologist guy on his death bed using the ruby he's just discovered to make a map; doesn't even send it back to his wife with the letter, he –

Oh my god.

I know where I've seen that writing before!

'Gimme that!' I demand, snatching the map off the desk. Anger rises in Wallace's eyes, but I ignore it. I'm right!

'These symbols,' I say. 'I saw them earlier!' I'm picturing it now. That seedy hotel room. Bible and papers and washbowl on the dresser. The gun going off. Blood splattering everywhere.

Bible and papers and washbowl on the dresser.

Bible and *papers* …

'It's the letter to Badger's wife – the one that came with the ruby! What if it's a code – a private form of writing that Badger invented himself?' Hey, I'm actually feeling excited about this! There's nothing like the thrill of the chase – even if all you're chasing is a bit of paper. 'If we get that letter, maybe we can work out the code!'

'Well, get it! Now!' Wallace yells.

'There's a dead guy in there …' I begin.

'I'll go with you,' Harry says. Look, I don't need my hand holding – my concern is busting back into what might be a crime scene by now. But I hold back a retort; I can cope with his company. He holds open the office door for me, then takes my arm. 'Hey Horace – don't forget to put that back in the safe!' he calls back over his shoulder, and Wallace gives him a thumbs-up. 'Not that he would forget,' he tells me, shouting to make himself heard over the woman in the teeny-tiny clothes who's now crooning Gershwin's 'Summertime'. 'He's paranoid about that map.'

'Plus he's got a million-dollar ruby in there,' I point out.

We make our way out of the club, and spend the journey swapping stories about our dealings with Wallace. Harry's real interested in all the stuff about the curse. 'You didn't know?' I ask.

'Only just got back from overseas,' he says. 'Like Wallace says, I got a roaming brief. Go round the world, checking out stuff he might be interested in.'

'Sounds like a pretty sweet deal,' I say, and I mean it. Harry agrees, and I fill him in on what else I know about this ruby. I'm just telling him about Mrs Peterson-Lee and that brilliant line: 'But darling, I was already dead by then,' which cracks me up every time I think about it, and he frowns.

'Peterson-Lee?' he says.

'That's her,' I say.

'I've heard that name before,' he says, and wrinkles up his brow so a would-be slicked back lock falls onto his forehead. I just stop myself pushing it back in place. And maybe stroking a finger down his cheek afterwards. Maybe running it across his lips …

I shake my head to clear it. We're at the Liberty Crown.

No police presence – could be a bad sign, the room might have been cleared out already. We take the stairs three at a time. No police tape, so we go straight in. There's Georgy-boy getting stiffer and stiffer, with his brains just peeking out from behind his head. No one's found the poor chump yet. Jeez that's sad. But not my business. I turn to the dresser. Washbowl and jug, Gideons Bible.

And the letter.

You know what, that was a surprise. That's not how things usually work – they don't go that smoothly. I'd been expecting the letter to be gone, or the corpse to be gone, or that someone had written some mysterious message on the wall in blood. Nope! This had all worked out just fine.

Harry picks up the letter, folds it and puts it in his pocket. He ain't got no more scruples than me about calling the cops, and we leave, still unseen.

We're heading back to the Pink Tiger club, and I'm wondering what clothes I'll need to pack for a trip to Egypt (no question I'm seeing this through to the end). As we're walking past the docks, Harry suddenly stops still.

'What?' I ask.

'That name - Peterson-Lee. I remember where I heard it. There was a dame with that name on the boat I came back on. Fifties, maybe? All sable and rouge.'

I shake my head. 'No idea. All I've seen is the name.'

We speculate until we get back to the Pink Tiger. The girl's now doing 'Meet Me In St Louis, Louis'. We head through to the office, guessing that Wallace is going to be pretty pleased with us, hopefully so much he'll get real generous.

Harry opens the door - and stops.

Horace P. Wallace is lying face down on his desk, and ain't going to be handing out bonuses any time soon.

Harry's just staring, frozen. I squeeze past him - maybe there's something I can do.

No. The guy is definitely, one hundred per cent dead, and there's a knife sticking out of his back.

This ain't the same situation as with George Junior, we can't deal with this by shutting a door on it. And tampering with a murder scene is out. Wallace is lying on the desk phone, so I tell Harry to go find a phone box and call the cops. He don't move. Well, I guess he's known the guy longer than I have, gotta be a bit of a shock.

'All right,' I say. 'Just give me a minute and I'll come too.'

I do a quick survey of the room, my PI instincts kicking in. Map – ruby – neither of them are on show. The safe is open and still got piles of cabbage in it – but the folding stuff takes up a lot more room than a ruby, even given the whole 'size of a pigeon's-egg' deal. Makes sense to leave it and just take the million-dollar sparkler.

Except why would your standard, everyday robber take the map too?

I spot something that I'm fairly sure hadn't been there when we left. A scribbled note, just by the dead man's hand – just three letters: 'SPL'.

Of course, two of those leap out, considering who we'd just been talking about. 'Peterson-Lee,' I say. 'Ever heard the dame's first name?' No answer. 'Harry! Get with it!'

He shakes his head, like he's trying to kick-start his brain. 'I'm thinking it's Susan,' he says at last. 'Yeah, that sounds about right. Susan Peterson-Lee.'

'Right.' That is what we in the detective business call 'a clue'. 'Come on,' I say. 'We'll go phone.' There's a key on the inside of the door, I take it out and lock the room as we exit.

'Hey,' I call out to the barman on our way out. 'Anyone been back there since we left?'

He don't even look up from the glass he's polishing (I swear he's been polishing the same glass for however many hours), and says, 'Not seen anyone.'

The canary stops singing and comes across to us. Her cutesy little-miss voice with a complete disregard for the invention of the letter R puts my teeth on edge. 'I saw a broad go in there. It was when Lenny was out the back.'

I look back at barman Lenny. He shrugs.

'This dame, what she look like?' Harry demands.

'Hey, I dunno. I was just coming out of the little girl's room, you know?' A look of ecstasy suddenly crosses her face. 'She had on this fur coat to die for. It went right down to the *floor*!' Then she frowns. 'It was a bit odd, you know? She was kinda looking around, like she didn't want no one to see her, you know?'

Lenny frowns too. 'What's this about? Someone been bothering the boss?'

'Something like that,' Harry says, which is a fair enough response. Being murdered *would* bother someone. 'Better not go disturb him, OK? We're gonna be back soon.' I'm glad to see he's starting to think clearly again.

I wait till we've left the joint, then I look at him and say, 'Fur coat down to the *fl-oh-rer*,' imitating the canary's cutesy voice.

'Peterson-Lee?' Harry suggests.

'Sure looks like it. I guess we need to tell the cops about her.'

But Harry shakes his head. 'We can't tell the cops about any of this stuff. The map and such, I mean.'

I remember the line I'd fed to Wallace when we met, about how he wouldn't want cops running the show cos everything'd end up in Evidence, and I saw where Harry was coming from.

'OK,' I said. 'We'll call them, gotta do that. Yeah, we'll get tied up in questioning, but we both got watertight alibis in each other, so it'll be sweet. We just maybe leave a few things out. Then we find Mrs P-L and do a bit of questioning ourselves. You in?'

'Yeah,' he says. 'You bet I'm in. She ain't gonna get away with this.'

And something in the way he says that makes me think I wouldn't want to get on the wrong side of Harry Durkin. No sir, not at all.

CHAPTER TEN

STORMCAGE, AD 5147

It took a long time for Ventrian to tell me everything, by which time I'd almost finished the book. I kept reading it to him, chapter by chapter, and in return he would tell me the next instalment in his own story. When I finally knew all of it, I wasn't surprised that he struggled with life in the day-to-day.

I'm going to set it out here as clinically as possible. Just the bare bones.

That's quite an unfortunate turn of phrase, actually. Because that's what Ventrian dug up to start his nightmare. The bones of a man – well, a humanoid at least. The bones of a man, and this Device, the thing he was now calling the Eye of Horus.

It might have been unclear what the Eye *was*, but what it *had* was immense power, and what it *wanted* was for Ventrian to use it.

This is what he figured out, eventually. Someone had brought the Eye to this uninhabited, tech-free world to starve it of almost everything it needed – then had died themselves, removing the last, living component that the Device needed to function. They'd put up a plague beacon to keep people away, but Ventrian's probe had given this Device access to technology once again, and it drew him in.

'The Device's power comes through other things,' Ventrian had said. 'It can't control people directly, but it can control technology and twist reality until the people are controlled anyway. And that's what started to happen. It filled my head with such dreams ...'

'Couldn't you just put it back where you found it?' I'd asked.

He'd laughed almost hysterically when I'd said that. 'It makes you want to use it! And every time you do ... it takes a piece of your life force.'

'Killing the host is an evolutionary dead end,' I'd pointed out, trying to bring a bit of rationality into this.

'Not if it heals you too,' Ventrian told me. 'The trouble is – it heals you by replacing your life force with its own. You slowly *become* it. Your thoughts are twisted to its own way of reasoning. Once the real you is lost, you can no longer stop it. And unstopped ... truly, it could destroy the universe.'

'Then *you* destroy *it*,' I'd said.

Of course, I should have known that things weren't quite so simple.

Ventrian had returned to his own world, never quite sure what was real and what was illusion as the Device feasted on all the technology around him. He tried to use the Device for good – or what the Device made him think was good. He piled up riches and his influence started to spread.

And another planet declared war. I'm not entirely sure how it came about, because Ventrian was only aware of it vaguely, amid the fog, so couldn't tell me. All he did know was that the Device wanted him to destroy the other planet. To weave it out of existence somehow.

He tried not to do it. He fought. And his wife, the only one close enough to see what was happening, fought too. And Ventrian killed her.

She didn't die straight away. Ventrian had a moment of complete clarity, where he understood what was happening to him.

He could have used the Device to heal her.

But healing used up so much more power than hurting. (Isn't that always the case?)

If he healed her, he would go over the tipping point. He would become the Device's puppet entirely. And he would have no way to prevent it destroying that other planet – and going on to do who knew what else.

He couldn't let that happen. So he let his wife die. He let her die in front of him.

And the moment she died, grief unleashed such horrors inside him that he destroyed the planet anyway.

He'd let her die for nothing.

He fled. He couldn't destroy the Device – the Eye of Horus – no person was strong enough. It would take him first. So he took it back to where he'd found it, and buried it again on a planet free of people, free of technology, surrounded by plague beacons.

He wanted to die there. He wanted to stay until his bones lay beneath the earth, like the Eye's last host. But he was a wanted criminal. People would come looking for him, and he had to lead them away from that world, away from the Eye.

He left, and he was caught, and he was sent to Stormcage.

'I told you it was like your Eye of Horus,' he said, when he finally got to the end of his tale. 'It brings nothing but death. It's cursed.'

I'd already told him what I thought about curses. But I agreed that word fitted perfectly.

I think referring to this Device as 'the Eye of Horus' helped him, somehow; he was watching events at one remove, the pages of a book were between him and reality – it was as though he could look on all the terrible things that had happened as fiction. At times I wondered if he could even tell the difference between fantasy and reality any more.

I was almost considering breaking my solo rule and getting him out of Stormcage. It'd cause me a few headaches down the line, but – and I couldn't quite believe I was thinking this – it was the right thing to do. Being with a certain Special Someone has definitely rubbed off on me.

Not only did Ventrian not deserve to rot in prison, but he needed help that he was never going to get in here. I was convinced, too, that there was still danger out there. Ventrian had breathed life into the Eye and it wouldn't give that up easily.

Also, a Device powerful enough to warp reality sounded like *fun*. I was in a warped reality once – strangely enough, Cleopatra was there too. I think. Don't really remember it that well, although I'm fairly sure I didn't bring up the subject of her tomb. It would have been rude. You know, if I hadn't been so busy trying not to kill the man I loved, I could have had so much fun. It'd be nice to have a do-over. All the things I could do if I were in charge of the universe!

For a start, I'd –

And that's how it would get me. Me, thinking I'm so much cleverer than silly Ventrian. So much more clear-sighted, so much more sophisticated, so much more experienced.

I would have to be careful. Put the Eye of Horus out of my mind. Concentrate on the next step I need to take in *this* reality.

The more I thought about it, the more the idea of a joint jailbreak appealed. Visions of escape plans danced in my head. No need to be hasty, I'd let them percolate for a few days. While much of my life is governed by a 'seat of my pants' rule, occasionally it's worth planning ahead. I may treat things lightly – earnest doesn't suit me, and I certainly have *no* intention of developing worry lines – but that doesn't mean I don't know when something's serious. I was going to be the grown-up for once. I'd think it all through carefully.

Plus I rather wanted to finish my book first. I was only a few chapters away from the exciting denouement – the murderer is revealed! I was looking forward to that. The only part of writing even better than starting a project is writing 'THE END'.

Unfortunately, waiting turned out to be a *really* bad move.

CHAPTER ELEVEN

NEW YORK, AD 1939

Dealing with the cops ain't my favourite thing, but we've crossed paths enough times and they know I'm straight. Me and Harry get the easiest ride being as we was alibis for each other. That canary gets all hysterical when she works out what's going on and throws herself in Harry's arms – you ask me, though, she's been looking for an excuse. Harry passes her off soon as he can, and when we vamoose she's crying on a cop's shoulder instead. Keep crying, canary – we want to be out of reach before she starts singing about the fur coat she saw.

We need to track down the Peterson-Lee dame before the cops fix on her as a suspect. Could be a lot of legwork, or we might get lucky. She don't know that anyone saw her in the Pink Tiger, maybe she don't feel the need to hide. Now, that map? It's a secret. No one knows about it but me and Harry and maybe a couple people way over in Egypt, that's what Harry tells me – and it's darn sure Wallace ain't going to be telling anyone about it any more. Peterson-Lee? Why did she take it, if she don't know what it was (and speaking as one who's seen it, ain't no one gonna work it out at first glance)? Well, I got a theory about that. Peterson-Lee was at the auction, she knew the ruby came with a letter. The map – it had all those little hieroglyphs on it, same as the letter did. So, there's the ruby on the desk, there's this paper with funny writing on it Egyptian-style – wouldn't you jump to the conclusion they're connected? That maybe that's the letter? So if you're taking the ruby, makes sense you'd take that too.

We go back to my office. I grab the directory and turn to the section on hotels. Not the first time I've had to do the rounds – it's a slog, but a private eye's job is 5 per cent guesswork, 5 per cent grey matter, and 90 per cent legwork. Maybe I could've phoned around and hang the cost, but trotting around the city with Harry appealed some.

So, I turn to A for Adelphi, and I'm just gonna start making a list when my eye catches a name just a couple of lines further down and I come to a full stop. I show the listing to Harry.

'What d'you reckon? Say you're the reincarnation of Cleopatra – where else would you go?'

He looks and he agrees. So together we set off for 250 West 103rd Street, just off Broadway, and the Hotel Alexandria.

It was an impressive building of 14 storeys – mind you, it had to be impressive, to charge five bucks a night. I'd slipped a mink over my workaday clothes before we left; not my style at all, and there'd been many a time I'd thought of hocking it for rent money, but it was worth its weight in – well, in mink. Put on a coat like that and you're somebody. So I assume my best 'I belong here' face, with

Harry hurrying after me like a well-trained secretary (or Boston Terrier), sweep up to the desk and demand Mrs Peterson-Lee's room number.

The desk doll starts to say, 'We ain't supposed to ... ' but I look at her like no one has ever said no to me in my life before and anyone trying to start now will be looking at the Help Wanted ads tomorrow morning. She caves.

I go over to the elevator and instruct the liftboy to take me to the fifth floor, calling over my shoulder to tell Harry to take the stairs. I just figure that's what a really rich dame would do – plus it's funny. His face as he said, 'Yes, madam' was a picture. It's even better when Harry then joins me on the fifth floor and I say, 'Took your time, didn't you?' as he gets his breath back and tidies his hair (one wavy lock tends to spill over his forehead when he runs, that's pretty much the whole reason I did this. It's pretty darn adorable).

We find the room. A maid with a trolley full of fluffy white towels is just coming down the corridor, so as the Peterson-Lee woman opens—

CHAPTER TWELVE

STORMCAGE, AD 5147

I was in the middle of revising the chapter where Melody goes to the Hotel Alexandria (there's a reason why the writer's curse is: 'May your rewrites never end') when Ventrian started screaming.

'What's happening?' I demanded through the air vent. It felt like a very long time before I got an answer.

'They're going there!'

That was unhelpful. 'Who is going where?'

'They'll find it! It'll find them! I can already feel it! Something's getting close …'

I told Ventrian, 'Calm down' a lot. After about the 80th time, he almost did.

But it turned out he had good reason to panic. We may well have a problem – a big one. *Universe* big. One of the guards had informed Ventrian that the authorities were attempting to retrace his steps. They wanted to find the weapon he'd used to destroy the planet. So of course Ventrian was terrified they would find the Eye of Horus Device, and he had good reason. But getting agitated does no one any good. I don't panic – I act.

'Listen to me,' I said, as my brain whirred. 'This is the plan. Tonight, I'll go and see what I can find out. If there really is something to worry about, I'll come and get you, and we will stop it. Listen to me,' I said again. 'We *will* stop it.'

'We can't wait that long!' he said, but unfortunately for him, we had to. The guards may be happy to look the other way on occasion, but without my hallucinogenic lipstick there would probably be a bit of violence involved, maybe a few alarms set off – basically a discreet exit would be impossible.

I spent the rest of the day making plans and tidying my prose. Looked like I wasn't going to finish my book in Stormcage after all, I'd have to wrap it up later. A pain, but I'd got most of it done at least.

Finally it was time for night-time rounds. After lights out, the warders come round to make sure all the prisoners are tucked up safely in their beds. I'd told Ventrian not to take his meal pill; he was to feign sleep and stay awake until I could report back.

'Goodnight, boys!' I called out to the guards as they passed, adding in a rather winsome little yawn to show I was all ready for beddy-byes. Each floor contains 50 cells, spread far apart, and they still had one more floor to check after mine. But following that, they would rejoin their fellows in the staff wing and the coast would be clear. I had planned what I would do next down to the smallest detail.

Suddenly there was a distant sound. Loud, but muffled. Perhaps a space shuttle backfiring – not that many shuttles make it into our little galactic blind alley. I tensed, waiting.

There was nothing else for a few minutes, and I was starting to relax when I heard footsteps. The two guards hurried back through the gloom, pistols unholstered. 'What's happening?' I called as they passed. One half-turned to look, maybe speak, then changed his mind. The other didn't even glance my way. Not normal. I'd expect a 'Mind your own business' at the very least.

Someone said something – it wasn't a guard's voice. Then the corridor lit up red, just for a moment. Then another moment.

Thud. Thud.

A sound I recognised very well. Bodies falling to the ground. Two of them, one after another. And the flashes – that had been energy weapons discharging. But not Stormcage-issue weapons: the beams were the wrong colour.

I moved over to the bars of my cell – quietly, slowly, keeping low – and tried to look down the corridor. There was something right on the corner of my vision that might have been a shoe, supine. *Urgent, man down, man down!* Surely the alarms would go off any moment? But no. There was no one else to set them off.

Look, if you work somewhere like this, you know the risks. And there aren't many prisoners I'd raise even a little finger to help. But (other) people breaking in to Stormcage and shooting the warders is irritating, to say the least. When it gets so you don't feel safe even in your own maximum-security prison, there's something very wrong going on.

I was tempted to forget my plans and just stay in my cell. Keep out of trouble.

The problem with that is, I like trouble.

And there was something else too. The few words I'd heard just before the shootings. I was almost certain they'd been 'Eye of Horus'. Possibly 'Where's the Eye of Horus?' Something like that.

The Egyptian symbol of protection, power and health? The fictional ruby of Melody Malone's story? Well, both seemed rather unlikely. Ventrian's powerful Device? Rather more plausible. Except – who could possibly know he was referring to it in that way? Was he still connected to it somehow? Did it have its claws so deep into his mind that it knew what he was thinking? That could cause a lot of problems. I needed to find out what was going on.

I would have to bring my breakout forward.

The cells in Stormcage are low tech, deliberately. They've learned the hard way that many criminals are able to hack, reprogram, fuse, sonic or otherwise break through electronic systems, whereas iron bars and bolts and huge locks with metal keys can't be overcome with the merest flick of a switch or click of the fingers. But there are ways. Normally I like to have a little fun, play a game, pit my wits against the guards to get out of my cell (seriously, they love it too, I know for a fact they keep a book on what method I'll use next time, so really it's a favour to them to keep it interesting). But now, of course, I just needed to get out with the least amount of fuss in the shortest amount of time.

I dug through my makeup bag until I found a small bottle labelled nail varnish. Notice 'labelled' – because labels can lie. This particular label should say 'fearsomely strong acid'. I remember this woman I was at a party with, One-Thumb Marlene – oh, actually, that rather gives away the end of the anecdote. Never mind.

I painted on the liquid with the handy little brush, and waited for it to burn through the metal. There were only a few drops of acid left in the little bottle when I was done, but I took it with me anyway. My arsenal was necessarily low due to my situation; the warders may turn a blind eye to some things, but heavy-duty weaponry isn't one of them. Apart from the dregs of acid, my resources consisted solely of a sharpened nail file and an under-razer-wired bra (and for goodness' sake, never go on a trampoline when you're wearing one of those). I quickly fastened the Vortex Manipulator around my wrist too – usually you can't teleport from inside the prison thanks to a powerful dampening field, but if intruders had made it in, there was a fair chance the field had been, or would be, disrupted somehow.

I crept out. I'd been right, two guards lay dead on the floor. Tomas and Ezra. Both not too objectionable, in their own ways.

Their weapons were missing. Oh, and someone had cut off their hands and dug out their eyes. I'm not squeamish, but I was still quite glad it was night-time and I didn't have to look too closely. It gave me a moment's pause though – maybe the words I'd heard weren't 'Eye of Horus', but something else. 'Where's the eye for us?' Could have been that, maybe.

The sensible course of action would be to assume I was mistaken and go back to my nice, cosy cell.

Oh, I don't think so.

I was assuming that the explosion I'd heard was the outer shell being pierced. And here's a thing. My time sense was tingling. Remember the 'marble drop doors' that had to be properly aligned if you didn't want to do an impression of Marie Antoinette at the guillotine? This intrusion had been planned, and planned well, because we were just coming up to the time of day when all the doors aligned on this floor. Unless it was an almighty coincidence, I guessed the intruders were heading to the staff wing, from where you can access all the Stormcage systems.

Most prisoners wouldn't be able to find their way through the prison labyrinth to the 'marble' doors. Luckily I'm not most prisoners. But even if I had been, I could have easily followed the interlopers' trail, scattered as it was with open gates and dead guards instead of breadcrumbs.

I reached the 'marble drop' door. There was still time to make it through, so I did. Unlike the rest of the prison where a soft blue night-time light was the only illumination, here it was as bright as day. I followed the open route to the staff quarters, wading through a sea of dead guards, most of whom I knew by name.

Finally I came upon the intruders. There were only five, all men, but they were huge, thuggish, and very heavily armed. Keeping low, I crawled forward. My hand came down on something squishy. I'm not squeamish, I've already told you that, but how would you like to find you'd just put your hand on a discarded eye ball? Especially when you knew its owner. I won't lie, I was tempted to say a few rude words. Still, waste not, want not. Maybe I'd need to get through an iris reader some time. I put the eyeball in my pocket and hoped it wouldn't stain.

Onwards. I couldn't see what was on the screen in front of them – but I could hear their voices, whispering to each other. A bit closer and I might be able to make out words …

I took out my sharpened nail file and held it between my teeth, like a pirate carrying a cutlass (did you know that's where the phrase 'armed to the teeth' comes from? Musket in both hands, knife between the teeth in case you don't have time to reload. We archaeologists are full of little tidbits like that. Life and soul of the party, I'm sure you'll agree).

A step. Another step. Then one of them said loudly, 'Well, how would you spell it, then?'

'Try F – E – N – T – R – Y – O – N,' said another. Slowly. Huge, thuggish, very heavily armed, but not necessarily blessed with brains.

Now, they don't let me have access to the prison rosters – I have asked, it'd be very helpful when compiling my Christmas Card list, but no – but I would be surprised if there were too many prisoners whose name sounded like 'Fentryon', however it's spelled (something I'd have to check with the man himself later).

So if they're looking for Ventrian, there's a very good chance they *had* said 'Eye of Horus'. It also meant – or so I reasoned – that there was no connection still between the Eye and Ventrian, because if there had been they'd at least have known how to spell his name.

These men had slaughtered their way through Stormcage, and they wanted the Eye of Horus.

And if the Eye of Horus had caused so much death and destruction in the hands of a good man – because I was sure

Ventrian was a genuinely good person; I'm not a good person, so I can spot a fake a mile off – then how much more dangerous would it be in the hands of people who are not good at all?

So that's how I suddenly realised I had to cancel my plans and do whatever it took to stop them.

CHAPTER THIRTEEN

STORMCAGE, AD 5147

'You sure you've got the name right?' demanded one of the men.

'It's what Sukri said. He kept overhearing this bloke talking with some bird. Only heard the name a couple of times, but that's what he told Deff. But he hadn't got no clue where the voices were coming from.'

Well, that solved another mystery: how they knew about Ventrian and the Eye. Our vent-to-vent conversations had been overheard. I briefly contemplated tackling all five of them there and then, my righteous fury at being called a 'bird' more than making up for any deficiencies in weaponry, but I was wearing white and you can never get the bloodstains out; it would be bad enough having to deal with the squishy eye goo that was already seeping out of my pocket.

I had to warn Ventrian. The trouble was, I didn't know where to find him either. Our earliest conversations had been rather like a confessional: words sent into the ether to an unseen audience, in some ways they hadn't felt *real*. I realised how foolish I'd been not to check in with him before I set off chasing the intruders.

So, should I stay here and watch these goons until they worked out Ventrian's location, then hope I could get to him first? That would be cutting things very fine. No, I'd try to locate him on my own, with my fingers very firmly crossed.

I reversed back into the vestibule. The doorway to my floor would remain open only a few minutes more. I had to hope the thugs disabled those defences or I'd never be able to get to Ventrian in time. The trouble being, of course, that once they disabled the defences the way would be accessible for them too.

Back to my cell. I pulled my mattress aside, and was about to call out when a thought hit me: what if we were overheard? That guy they mentioned – Sukri. He was obviously an inmate, but he wasn't with them. *He could still be listening.* I had to watch what I said.

'Ventrian! Ventrian, are you there?' I hissed through the vent.

No reply. Surely he hadn't gone to sleep?

I tried again. 'Ventrian?'

Aargh! He just couldn't hear me. There was no choice, I had to shout. 'Ven-tri-aaaaaan!' I yelled. The ducts took my words and threw them around, the echoes churning inside the pipes. I did it again. 'Ven-tri-aaaaaan!'

That reached him. A sudden, surprised, 'River? It is time already?'

'No. Just listen. You're in danger. Someone's coming for you.'

'Who? Why? I don't—'

'No time for that. Tell me how to find you.'

'I'm in—'

'No! Stop! We could be overheard.'

'I don't know what to do!' I'd put the poor man in a panic. Not surprising. But there had to be a way through this.

My personal pied-à-terre is Cell 426. A nice even number. 'You can find me at the fall of the Roman Empire minus 50,' I told him. 'Get that?' One of those dates that all Earth historians know, and

I'd talked about Rome with him. Not that it mattered if he remembered it was AD 476 or not, I was just giving him the idea. He had to tell me his cell number in a way that only I would understand.

'Oh!'

'Don't get flustered. Just give me a sum.'

There was silence for a few moments. My foot was tapping in irritation. Finally he said, 'I'm, er, in … oh yes! Alexander the Great conquers Egypt … plus Julius Caesar is assassinated!'

What a clever boy! He'd definitely been listening. I felt quite proud of myself. I was obviously an exceptionally good teacher. So – Alexander the Great conquers Egypt: that's 332 BCE; Julius Caesar is assassinated: 44 BCE. Both negative numbers, strictly speaking, but I'm fairly certain we don't have negative cells. So 332 plus 44 equals 376. I threw my hands in the air in frustration. He could have just used my example of the fall of the Roman Empire minus a hundred. I almost went to berate him, then decided that would be better kept for later.

'I'm on my way,' is all I said.

With 50 cells to a floor, he must be right underneath me. Obviously that made sense, our vents were connected, although if I had to guess I'd have put him further away. If only I'd packed a bucket of acid instead of just a few millilitres, I could have burned through the floor and reached him like that. As it was, I had to take the long way round.

I retraced my steps until I got to the 'marble doors'. I'd just make it. No time to think twice, I just dived through. If Ventrian's floor was below mine, the likelihood was the next alignment would take me to him.

I was counting down the interval until the next passage opened, when I heard someone coming from the direction of the staff wing – and as far as I knew, the only people still alive in there were the thugs. I'd have to cross the threshold the instant it became viable – it didn't matter where it took me, I had to get out of there. Closer and closer came the footsteps. It wasn't going to work! The entrance wouldn't align in time. Could I make it out the other way? I didn't have my special mirrors with me, the laser maze would cut me to pieces.

'Hey!' The thug had seen me now, and he was running. And I had nowhere to go.

Except … I started to run too. I glanced back over my shoulder, looking scared, looking like I really feared he would catch me … he was getting closer, he was going to catch me, I had to speed up, so he had to speed up … then I turned back to the doors, exclaimed, 'Oh, thank god!' and dived.

And ducked. And stopped just this side of the entrance, as he kept going.

I was going to say 'kept going right through', but that wouldn't be one hundred per cent accurate. Looking at what remained this side of the doorway, 50 per cent accurate would be about right; he'd carelessly left half his torso and both legs behind. At least the floor was covered with a nice wipe-clean low-tech linoleum.

At last the clock in my head told me it was safe, and I dived straight through for real. I looked at the first cell – 450. Damn! I needed to go down, but I'd gone up. I'd have to go back.

I stepped back through the entrance – and something happened. My whole body was shaking, juddering, teeth chattering, bones rattling. Had I got it wrong? Was I being torn apart?

Was this really the end of all my fun?

And then it was over. I was back in the vestibule – the semi-body on the floor told me as much. And I realised what had happened – the incomers had managed to turn off the security and the doors had all opened, just as I was heading through one. Not an experience I'd like to repeat, but much better than being cut in two. I looked around quickly – all the doors had separated out, it was rather like being inside a giant colander. Yes! There was the entrance to the next floor down. I headed straight through.

But I was seen. Shouts came from behind me once again. Spears of red light shot past me. But I had a guard's eyeball. It wasn't just computers it unlocked. I could access environmental controls.

I turned off the lights. I didn't hang around to find out exactly what happened, but the curses that came to my ears suggested my pursuers had just slipped in a pool of blood left by their half a friend. Plus it would take them a while to develop night vision – which they would destroy every time they fired at me. And while they may have got directions from the computer, they weren't used to the labyrinth. That all gave me a head start, at least.

Down the corridor I ran, ignoring the shouts of prisoners wanting to know what the hell was going on, until I found Cell 376.

The small man inside shrank back into the far corner, clearly terrified. 'It's OK, it's me,' I whispered. 'River. Let's get you out of here.'

He hurried over to the bars. 'River! What's happening?'

I pulled up my top to remove my bra. Even with the dim light, the poor man looked like he was going to have a heart attack. 'Wire saw,' I explained, handing it over. 'Start sawing.' I got out the remainder of the acid – it wasn't enough to burn all the way through the bars, but was better than nothing. 'Someone overheard us talking, and they want the Device,' I told him, finally answering his question. 'And judging by the number of dead guards they've left behind them, they're not going to say please.'

He froze. 'No,' he managed to say. 'No, that can't happen. I must find a way to destroy it, I must!'

'Look, these hoodlums are coming to get you, and the cops are on their way to the "Eye". It's a race, and it doesn't matter if the bad guys or the good guys win, because the good guys will turn into bad guys, if everything you say is true. So we need to get you out of here, then fetch the Device. Take it somewhere completely tech-free. I've got a few ideas. Then you can keep on trying to find a way to destroy it, in safety.'

He was still frozen. It was all too much for him to take in. That was understandable. But it was not acceptable. There was more than one life on the line here.

'Keep sawing!' I ordered. But I could hear distant footsteps. There was no way we could work fast enough.

There was no time. No time at all.

Time …

'The important thing is to keep it out of all of their hands.' I took a deep breath. 'I suggest hiding it in time, rather than space. Take it somewhere completely non-technological. The Device will be neutered to a certain extent and I'd be surprised if these gentlemen have time-travel capability.'

Now he was staring at me as though I'd suggested taking it in a hot-air balloon to the sun. 'Hide it … in *time*?' he said. 'That's … impossible.'

'It's not,' I said, 'and you're just going to have to trust me on that.' I peeled the Vortex Manipulator off my wrist and I handed it to him through the bars. 'It's got voice controls,' I told him. 'Tell it where and when you want to go. Fetch the Eye, and meet me here.' I told him where and when – deciding on my office, in the twentieth century. He gaped as I told him the address and the date, and my preferred time of day. I shrugged. 'I'll meet you there, and we'll work out the best hiding place.'

'But what are you—'

'It only carries one. I'll get a lift home. I've got friends,' I said, mental fingers firmly crossed. 'Go! Now!'

His finger hovered over the button – I think he suspected I was playing some elaborate joke on him. Or that it was a trap, that I was one of the bad guys.

'Now!' I shouted.

Ventrian vanished; the thugs arrived; I ran.

Oh, how I ran. To my shame, I lost my way. I wasn't thinking, wasn't planning, I was a fleeing animal operating on instinct and desperation. And the predators were on my heels.

And then I turned a corner …

… and there was nothing. Actual nothing.

This was where they'd broken in. There was a temporary seal over the hole with what the hubby used to call 'space cling-film' (it's rather an endearing little affectation he has, likening things to Earth objects from the twentieth century), but through it was a field of nothingness. The sort of nothingness that includes absolutely no air. There was no ship visible. There was no way out.

They were laughing as they reached me. They knew I had nowhere to go. I couldn't fight my way through four of them, not when they all had guns, and poor little me only had a sharpened nail file.

That's probably why they couldn't understand why I was laughing too.

Because who would be mad enough to use a sharpened nail file to cut through space cling-film? When there was just a void on the other side?

Hey, fellas, I think that would be me.

I took a very deep breath.

They were still smiling for, ooh, almost a second before they realised. Before they were sucked towards the rapidly increasing opening.

And I too was pulled out – into uncertainty.

If I survived, I would send a message to the Doctor, and he would pop back here to rescue me.

If I didn't survive, I wouldn't be able to send the message. So my Beloved wouldn't be able to rescue me. So I'd die.

And I had no way of knowing which future awaited.

I was floating, falling ...

A muscled arm grabbed me, curling around my waist from behind.

It wasn't Beloved's arm. Not any of him.

And I was so surprised, because things have always worked out before, somehow. I really thought they always would. Forever. I never really expected there to be an end.

Shame I wouldn't get to say goodbye.

'Sorry, my love,' I whispered. Maybe the words would get to him somehow. River's last goodbye.

I still had the nail file in my hand. I only had moments to live. Even if it took the last scrap of energy I possessed, I was going to take someone with me.

Chapter Fourteen

Space, AD 5147

Then I saw a face. *His* face. Not him, solid, holding out a hand to guide me into the TARDIS. Just the vague ghost of his face, hanging in the void.

Oh, I thought. I'm seeing things. My life passing before my eyes. My loved ones waiting to greet me at the gates of … wherever.

If there had to be an end, I could cope with that being the last thing I ever saw. His silly old face with that silly old floppy hair, that silly old fez and that silly old bow tie …

That silly old, wonderful old face.

I stared into its diaphanous eyes, and stabbed backwards, as hard as I could.

A hand caught my wrist. A voice exclaimed, 'Hey!' It sounded annoyed.

I wondered how someone could be talking to me in the vacuum of space, and how I could hear them. In space, no one can hear you scream. Or chuckle. Which is what this voice went on to do.

And then I realised I was breathing. Lovely, lovely oxygen. I was inside an air bubble, alongside my … captor? Rescuer?

'Thing about being immortal is I age very slowly. Which means hair, nails, stuff like that – real slow too. So let's cancel the manicure, OK?'

Oh, I knew that voice. So I repositioned the nail file carefully.

'OK, you do not wanna do that! Do you know how many hearts would be broken?'

'It's not hearts I'm aiming for. Didn't anyone ever tell you it's rude to grab a lady from behind?'

'But it's a behind in a million …'

I reholstered the nail file and spun around in the artificial gravity of the bubble. Couldn't help smiling as I looked up at him. 'Hello, Jack.'

'Hey, River.'

'Did you just happen to be passing?'

He pointed to the Doctor's face, still hanging in the Stygian darkness of space. The vision suddenly opened its mouth and said: 'You've reached the Doctor's emergency line. I'm sorry I'm not able to deal with your life-or-death problem right now. If you confirm your coordinates, someone will be there to rescue you shortly.'

WHAT? He'd rerouted my eventual call to his answerphone? He'd palmed off my rescue to someone else?

'Yup,' said Captain Jack Harkness. 'I'm your replacement bus service. The man himself is a bit busy. Saving the universe – or was it a Girl Scout cook-out?'

'Well, he does love his smores.'

A sudden flash of colour in the gloom. A spaceship, pulling away from Stormcage. It had been out of sight around the far corner. Jack turned to look too. His face took on a grim expression. 'That's one of the Gain Gang ships. Is that who you've been messing with to end up floating about in space like this?'

'I don't "mess",' I said. 'And I've never heard of them. Gain Gang?'

'Yeah. You've heard "No pain, no gain"? Well they've reversed it. Where there's Gain, there's pain. Gangsters, racketeers, space mob – whatever you want to call it.'

Having seen the heavies who'd broken into Stormcage, learning they were mobsters didn't surprise me. At least they were now dead mobsters: no one had given them an air bubble and they were floating around space like dead fish in an aquarium. My mind immediately went to Melody. I'd been living in 1939 America, it hadn't been hard to find people to talk to for research into mobsters. I'd met witnesses to the St Valentine's Day Massacre, spoke to one of Lucky Luciano's runners, and – due to a slight misremembering of a kids' movie I'd seen at a drive-in in the 1970s – given Bugsy Siegel a custard pie. Although actually, it worked out fine, he rather liked it.

But despite organised crime being a way of life back in thirties America, I wasn't a fan. Random crime is much more fun in my book.

My book. Damn it. I almost said some very rude words, but I didn't want to shock the delicate ears of Captain Jack Harkness. My typewriter was back in my cell, and my Vortex Manipulator with the back-up was on the wrist of a frightened archaeologist with a decidedly sweaty grip on reality. Worse thing of all, I'd nearly finished it. Acquaintances have told me of painful things they've experienced – gallstones, childbirth, decapitation – but I'm practically certain none of them is anywhere near as painful as a writer losing a nearly completed work in progress. OK, so I'd just been saved from almost certain death, but this really put a dampener on the day. It was time to go home.

'Well, thanks for the rescue,' I said, 'but I can't hang around here all day. Have to meet a friend of mine back in 1939.'

'Someone special?'

'Oh, incomparable. Fancy giving me a lift home?'

'Do I get to come in for coffee?'

'Oh, we'll see ... ' I gave him the coordinates and he input them into his Vortex Manipulator. 'Ooh, looks like the latest model,' I said. 'Carries two, I see.'

'Only problem is you can't hang out with twins,' he said, and pressed the button.

CHAPTER FIFTEEN

NEW YORK, AD 1939

Travelling by Vortex Manipulator is not pleasant, even with the latest model, and travelling to 1930s New York is ten times worse than a standard trip, for reasons I've already explained. The instant we arrived in my office, I checked in the wall mirror to see if my stomach was actually on top of my head, my intestines wrapped around my ankles and my lungs upside down somewhere around knee-level. To my immense surprise, there were no internal organs on the outside of my body at all. Physical sensations can be deceiving.

'Ventrian?' I called out. 'Are you here? It's me, River.'

Jack smiled. 'That the guy you've got the date with?'

'That's right, Captain. And the date we're supposed to have together is the twelfth of April 1939 at noon – is he off, or is it us?'

Jack checked his Vortex Manipulator. 'Right time, right place,' he said. 'How's your date getting here?'

'Also Vortex Manipulator. Although *not* the latest model.'

He shrugged. 'Don't sweat it. You know what these things are like. They're often out by a bit, space or time. Turned up late to my own wedding once.' He smiled and I raised my eyebrows, indicating I wanted to hear more. He obliged. 'I'd met this guy just after Woodstock. August of 1969. Peace and love – two of my favourite things. I said it was the VM that made me late, and he was so mad he grabbed it off my wrist and scooted back in time to stop himself from meeting me in the first place. Unfortunately, long story short, he got there too early and popped up right in the middle of the stage. People were so high they just applauded. He liked the adulation, the wedding never happened, and he went on to have six hit albums.'

I rolled my eyes, but with a smile. I was extremely fond of Jack.

'Anyway. Want me to help you look for the guy?'

'No,' I said. 'I'll handle it. But thanks.'

'OK. But I'd steer clear of the fifty-second century for a while. You're not going to be Deff's favourite gal.'

Jack and I made a rather enjoyable farewell, then he zipped off to who knows where or when, complaining that he was needed for a lot of jailbreaks just at the moment.

The name Deff had rung a bell. Yes ... 'Sukri' (who I'd guessed was a prisoner) had passed on my and Ventrian's conversations to a Deff – presumably Don of the space Mafia. Jack's warning was justified: there was a very good chance he knew my name. Next time I went to the 51-hundreds I'd have to watch my back. I can handle myself, of course, but there's no point looking for trouble.

Oh, who am I kidding. I *always* look for trouble. After all, like calls to like.

Talking of calls – and talking of trouble – I'd better make that call to the Doctor. I patched into his emergency line, confirmed my previous coordinates – and rerouted the automatic answer to them as well. As a Child of Time, paradoxes bring me out in hives; I have to be very careful.

That done, I had to decide whether to sit and wait for Ventrian to turn up, or to carry out a search in case he'd arrived early or displaced. Well, I'm not one for sitting or waiting, so the latter seemed preferable. I left a note on my desk, propped against a framed photo of my parents. Nineteen-thirties fashions rather suited my mother, but unfortunately my father had decided to adopt a pencil moustache which he thought would make him blend in. Oh, Dad. I do love you, but no. Just no.

I visited some of the other floors of the building, popping into a few offices to ask if anyone had seen a small confused man wandering about. No luck. I went down to the street and canvassed the locale, still nothing. Conceding defeat, I returned to my office. Still no Ventrian, and my note was still lying on my desk. So he hadn't –

Hold on. The note was *lying* on my desk. I'd left it propped up against my parents' photo.

The photo was gone.

I shifted immediately into alert mode. Someone had been in here. No sign of anyone having forced their way in, implying matter transmission of some sort. Ventrian? Well, that was the logical answer, of course, but why would he have taken the photo? And why not wait for me here, the note clearly said I'd be back soon.

A knock at the door. Perhaps Ventrian returning, or one of my neighbours coming to tell me a man had suddenly appeared in their broom cupboard. I genuinely had no presentiment of evil. As far as I knew, I had no enemies in this city in this time period.

Silly me.

I opened the door.

It wasn't one of my neighbours. The way I knew that was that all of my neighbours were under eight foot tall; also the majority of them were human.

Actually, it's possible the person on the other side of the doorway had once been human. Humanoid, at least. But he had been majorly modified. One arm looked human, the other ended in what appeared to be the huge claws of a Raxacoricofallapatorian. What I assumed to be his original eyes were all-white, and a pair of completely circular black eyes now sat above them. At first I thought he was wearing a particularly unfashionable hat, but a second look showed me it was the horned forehead of some arachnoid race, perhaps the Skithra. One leg was definitely robotic, and I'm just not going to guess what might be going on under his clothing. Basically: one very big and definitely scary dude.

Oh, and his human hand was pointing a plasma pistol at me.

Obeying his gestures, I walked backwards until I was up against the desk. He reached behind himself and pushed the door shut without looking away.

'Have we met?' I said. 'You'll have to forgive me, I'm terrible with faces.'

'Name of me is Deff,' he said (I'd already guessed that, of course, I was just messing with him). 'Where is it?'

'Where is what?' I said, which seemed to annoy him, although it was a perfectly reasonable response.

'You knowing already,' he said.

Honestly, I like guessing games as much as the next person, but I need to be given a few clues.

'How about we play 20 questions?' I suggested. 'Is it alive?'

'Is what?'

'The thing you're looking for, is it alive?'

'Not of life.'

'Yes or no answers only, please. I'll take that as a no. Is it … bigger than a police box?'

He thrust the pistol right into my face, and I saw something on his wrist. Looked like the edge of a Vortex Manipulator.

'You have enough lips.'

A true observation, if a non sequitur. I suspected a translation device was in play, perhaps 'enough lip' or similar had been his intention. But I gave a little kissy moue to demonstrate that the number of lips I have was indeed sufficient.

He was big and had a lot of pointy bits, but I still had that sharpened nail file in my pocket, and I also have a heliotrope belt in Venusian karate. I rather wanted to see this composite horror horizontal and maybe crying for mercy a little bit. I tensed ...

And he reached into his pocket with his claws and threw something on my desk.

A photo of my parents.

But not the photo that had gone missing. A new one. Mum and Dad out in the front yard of their Manhattan garden apartment. Dad pushing an ancient lawnmower, Mum pruning roses.

'Progenitors of you,' he said. 'My Homo sapiens has eyeballs on top of them. So do not get any intelligent ideas, sugar-ventricles.'

'Don't you get any clever ideas either, *sweetheart*,' I replied, stony faced. 'Anyway, I don't believe you've got a man watching my parents. Vortex Manipulators only carry one.'

He rolled back his sleeve. 'Carrying two. Latest mannequin, so said the sage. Before I spanked him.'

The interesting images conjured there meant it was a few moments before I untangled his speech enough to realise I'd heard a 'wise guy' say something similar recently about the latest model of Vortex Manipulator.

A terrible sinking feeling in my stomach, almost as bad as my last trip by VM. Please no ...

No. I knew almost immediately that I didn't have to worry – Jack was immortal. It couldn't have been him. Some other poor time agent had fallen into this thug's clutches. But that moment of fear had been surprisingly painful. It would be a much duller universe without Captain Jack.

That fear might have subsided, but I was still concerned about my parents. They can handle themselves – well, you don't survive even a day with the Doctor if you can't – but they thought they were safe here. They were settling in, settling down. Carving new lives for themselves. Talking about adopting a little brother or sister for me. They'd given up so much to be together, and while I can't shield them from all the unpleasantness of life – there's a second world war coming, after all – I didn't want this for them. I didn't want to bring danger back into their lives. I may not be the best daughter in the world, but by god I will protect them where I can.

If this guy was any kind of mobster, he should know that. You don't mess with family. I might be beaten for now, but I wouldn't forget.

'Homo sapiens Ventrian is here meeting you. I have prisoner ears.'

Outwardly calm and cool, my thoughts were racing. Someone – probably that Sukri who'd listened in before – had heard what I said to Ventrian and reported back to Deff. Deff, with all his eyes and ears, had found a time agent and taken his Vortex Manipulator. He might have arrived here minutes after me, but could have spent months tracking me down. And, of course, I knew exactly what he was looking for. The 'Eye of Horus'.

'All right,' I said, in a conciliatory tone. 'I can guess why you're here. But Ventrian hasn't arrived. A million things could have gone wrong; he may never turn up. How long are you planning to camp out in my office? It could get rather awkward. We're decades too early to be able to call out for pizza and there's nothing good on the telly until 1963.'

'I making entertainment of my own,' he said, and pointed again at the photo of my parents. I kept calm by imagining the popping sound his all-white eyeballs would make as I stuck some 1930s art deco-style novelty cocktail sticks in them. My clothes already had eyeball juice on them. A bit more would make no difference.

There was a knock on the door. A proper *rat-tat*. 'Package for Miss Malone!' called a boy's voice.

'Hold on!' I called back.

'Not name of you!' growled Deff.

'For business purposes it is,' I said. 'This'll just be a delivery boy. Paper. Typewriter ribbons. You know?'

'I assassinate.' He raised his plasma pistol.

'No!' I tried to get through to him. 'You want the Device. You kill someone, the Earth authorities'll turn up – oh, you can kill them too, but you'll scare off Ventrian. He'll zap away and you'll have no idea where in time or space he'll end up.'

Unexpectedly, Deff responded to this logic. He backed into the broom closet and indicated that I could open the office door – but that his plasma pistol would be aimed straight at me while I did.

'Package for Miss Malone!' the boy said again as I opened the door, holding out a brown-paper-wrapped parcel. 'I had to wait to deliver till just this minute.' My address was on the wrapper, and written in large black letters alongside it was 'OPEN NOW – RIGHT NOW, 12.27pm – URGENT'. And I knew the handwriting. It was my mother's.

I winked at the delivery boy. 'I'll get your tip,' I said loudly, retreating to my desk and hoping Deff would stay out of sight while we had company – while he was in the cupboard, he couldn't see clearly what I was doing. 'I'm sure I've got some money here somewhere … ' I tore open the paper on the parcel. 'Where did I put it …?'

The delivery boy lingered, looking as bewildered as I did as I took in the parcel's contents. There was a book, what seemed to be a set of publisher's bound proofs, a mock-up of what the finished product might look like. The soft cover showed a dame on the cover, not entirely unlike me, in slinky red dress with a ruby at her throat, a gun in one hand and a cocktail glass in the other. At the top it said *THE RUBY'S CURSE: A Melody Malone Mystery*. My book. Written by me. Except I'd never finished writing it, let alone sent it to the publisher.

I put that mystery aside to look at the other item in the parcel. It was my Vortex Manipulator. No question that it was mine, all those mods I'd made meant it stood out in a crowd. But that VM should still be on the wrist of Ventrian. What had happened to him?

Alongside these was a handwritten note, headed by an Upper West Side address. I pulled a five dollar bill from under the blotter on my desk and held it out to the delivery boy, who came in to collect while I scanned my mother's familiar script.

Darling girl,

What are you up to this time? A Vortex Manipulator and a pile of papyrus scrolls suddenly appears in the living room with instructions that I'm to turn the latter into a book – the scrolls had even been marked with page numbers! – and that both VM and book must be delivered to you on 12 April 1939 at 12.27pm, not a minute either way. Not the strangest thing that's ever turned up in the living room ... but enough about your dad. Anyway, I've done as asked, presuming there'd be some terrible paradox if I didn't, but we want to hear all about it. Come to tea soon. Tea's better than dinner, Rory's been practising making Woolton pie even though I've told him rationing won't start over here until 1942, and I'd like to spare you that horror if I can.

Your ever-loving mother,

Amy

PS I was also told to tell you to put on your Vortex Manipulator now and give this letter to the man who's going to force his way into existence in exactly three minutes.

As the delivery boy left with a beaming 'Thank you!' I strapped the VM on to my wrist just as Deff emerged from the cupboard. 'What is in lovely present?' he demanded.

I held up the book. 'My latest magnum opus,' I said. 'Didn't Sukri tell you I was a writer? If you like, I can read you a few pages – just don't post any spoilers on the internet, there's a good gangster.'

My brain was racing, even as I spoke. Who'd sent the manuscript to Amy? Me? Papyrus suggested ancient Egypt, of course, but I currently had no intention of going there.

I assumed the person about to materialise was Ventrian. He'd be disorientated from his journey through the Vortex, a sitting duck for Deff. I needed to buy him some time. Deff was nasty – but he wasn't clever. That was my big advantage.

'If you don't want to scare away Ventrian,' I told Deff, 'you'll get back in that cupboard. Look, he trusts me. I can get the Eye of Horus for you. You know I won't double cross you – not with my parents' lives on the line.'

'If you not give me Optic of Horus – I am butchering them.'

I didn't know if that was a mistranslation or an accurate summation of his plans. I didn't want to find out.

There was a shimmer in the air. Right on time. An outline, twisting and turning. Faint cries coming and going. Someone was trying to materialise, and 1939 was not making it easy for them.

'That's him!' I told Deff. 'Please – I'll get you the Eye.'

He retreated into the cupboard again, like a good little gangster.

The outline became solid, revealing Ventrian, his face green with nausea. My eyes went straight to his wrist. Yes, that was still my VM he was wearing. I took a step back just in case. Blinovitch doesn't usually kick in with inanimate objects, but it's not worth taking the risk. I'm very attached to my arm and would hate to see it explode.

'R-river,' he stammered.

'It's all right,' I said. 'It'll wear off in a few minutes. I should have warned you it might be a rough ride – but there wasn't a lot of time.'

While I spoke I was scanning him up and down. There was nothing in his hands, but I had no idea what size the 'Eye of Horus' Device was. It could easily be in a pocket, and he had several.

I needed him out of here. I manoeuvred so I was between Ventrian and the broom cupboard and tried to tell him with my eyes that he needed to leave. He didn't get it – he was still groggy from the trip. I got more insistent, now bringing up my wrist as slowly and carefully as I could so Deff wouldn't see the movement, and pointedly indicating the VM.

I kept on talking, keeping my voice calm. 'Anyway, welcome to the twentieth century. You'll like it, I think. Maybe you'll never want to *leave*!' And on the word 'leave', there I am, tapping like crazy on the Vortex Manipulator again. Ventrian's still blank. I wouldn't want him on my team for charades at Christmas.

But then he seemed to pull himself together. 'River,' he managed to say. 'I got it …' And he reached into a pocket …

'No!' I shouted, and dived forward.

I heard the closet door open. Ventrian's eyes were suddenly wide with fear. An energy beam nearly grazed my shoulder. It didn't entirely miss its mark – Ventrian was hit, but he wasn't down. Remembering mother's message, I thrust her letter at him then slammed my hand heavily on Ventrian's wrist – the fast return switch. He vanished. I hit the fast return switch on the VM I was wearing. I guess, from Deff's perspective, I vanished too.

But where would I reappear?

Chapter Sixteen

Egypt, 30 bce

The room I was in was unlit, but even so I could tell it was a crude, simple place. The first thing I saw in the gloom was Ventrian, who was lying on a wooden bunk. He looked up at me and smiled. And said, 'I've used it too much, but it had to be done. I'm going to die now ...'

I dropped my book on the floor and knelt by the bed. 'Hold on, I can help ...'

A weak shake of the head. 'No. This is the right time and place for me to end. I just had to keep going until I'd found a way ... I wish I could have destroyed it myself, but I'm too close to it. Still, I've told you how. Destroy the Eye, River.'

The 'er' at the end of my name turned into a long, drawn-out syllable, a rattling exhalation. No inhalation followed. I pulled back the sheet and laid my head on his chest, but could detect no movement.

Of course, I tried to resuscitate him, but without success.

I'd thought at first that this was where the Vortex Manipulator had brought Ventrian, and he'd been too badly wounded by Deff to survive. But as soon as I'd got close enough to see him properly, I'd realised that couldn't have been the case.

When he'd arrived in my office, Ventrian had been in prison overalls, but the body was wearing a linen tunic. Linen strips had been used as bandages, but they couldn't cover up the extent of the wound. Pus had soaked through the fabric; jagged red lines shot out from the covered flesh like miniature lightning bolts. The smell of rotting flesh filled the room. This was not a wound that had been inflicted mere moments ago.

But where was I? And when?

There was a faint glow coming through the room's one window, leavening the gloom.

I looked out. The light was coming from some distance away, across water. A tall structure – maybe half the height of 30 Rockefeller Plaza – stood out there, and the light came from a fire burning at its top.

Oh yes. I knew where I was. That was one of the Seven Wonders of the Ancient World: the Pharos lighthouse, standing on an island in the harbour of Alexandria. Built in the third century BCE, eventually destroyed by earthquakes.

This was undoubtedly Ancient Egypt.

I'd told Ventrian to hide the Device somewhere with no technology, and my Vortex Manipulator had voice controls. Only last night – how ridiculous that it was only last night! – I'd read him the latest chapter of my book – the book about Cleopatra's ruby. Egypt would have been right there in his head. The fast return switch had taken him away from Deff, and he'd had to think of a hiding place without my help. So he'd chosen to come here.

Alexandria was on the Mediterranean Sea at the end of the Nile Delta – by 1939 much of it would be underwater, causing many problems for archaeologists. A mere hundred or so miles away would be the Great Pyramids and the Sphinx, and enough sand to make a life-size sandcastle or two.

Maybe tomorrow I'd have time to be a tourist. Now I had to figure out what was going on right here.

I examined the room by the light of the distant flames. It was surprisingly similar to a Stormcage cell. There was the wooden bunk with linen sheets bunched untidily at the foot, a wooden stool and a table with what I took to be an oil lamp made of clay on it, a dish of something black and oily, and some food. There, this primitive dwelling beat the prison hands down: there was bread, figs, dates and pomegranates, as well as a jug of rather lumpy-looking liquid that smelled fermented. Not quite the Manhattans that Melody Malone drank, but better than nothing – I'd not had anything but food pills and recycled water rations for quite some time, so this was a feast. Poison didn't appear to have played a part in Ventrian's death, so I had no qualms in tucking in to a few dates. I was just contemplating peeling a pomegranate when I spotted something under the table. A few rolls of papyrus – most blank, but some with writing on.

Underneath them was Amy's letter, grubby now, as though it had been consulted over and over again.

I picked up one of the papyrus rolls. I could make out some words, some sentences, with lines through them. 'I was wearing the red dress again' – crossed out. 'I got ready for the meeting with Wallace' – crossed out. '"Gee, Miss Malone," Phil said, "You look' – crossed out.

What I didn't find was anything that resembled a catastrophically powerful device of any kind.

Of course, I didn't assume it would have flashing lights and a big arrow pointing to it. Having checked Ventrian's clothing and found nothing, I examined every single thing in that room. Remembering a scene from *The Ruby's Curse*, I delved deep, straining the liquid in the jug and the dish of what seemed to be ink, in case something was hidden inside. There was nothing inside the oil lamp, nothing baked into the clay of the few pieces of crockery. Could the gadget disguise itself as a piece of fruit? Well, it wasn't impossible. I guessed I'd find that out if eating some gave me indigestion and dominion over all – but it didn't seem likely. My money was on the nominal Eye of Horus being elsewhere.

'I've told you how. Destroy the Eye, River.'

I don't like being told what to do.

After all, this situation wasn't my fault. I hadn't dug up this Device, I hadn't used it, I hadn't destroyed a planet (well, not that particular planet, at least). Yes, it was my conversations with Ventrian being overheard that had brought Deff to the prison, but that was on Deff, it wasn't on me.

Why shouldn't I just go back to 1939? Yes, there are issues about time travel to 1939 New York, but I'd get to the right spot eventually. Go to the Upper West Side before Deff's goon turns up to threaten my parents. Return to my office and I'd have the advantage over Deff any day. I'd be on my home turf, and I'd be angry. He wouldn't stand a chance.

But what of the Eye? Ancient Egypt may not be a place of electronics and computers but those advancements would come. The Eye would just bide its time. If I left here now, there might not be a 1939 to get back to. It's why time travel is – or should be – such a responsibility. Tread on a butterfly and the future changes entirely. I once destroyed the whole of time in order to keep someone I love alive. Luckily, it got better (and it did make my wedding day especially memorable).

None of this was my fault. But perhaps it would have to be my responsibility.

I sat down on the wooden stool and thought. What might have happened here?

When I'd last seen Ventrian – perhaps 15 minutes ago for me, and who knew how long for him – he was fleeing with the Eye of Horus Device. The Vortex Manipulator had brought him here –

and stored on the Vortex Manipulator was the almost finished manuscript of *The Ruby's Curse*. I'd read most of the book to him back in Stormcage so he knew it well, and he could have accessed the file in voice format. In short, he had virtually the complete novel at his fingertips.

So – was he the one who finished writing it?

The book was still lying on the floor where I'd dropped it. I turned to the last page. 'The End'. Well, it had been finished by someone, anyway.

Back to the first page. A – dedication? There was no name. A quotation? Not one I knew.

Beware the Ides – now Caesar's gone

The Eye's the only Rubicon.

A riddle perhaps? I hadn't written it, and with a risible rhyme like that, I don't think I ever would. Someone else had put it there.

The events slowly took shape within my mind.

Ventrian arrives.

He accesses the file of The Ruby's Curse *and writes it all down.*

He finishes the story. (Why? Boredom?)

Meanwhile, his wound has become infected. They don't have the medical technology to deal with it here. He's dying. He has the Eye of Horus Device with him. 'I've used it too much,' he said. But he wouldn't use it to heal himself. I'd heard him talk about his wife. He'd never do that.

Just before he dies, he bundles up the scrolls and attaches the Vortex Manipulator. He has Amy's address, it's on the note from the parcel. He knows the time and date from that too. He writes down instructions for her to follow and sends it, using the VM's voice controls.

Why not just use the VM's fast return switch? Why not send the papyrus to me?

No, he was right not to. The fast return switch would take it straight to Deff. Plus I'd have been lumbered with a few dozen rolls of papyrus which would have been rather awkward to carry through time and space, to say the least.

But the question remained – why go to such a lot of trouble at all? And had he really just finished my book out of boredom, and written a cryptic credo for fun? He could have left, gone to any place or time. So was there a deeper purpose at play …?

I've told you how. Destroy the Eye, River.

He must have faced so many hardships, knowing all the time that he was dying. Refusing to heal himself – and, I suspect, not wanting to heal himself. The only reason he had to keep on living was to safeguard others from the Eye of Horus Device.

But he'd finally found a way to destroy it. He couldn't do it himself – so he'd got in touch with the one other person who knew about it. The one person he seemed to think he could trust to do what he couldn't. Me.

And he'd sent me instructions – instructions disguised as a 1930s hard-boiled crime novel.

What I needed to do was read the book from the start and see how it had changed. Not only did I need to see what clues Ventrian had left for me, I was rather interested to read the ending. Ventrian had no idea how the mystery was supposed to conclude, no idea who Melody was going to reveal as the murderer. I'd planned a huge showdown on board a flying boat – the first transatlantic passenger flight was due to happen in summer 1939, and I thought I'd cash in on the publicity. I shuddered to think what strangeness Ventrian might have introduced. But then there was more than my authorial name at stake, and a kicking on Goodreads couldn't happen for another half-century.

Twilight had passed and dusk had fallen. I'd had to break the oil lamp during my search and my eyesight is precious. It made sense to bed down here for the night; I'd start my research in the morning.

My old man has been heard to remark that sleep is for tortoises, but I still need my 40 winks of beauty sleep if I'm not to get all grouchy in the morning – and coffee doesn't arrive in Egypt until the sixteenth century, so I'd be a monster. Seriously.

Not fancying a corpse as a bunk mate, I covered up Ventrian, and took the remaining linen sheets from the bed to make myself a nest on the floor. It reminded me of some of the more uncomfortable dig sites I'd camped in over the years, but those experiences, not to mention my many years of incarceration, had taught me to sleep anywhere. I treated myself to that pomegranate, a hunk of bread the consistency of pumice stone, and a ceramic cup of lumpy beer, and settled down for the night.

My time sense kicked in as usual, and I rose with the sun. A quick breakfast of figs and I was ready for the day.

The first thing I would do was find someone who could make arrangements to remove the body, preferably someone who wouldn't declare me responsible and make a song and dance about it. Every schoolchild (well, those at Leadworth Secondary, anyway) knows that the Ancient Egyptians made a big deal about death. Brains pulled out of the nose by a hook. Organs in canopic jars. Months of drying out the body, packing it and wrapping it with linen. Coffin, sarcophagus, tomb. Fill the tomb with food and games and possessions and maybe a few dead slaves and cats, ready for the afterlife.

Sorry, no. That's a myth. Most Egyptian people were just buried in holes in the desert and mummified by the heat. And Ventrian needed no ceremony to enable him to traverse the underworld; he was just ... gone.

I could see why people clung to their beliefs and rituals, though. How comforting to think that your spirit would survive death, that you would continue to exist, perhaps meeting again with friends and family. I have no intention of dying for some considerable time, but if I had to go – yes, those thoughts would comfort me too. A happy afterlife, surrounded by friends, lost no more. For a moment, it almost felt like something that could happen, and I smiled.

But I knew it wasn't a reality. Just a dream.

I found a spare linen robe and changed into it. There was no kohl – an Egyptian essential – and I decided against using the dish of ink instead; with no mirror I was likely to achieve a look more 'hungover panda' than 'glamorous Nefertiti-alike'. Perhaps I'd try to pick up some actual make-up if it looked like I was going to hang around here for long.

I wrapped up my book in a bundle, together with the remaining food and anything else I could find in the room that might be worth something to someone – I'd have to barter for goods and services, no doubt – and headed out.

I've been to many times and places, so I'm not going to say Alexandria was unlike anywhere I'd ever been. But it managed to cram so many experiences into a single city. In Earth terms it felt like Rio Carnival, Times Square on New Year's Eve, Istanbul's Grand Bazaar and a hen party in Newcastle all mixed together, surrounded by more art than you'd find in the Louvre and smelling like cinnamon, cardamom and salt. I wanted to dance, I wanted to party. But I also wanted this place and all the people in it to survive, and possibly – just possibly – that was up to me. The partying could come later.

A small amount of initial research was required, and no time traveller has yet come up with a way of asking 'Madam, what year is this?' and not sound ridiculous. Waking up after a night on the town and not being one hundred per cent sure if it's Wednesday or Thursday is one thing, accosting passers-by and asking if we've got to Anno Domini yet is clearly another. And if you do find a way of framing such a question, you might not get an easy answer. Be very, very suspicious of anyone who says, 'Yes, mate, it's 50 BC.' In this case, however, being a white woman in Africa was an advantage – oh, there were people of many skin tones to be found, I wasn't out of place, but I could reasonably claim to be a visitor who knew little of what had been going on in the city recently.

What I found out seemed extremely significant. Cleopatra was dead. Egypt was now a Roman province, captured by the man currently called Octavian, who would become known to history as Augustus, the first Emperor of Rome. Remember my little history lesson to Ventrian, all those chapters ago? But the Roman victory and the death of Cleopatra and her paramour Mark Antony were recent events – only a few weeks had passed. The people seemed to have returned to their normal day-to-day lives – Octavian had left the city almost immediately after the queen's death – but there was a general sense of awareness in the air that they were now subjects of Rome.

I wondered – I wondered very much – if Ventrian had arrived before or after such a momentous occurrence. Perhaps something in the book would tell me.

I wandered down to the green banks of the Nile, relishing the breeze. Bald, naked children were playing in the water, splashing the adults who'd come there for their daily bathe. Boats and barges sailed past – or rowed past, depending on their direction of travel. I decided to perch myself down by the riverbank, hoping I could persuade a couple of young men to waft feathered fans over me while I read. If I asked very nicely, they might even peel some pomegranates for me too. I was (probably) on a life-or-death mission, true, but aside from that, going by first impressions, I'd definitely recommend Ancient Egypt for a getaway break.

I settled down to read …

CHAPTER SEVENTEEN

NEW YORK, AD 1939

Dealing with the cops ain't my favourite thing, but we've crossed paths enough times and they know I'm straight. Me and Harry get the easiest ride being as we was alibis for each other. That canary gets all hysterical when she works out what's going on and throws herself in Harry's arms – you ask me, though, she's been looking for an excuse. Harry passes her off soon as he can, and when we vamoose she's crying on a cop's shoulder instead. Keep crying, canary – we want to be out of reach before she starts singing about the fur coat she saw.

We need to track down the Peterson-Lee dame before the cops fix on her as a suspect. Could be a lot of leg work, or we might get lucky. She don't know that anyone saw her in the Pink Tiger, maybe she don't feel the need to hide. Now, that map? It's a secret. No one knows about it but me and Harry and Phil and maybe a couple people way over in Egypt, that's what Harry tells me – and it's darn sure Wallace ain't going to be telling anyone about it any more. Peterson-Lee? Why did she take it, if she don't know

119

what it was (and speaking as one who's seen it, ain't no one gonna work it out at first glance)? Well, I got a theory about that. Peterson-Lee was at the auction, she knew the ruby came with a letter. The map – it had all those little hieroglyphs on it, same as the letter did. So, there's the ruby on the desk, there's this paper with funny writing on it Egyptian-style – wouldn't you jump to the conclusion they're connected? That maybe that's the letter? So if you're taking the ruby, makes sense you'd take that too.

We go back to my office. I grab the directory and turn to the section on hotels. Not the first time I've had to do the rounds – it's a slog, but a private eye's job is 5 per cent guesswork, 5 per cent grey matter, and 90 per cent legwork. Maybe I could've phoned around and hang the cost, but trotting around the city with Harry appealed some.

So, I turn to A for Adelphi, and I'm just gonna start making a list when my eye catches a name just a couple of lines further down and I come to a full stop. I show the listing to Harry and Phil.

'What d'you reckon? Say you're the reincarnation of Cleopatra – where else would you go?'

He looks and he agrees. So together we set off for 250 West 103rd Street, just off Broadway, and the Hotel Alexandria.

It was an impressive building of 14 storeys – mind you, it had to be impressive, to charge five bucks a night. I'd slipped a mink over my workaday clothes before we left; not my style at all, and there'd been many a time I'd thought of hocking it for rent money, but it was worth its weight in – well, in mink. Put on a coat like that and you're somebody. So I assume my best 'I belong here' face, with Harry and Phil hurrying after me like a well-trained secretary (or Boston Terrier), sweep up to the desk and demand Mrs Peterson-Lee's room number.

The desk doll starts to say, 'We ain't supposed to … ' but I look at her like no one has ever said no to me in my life before and anyone trying to start now will be looking at the Help Wanted ads tomorrow morning. She caves.

I go over to the elevator and instruct the liftboy to take me to the fifth floor, calling over my shoulder to tell Harry and Phil to take the stairs. I just figure that's what a really rich dame would do – plus it's funny. His face as he said, 'Yes, madam' was a picture. It's even better when Harry and Phil then joins me on the fifth floor and I say, 'Took your time, didn't you?' as he gets his breath back and tidies his hair (one wavy lock tends to spill over his fore-head when he runs, that's pretty much the whole reason I did this. It's pretty darn adorable).

We find the room. A maid with a trolley full of fluffy white towels is just coming down the corridor, so as the Peterson-Lee woman opens the door in response to my knock, I go 'Susan, honey! It's me! Thought I'd surprise you!' Then I sweep past her, followed by Harry and Phil, while she's still standing there, kisser wide open in shock.

A few seconds later she's composed herself. 'You seem to know my name, but I've never seen either of you before in my life. What precisely is the nature of your business here?' she says, in that hoity-toity tone.

'I'm a private detective,' I say, and she looks real sore. Something to hide?

But she raises her chin high. 'And that gives you the right to barge into my hotel room, does it? State your business at once, or I will call the manager.'

'Oh, I think you know what our business is,' I say. It's not like she's covered in blood and I'm pretty certain she ain't packing heat, but there's still that wary look in her eyes, for all she's acting the grand dame.

'I have no idea.' But she shoots a quick, questioning look at Harry. 'Have we met before?'

'RMS Caesarion,' he says. 'We both crossed on the same ship. Although you wouldn't have found me in first class.'

That seems to relieve her. Maybe there are places she'd rather not be recognised from – like the Pink Tiger club. But all she says is, 'I see. I have naturally tried to forget all about that terrible journey. What are you doing?' This last, strident question is aimed at Harry, who's ankling into her high-class en-suite bathroom.

He comes out again a few moments later, carrying her sponge bag in one hand and what looks to be a pot of something – face cream maybe – in the other.

'Unless you leave immediately I will call the real detectives in the New York Police Department and have you removed,' she says.

'Fine,' says Harry. 'Just before you do that, though, I'm guessing you won't mind me giving this the up and down.'

He holds up the pot of cream. Yeah, I can see now it is face cream, and a real high-end brand at that.

'Do you know how much that costs?' the dame demands.

Probably about three months' rent, would be my answer.

But Harry says, 'yeah, it's pretty damn valuable. Let's have a look-see.' He untwists the lid, and to both my and Peterson-Lee's astonishment, digs his fingers into the cream. Out comes something dripping with globules of thick white lotion. Harry wipes his hand on a handkerchief, then wipes the object.

It's the Eye of Horus. Can't mistake that. Not many rubies the size of pigeon's eggs hanging around.

Mrs Peterson-Lee, eyes wide, collapses on to her satin counterpane. 'But … but … how did that get there?' she asks.

'You tell me!' I say, reaching out to take the stone from Harry. I lift it up and examine it closely. Yeah, it's the real deal. I've already stared into its soul once; ain't no question this is the same ruby I picked up from George Badger Junior.

She's staring at it too, now. 'Is that … it?' she says. 'Is that *the* ruby?'

I don't know what she's trying to pull with this 'is that the ruby?' rubbish - no, wait, I know exactly what she's trying to pull. Playing dumb - that's a trick I've tried myself on occasion. It don't ever work.

'That's an old trick, lady,' says Harry, putting down the tub of cream. 'And believe me, I know all the tricks. Hey, Malone, why don't you have a look around, see if I missed anything.' By which he means look for the map, of course.

'What are you looking for?' Peterson-Lee demands, although it looks like she can barely drag her eyes away from the ruby.

'As if you don't know.'

I start on a thorough search. Bed, wardrobe, curtains, rug, dresser - nothing.

'I didn't get all the way through the bathroom,' Harry says. 'Maybe try in there.'

Fair enough. I head into the bathroom, which is bigger than my entire joint. Stick a couple of pillows in the bath and I'd bunk there, no problem.

Like Harry, I know a few tricks - but turns out I don't need them. There's a mirror screwed to the wall, and the map's been folded and pushed behind it. Pretty obvious place to hide something.

I go back to the bedroom and give Harry a nod. 'Got it,' I say.

'Got what?' demands Peterson-Lee. She's still staring at the ruby, like she's hypnotised, then it's like she wakes up. 'I am calling the police!' She stands up – and sits down again as Harry whips out his bean-shooter and points it straight at her.

'Hey, Malone,' he says to me, 'the lady here wants the cops called. I reckon we should oblige.'

I agree. I go over to the phone and pick up the receiver.

'Tell them we got some information they're gonna want to hear about a certain murder they're looking into,' Harry says to me.

'Murder!' shrieks Peterson-Lee. She's putting on a good act, but I don't know why she's bothering. She jumps up, like she's going to run, but Harry waggles the Colt .45 a bit and she collapses again. The lady takes several deep breaths and says in this fake-calm voice, 'I have no knowledge of any murder or of how that ruby got here. You have to believe me. Please. I would never hurt anyone, let alone murder someone!'

'I thought you were a reincarnation of Cleopatra,' I say, still holding the phone. 'It's not like she would have a problem with murder. Who did she bump off, couple of brothers, couple of sisters, right? One *real* femme fatale. So are we supposed to think it's a coincidence, you coming all the way across the pond right now and hey, look what happens, your rival Wallace gets murdered and the ruby gets stolen?'

She just gapes at him. 'Wallace? Wallace who?'

'Mr Horace P. Wallace, lady.'

She shakes her head in horror. 'Horace P. Wallace? But I was only speaking to him a few hours ago!'

'Speaking to him ... stabbing him ...'

'No!' She sounds shocked, but it's kinda weird. There's this sort of glow to her face. A kind of ... horrified ecstasy. 'The curse!' she breathes. 'The curse has claimed another victim!' And she *liked* that. She was a pagan priestess, exalting in the power of her god. 'I had hoped to prevent this. I had hoped the girl would be the last ...'

'Girl?' I say, cos I can't think of any girls associated with the thing. 'What girl?'

She looks at Harry. 'You know, surely? You were on the ship.'

Harry's eyes spring wide open. 'A girl – from the ship? Dead? Who? Tell me who, dammit!'

Oh, like that, is it? I raise an eyebrow, but he's not looking at me.

'The daughter,' she said. 'Oh, I suppose you might not have heard, they didn't want it talked about. But Badger's daughter, Ruby. She threw herself over the side of the ship.'

I didn't take my eyes of Harry's face, and there was definitely relief there. There'd been some shipboard romance, I guess, but not with Ruby Badger. Well, jealousy ain't my colour. Not like I'm looking for him to put a ring on my finger.

'Poor kid,' he says.

'So why do you want the stone, seeing as it comes with a free curse?' I ask Peterson-Lee.

'The curse is hardly going to affect its rightful owner,' she says, as if it's obvious.

We're both getting pretty sick of this nonsense. Enough digressions. I turn my attention back to the telephone and ask to be connected with the police department.

'Look, we know how it went,' Harry says. 'You wanted that stone, Wallace got it instead. You jump on a ship to New York to rub him out. Maybe you didn't mean to – who knows. Maybe you just saw red.'

Saw red. Appropriate. I get my connection and ask for a cop to be sent up here.

'I … I did travel in the hopes of meeting with Mr Wallace,' Peterson-Lee says. 'And I did telephone to his office earlier to make an appointment to see him. But I did *not* see him, and I most certainly did not kill him, nor did I steal the ruby. Apart from the auction in London, I have not seen it since it lay on my breast, the day I … left this world.' Well, ignoring the fact that she's clearly two bricks short of a pyramid to start with, the way her eyes keep being drawn to it, the hungry expression on her face – I can tell, that stone has one hell of a hold on her.

'How d'you think you'd get away with it?' I said, putting the phone down. 'I guess the English police treat you with kid gloves, being rich and all, but you're in New York now, that sort of thing don't fly over here. The cops'll be here soon, and you're gonna be lucky if you're not sleeping out on Riker's Island tonight. Won't be as sweet as this room, but at least you'll still get a private bathroom. Well, your own bucket, anyway.'

Harry and Phil and I wait for the cops to arrive. It's fair to say they're not happy with us for doing their job for them. Stern is not the word. Not that I mind a little bit of stern, under the right circumstances. I'm guessing Harry could be quite the disciplinarian if he put his mind to it.

We tell our tale. The cops are real interested in the ruby, not to mention the fur-coated dame at the Pink Tiger and Wallace's note of 'SPL', but their general position is that we should have told them of our suspicions and let them deal with it. We explain, eyes wide, that we didn't want to bother them with what was no more than a hunch, a mere guess that the police would not have wanted to act on. A cop takes charge of the ruby and the tub of face cream then Mrs Peterson-Lee gets led away, protesting her innocence and demanding to speak to the British Ambassador – but our grilling continues. On and on it goes, and in the end I agree they're right, it was a real dumb thing to do, and I'll never do anything like it again, promise, officers. I nudge Harry and he reluctantly says something along the same lines. So does Phil. He's not used to having to placate authority figures, I can tell, but sometimes it's the smartest move, even if it hurts your pride a bit.

Finally they let us go, although of course they've taken our names and told us we'll get called on again. Gee, can't wait.

No point in playing the rich bitch any more, so I let Harry and Phil ride down in the lift with me. 'Good stuff,' I tell him. 'Looking in that face cream – that was a real good call.'

'Yeah, well, working with Wallace – you pick up a few tips. You got the map?'

I produce it from its hiding place in my cleavage, although that wasn't the best place I could have chosen to stash it; a couple cops had been staring so hard I'd begun to think they had x-ray vision like that gink from the comic books. 'Back to my office?' I suggest. Harry and Phil agrees.

So back we go. Harry gets out the map and the letter we rescued from Badger Junior, and lays them both on the desk. Now we get down to the serious work.

Funny thing, I'd thought that once we had the map and the key, the rest would be a piece of cake. I'd not really considered we'd have a problem deciphering the code. Of course, I don't expect the letter to actually contain the key or nothing – but I have enough faith in my abilities to be pretty sure I'd work it out anyway.

Seems I overestimated myself a bit.

We pore over it until late. Harry suggests breaking to go pick up something to eat, or a drink at least. No way. No way am I gonna let this beat me. He can go if he wants, I tell him, Phil and I am going to make do with the flask from my pocket and a Baby Ruth candy bar I found in the desk drawer. Harry shrugs and decides to stick it out too.

Trouble is, as the night wears on, it starts to look more and more like I'm out of my depth. Out of my depth is not somewhere I like to be, and it ain't a place where I often end up. But I'm circling the drain right now.

In the end, I throw back my chair and admit defeat. Temporary defeat, anyway. Harry wants to go out on the town – together. I want to go straight to my bed – alone. I get my way. Sorry, Harry – under other circumstances, you know? Well, I know you know. I've seen you looking.

And I guess I've been doing a little bit of looking right back at you. But not tonight.

CHAPTER EIGHTEEN

EGYPT, 30 BCE

I laid aside the book, frowning at that chapter I'd just read.
   I had one question only.
   Who the hell was 'Phil'?

Chapter Nineteen

Egypt, 30 bce

The book that I'd written had no character called 'Phil' in it, anywhere. I flipped back to the start of the chapter and skimmed it again. This Phil didn't actually do anything. He'd just been inserted in randomly and rather inelegantly.

... with Harry and Phil hurrying after me like a well-trained secretary ...

It's even better when Harry and Phil then joins me on the fifth floor and I say, 'Took your time, didn't you?' as he gets his breath back ...

I let Harry and Phil ride down in the lift with me. 'Good stuff,' I tell him.

'Back to my office?' I suggest. Harry and Phil agrees.

He can go if he wants, I tell him, Phil and I am going to make do with the flask from my pocket ...

You see? Those lines were clearly talking about one person. Someone had added in an 'and Phil' or a 'Phil and' to all of them, without changing the grammar of the sentences to agree. I wasn't cross; for someone stuck 50 centuries or so before their own time, reluctant guardian of a potentially universe-destroying Device and dying of blood poisoning, syntax probably wasn't Ventrian's absolute number one priority.

Well, not too cross. I'd have them corrected for the second edition, I'm not a monster.

Of course, I'd expected to find some changes in the book. If Ventrian had left me clues, that's surely how he'd do it. But I was expecting something more along the lines of letters at the beginnings of lines spelling out words or perhaps some sort of code; even symbols such as those featured on the map in the book itself. Not a random character named Phil.

Perhaps Phil was a real person. Maybe Ventrian was telling me to find him. 'Phil' probably wasn't the most common name in Ancient Egypt, but there were about 600,000 people in Alexandria at this point in time, and no telephone directories.

I needed more information.

A large, sleek cat came and settled beside me on the bank. It obligingly raised its head so I could rub it under the chin, then rolled over to show its stomach. I felt gratified at its trust, and did not fall into the trap of rubbing its belly. At the back of my mind I seemed to remember that in Ancient Egypt, the punishment for killing a cat was death. Rubbing a cat's belly probably wouldn't bring quite such an extreme penalty – maybe tarring and feathering, or being pilloried – but better to avoid it all the same.

Holding the book in one hand and tickling behind the cat's ears with the other, I carried on searching for clues.

Chapter Twenty

New York, AD 1939

Late night follows late night, and we don't get nowhere.

Wallace's nightclub had been closed for a couple days while the cops investigated, but it was open again now. Turns out it had been in a bit of a muddle, finance wise, which no one had suspected. But Harry had jumped in to sort things, and it was quickly getting back on its feet – mainly cos everyone wanted to hang out at the 'murder club'. Nothing like a bit of homicide to raise a profile. Harry had got rid of the peroxide blondes and was going in for moody lighting and torch singers instead, and the place was raking it in. Clever man, Harry.

Clever *and* cute. Dear Santa, please remember I've been a very good girl this year.

Harry being busy, Phil and I've done a lot of sitting and staring at the documents all alone. I'm getting real sick of it, and it's denting my usually rock-solid self-confidence. I'm a detective! This should be easy for me!

'Trouble is,' Harry says one time he pops in, 'we're not in Egypt.'

'I don't see how that would help,' I say, because I don't.

He shrugs. 'Just a hunch. If we had the landscape in front of us, it might give us some clues. I've been there, two, three times, but that ain't the same thing.'

I'm not convinced. We need to crack a code, knowing there's a sand dune one way and a couple of pyramids the other way isn't going to help with that. Still, I guess, if all else fails … No, scratch that. No way can we afford the trip. At least *I* can't, and Harry and Phil had to confess to having empty pockets too.

The thought that cash might hold us back drains all my enthusiasm away. I'm not in the mood for yet another late night. Mind you, I'm not in the mood for an early night either. 'Let's get rid of the cobwebs,' I say to Harry and Phil. 'Fancy a dance? Anywhere but the Pink Tiger. I want to get away from all this.'

Now, Harry and I had shared a hell of a lot of lingering looks since we first met. Sometimes I'd swear you'd see steam coming out of my ears, the heat he was shooting at me. There was an unmistakable promise in his eyes, and a hint in mine that I might not be unreceptive. He's been angling for a night on the town every time he stops by. So to say I'm surprised when he shakes his head is an understatement. I'm the person who says no – no way am I the person who gets said no to.

There's a look in his eyes, though, a suppressed excitement. He's meeting someone else, maybe? I don't know how I feel about that. All he says, though, is that he has an idea. He'll tell me if it works out.

'Great,' I say. 'Well, *doesn't* that give me something to look forward to.'

He doesn't even spot the sarcasm. I get a peck on the cheek, and he heads off.

I sit at my desk for hours after he's gone, trying to figure things out. Trying to figure him out. Trying to figure *me* out. Do I want Harry? Or do I just want Harry to want me …?

It feels like my head has barely hit the pillow when some-one begins thumping at my door. I stagger out of bed, sweep up half a cup of cold coffee on the way, and pull it open. Guess I'm not looking at my best, which is reflected in the expressions of the people standing there.

Older guy, younger girl. Business suit on him, twin set on her plus hair up, glasses – you know, the whole 'Take a letter, Miss Jones' vibe as she scurries behind him.

'Yeah?' I manage to croak gruffly.

'You Melody Malone?'

I wave at the sign on the door. 'If I'm not I'm having a hell of a time with her man.'

The woman rolls her eyes in disapproval. Hey, I don't come to your place and drag you out of bed at the ungodly hour of – half past two in the afternoon. Oh. Well, I don't come to your place and drag you out of bed. Let's leave it at that.

'Come in,' I say.

They come in. I indicate the chair in front of the desk, and pull out another for the – look, I'm not going to straight away say 'secretary', jumping to conclusions, votes for women and all that – I'll just say lady.

I sit down on my side of the desk. 'What can I do for you?'

'Cuttling,' he says. 'Calvin Cuttling.'

I'm not sure what to reply. That don't seem like a proper sentence in actual English. Then I get a feeling I've heard the words before. Yeah, I have. Him and Mrs Peterson-Lee – they were the rival bidders for the ruby. Collector from

Chicago, that's him – and I'm not saying every Chicago businessman is in the Mob, but I'm thinking I need to be careful what I say. Thankful Harry took the goodies – by which I mean the map and the letter – away with him. Having what could be a clue to an incomparable historical discovery nearby can make a girl a bit on edge when an obsessed mobster comes calling.

Phil and I offer coffee – hot this time – but Cuttling shakes his head as though I'm offering him rat poison. I pour myself a cup anyway. 'And what can I do for you, Mr Cuttling?' I ask.

'I got a lot of eyes and ears down this way,' he says. 'Most every place, I've got them, ain't that right?' He looks at his female companion, who nods. 'And I'm hearing that you might have got eyes on something that I have a very particular interest in. A big interest, with money to match.'

He can only mean either the map or the letter. The thing is, though, no one should know about them. Harry and Phil and I haven't told a soul – or I haven't, at least.

'Not sure what you're getting at,' I say.

'Look, lady, I've spent the last 16 hours on a train from the windy city,' he says. 'Don't mess with me. Miss Jones?'

Holy moly, that was actually her name. 'Your secretary?' I ask innocently.

'Kinda. Read out that message.'

She pulls out a notepad and flips straight to a page, making a show of her efficiency. '"If you want to know how to find Cleopatra's tomb, go see Melody Malone, Floor 33, RCA Building, Manhattan. She's got something that'll lead you there."'

I stare at her. 'You … got that message? From who?'

'The gentleman didn't say,' Miss Jones replies.

'Who was he?'

'He didn't say.'

'Fat lot of use you are,' I mutter under my breath, then say in normal tones: 'What was this? A phone call?'

She nods.

This seems impossible.

Then there's another knock on the door. I hadn't locked it again, so I just call out, 'Come in'.

In comes Harry. 'Hey,' he says. 'You got our message, then, Mr Cuttling.'

Harry introduces himself to Cuttling and Miss Jones. Miss Jones suddenly becomes all kittenish. I roll my eyes.

'Could I see you in private for a moment?' I say to Harry, adding 'Do excuse me,' to the visitors.

Harry follows me into the back room with its sticks of furniture. It's not the way I'd expected him to enter the place where I keep a bed. Maybe that's why I find myself adopting a sort of nagging wife pose, arms folded in front of me and no smile at all.

'Well?' I say.

To his credit, he looks a bit ashamed. 'Yeah, I put my foot in it a bit.'

'Tell me about it.'

'Look, Malone, you know the bouncer at the Mastaba Club?'

'The one they call Silent Joe? Always on duty at the door, throws you out and don't say a word?'

He nods. 'Well, he's been talking.'

I laugh.

'Oh, I get it. I'm stupid.'

'Don't be so hard on yourself. I mean, *Silent* Joe? Who woulda guessed?'

'Thing is, cos he don't say a word ever, you kinda get to thinking he don't hear anything neither. I been having a few meetings, hinting I might have something big going on and might be looking for someone to bankroll it, and I guess I never thought about him being there.'

'Looks like you better pay a bit more attention next time, maybe.'

'But last night it hit me! Word is gonna get around, so we gotta be there ready! And we need someone who'll pony up. Cuttling's perfect. I just went for it, called that dumb Dora who works for him and made it a bit sorta mysterious so he gets intrigued. But I shoulda told you.'

'Finally caught on, have we? Yeah. We're partners now, right?'

'Yeah. And look – that Jones dame? Am I imagining it, or …?'

'No. You're not. You're not imagining it at all,' I say. It's pretty funny to see Harry look like a frightened rabbit at the thought of this dame going all gaga over him.

'Maybe this was a mistake,' he says.

I laugh. 'Oh, we'll find a way around it.'

We go back to the office. 'Sorry about that,' I say to Cuttling with my most winning smile (real gold-medal standard).

He doesn't smile back. I guess he's still a bit offended by the lack of warmth in my initial greeting.

'A slight misunderstanding,' I continue. 'All sorted now. So – shall we get down to business?'

I sit there and think it over while Harry sketches out the background. Where exactly were we right now? The ruby was still in police custody, as far as we knew, as was Mrs Susan Peterson-Lee. What exactly would happen to it in the end we weren't certain – I guess it would go up for auction again, with the proceeds going to Wallace's estate. That was the big deal, the ruby.

Some old map, some stupid letter? Harry and I had found both of them ourselves. Technically neither of us was in Wallace's employ at the moment of recovery, as he was dead (give or take a few minutes). Anyway, finders keepers is a thing. If we happen to stumble upon a meaning that has escaped everyone else, then wow, aren't we just amazingly lucky?

I kept telling myself that the last few weeks, and to be fair, I'd done a pretty good job of convincing myself. I can cope with skating along the edge of the law in a good cause, and my bank balance is a very good cause. But deep down I know we've skated right over that edge and are deep in dodgy territory.

Someone like Cuttling, though – yeah, he'd provide the money, Harry was right. And we'd be safe, because Cuttling's millions would make damn sure there was no comeback.

Heading off to Egypt with Harry would be something I could live with. I'm also keen on the whole 'track down Cleopatra's tomb, cash, fame and a damn big advertisement for Melody Malone Inc. in the papers' part of the thing.

OK. I guess I forgive him for jumping in without telling me.

Harry had brought the letter with him. Not the map, though. Enough to give Cuttling a taste of the goods on offer, not so much that he was getting a free sample before we'd done a deal. He was a businessman, he might not be happy about it but he understood.

'Never dreamt that British dame had stuff like that in her,' he comments, when Harry gets on to Peterson-Lee.

'Met her a few times. Crazy, of course. Real looney-tunes. But I never dreamt ... ' Then he clearly runs out of sympathy for murderer or victim. 'Right. All about the tomb. Now!'

Harry obliges. The story, as he tells it, has a ... *complex* relationship with the truth. He acquired the map in Egypt (true) and brought it back to the States (also true). Then we miss out a great big chunk regarding Wallace (there's a reason why courts insist on the *whole* truth) and pick it up again when the letter arrives as part of the lot along-side the ruby (true), how Wallace gave it to Harry as a reward for services rendered (now none of that is true at all. But we sure as heck aren't going to mention Badger Junior), how we spot it might be connected to the map (I guess that's in the ballpark around truth) and were going to show it to Wallace as we were trying to interest him in funding an expedition (nope), when – whoa! The guy gets a knife in the back! So would Cuttling be interested in the deal instead?

Cuttling starts firing out questions, of course – when, where, and most importantly, how much? Harry answers it all. Then comes the bit where he has to confess we ain't solved the cipher yet.

Cuttling sticks out a hand. Harry does this bit about, 'You're an honourable man, I know we can trust you with this,' and I'm guessing he's straying from the exact truth there yet again as he hands over the map and the letter.

We sit in silence as Cuttling stares at the papers.

'I can get my guys on this,' he says at last. 'I'll give you 20 large for them.'

Twenty thousand dollars! I barely scrape a thousand a year. Even split with Harry that'd pay my rent for a decade and make sure I didn't starve along the way. It was a pretty damn attractive offer.

Talking of pretty damn attractive, here's Harry.

And talking of Harry … whoa. Miss Jones *really* cannot take her eyes off him. He don't give her a second glance, but she is a puddle on the floor.

'That's not the deal,' Harry says. My vision of a non-hungry life with endless coffee on top pops like a soap bubble.

'So, I guess you need to tell me what the deal is, according to you,' said Cuttling.

'You send Melody and me over to Alexandria. You want someone to join us on your behalf, no problem.'

'I'd be happy to go!' Miss Jones leaps in.

Ahem! Miss Jones don't look like no explorer type. I'm guessing the main thing she wants to explore is Harry.

Harry does a sort of chin twitch of reluctant acknowledgement, then keeps on. 'I know the area where we need to be, and I can hire a team out there. We're close to cracking this thing, and we need to be on the spot. The ruby, the murders – they've all been stirring up interest. Someone's gonna jump our claim unless we're on the spot.'

And I don't know how he does it, but this unexpected meeting ends with a plan to take all four of us to go tomb-raiding. 'Look into those new flying boats,' Cuttling tells Miss Jones. 'Non-stop flight, that's what we want. No time to lose.'

Well, hold on to your hats, boys! Looks like Melody Malone's off to Egypt!

CHAPTER TWENTY-ONE

EGYPT, 30 BCE

The cat had curled up on my lap. Cats appeal to me. They answer to no one and go where they please, seeking company if they happen to desire it but remaining perfectly content with solitude. Not a bad way to live your life.

I wasn't planning to read *The Ruby's Curse* all the way to the end in one go, but after that part where we all get set to go to Egypt, I found myself hooked. Plus, I didn't want to disturb the cat. I read to the end and – I have to say – I put it down feeling fairly unsatisfied. Not so much as an author horrified at the mangling of her darling, but as someone hoping to find an answer which still eluded them.

Ventrian's denouement was different to my intended one and he'd not spotted all the clues I'd laid out for Melody to find, but none of that mattered. I knew I had to find the message he was sending me.

But nothing was leaping out at me at all. I rapidly flicked through the 160-odd pages again – still nothing.

Of course, a major part of the story is a cipher, and it was some sort of code or cryptogram I'd been hoping to find. Not that I had gone so far as to actually *create* a cipher – I mean, this is pulp fiction, no one's expecting to dig up a golden hare at the end of it. Alas, it seemed that Ventrian hadn't added one either. At least not obviously. But I kept going back to that strange verse at the beginning:

Beware the Ides – now Caesar's gone

The Eye's the only Rubicon.

If it wasn't a red herring, it must mean something. It would need to be solved.

But perhaps I needed more information?

While the story concerned itself with murders and jewels, and Melody's function in the plot was to uncover the killer, the ultimate goal, outside of plot constraints, was given as the discovery of Cleopatra's tomb. And here I was in Alexandria, place of Cleopatra's death, mere months after that death had taken place.

Her tomb had never been discovered – Ventrian and I had discussed that. I may even have mentioned my disinclination to use time travel to solve archaeological mysteries. But here I was, right place, right time. Surely, that had to be my goal?

I had to find Cleopatra's burial place.

I spent the rest of the morning canvassing locals. An approximate location should've been easy enough to find; Cleopatra may have been dethroned and the Ptolemy dynasty ended by Rome, but she would not have been laid to rest in secret. There were probably hundreds of workers around who had worked on building the tomb – I knew from ancient sources that Cleopatra had ordered its construction before her death.

What I learned made me convinced I was on the right path. Yes, the tomb had been built; it was unfinished at the time of her death, but the workers had been dismissed once the body had been interred and the project had been taken over by a newcomer, a man with skin as light as mine. It was clear to me that the man in question was Ventrian.

(Incidentally, none of the people I spoke to knew anyone called 'Phil'.)

The location I was pointed towards was a spot not too far from my current position in Alexandria. I knew that in reality my Vortex Manipulator would take me back to the New York office exactly at the moment I'd left it, however long it took me to track down the Eye of Horus Device, but the mind is incapable of regarding such things dispassionately – my parents were in danger, and my sense of urgency wouldn't submit to logic. I was consumed with the need to solve this riddle as soon as possible. I needed to go straightaway – perhaps I would find the Device and be home by sunset. (Alexandrian sunset or New York sunset – I wasn't picky.)

I moved along the bank of the Nile, looking for someone with transport to hire. The cat kept pace with me; she seemed to have adopted me as her new owner (although in Egyptian times, the cats tended to own their people). She was silver-grey with darker spots, and had what I believe is called 'the mark of the scarab' – a distinctive 'M' marking above her eyes. 'Well, I know what I'm going to call you then, don't I?' I told her. 'M is for Melody. Or maybe Malone. But don't think you're going to get anything out of this relationship other than some tickling under the chin. I don't have the time to provide you with a scratching post and we're a couple of millennia away from a tin of Whiskas.'

Enquiries quickly led me to a young man called Nebi who was willing to both transport and guide me to where I wanted to go for the very reasonable sum I negotiated (that included the fluttering of eyelashes and a *particularly* dazzling smile, if I do say so myself).

We set off on his boat and, although the heat and the insects made it not quite as perfect as it could be, the journey down the Nile and around Lake Mareotis was perfectly pleasant, and I also learned some very good Egyptian swear words whenever a cargo barge passed in the opposite direction and wanted us to get out of the way.

History can be unexpected. It wasn't that long since I'd been sitting in my cell, considering the matter of Cleopatra's tomb, thinking all I'd have to do was go back to 30 BCE to solve the mystery of its location. But here we were, actually in 30 BCE if my sums were right – in any case, not long after Cleopatra had died – and yet no one here and now could point me to where their late queen was laid to rest. I wondered at first if it was simply a reluctance to tell me, a stranger, a foreigner, but I really didn't think that was the case. They literally did not know.

We tethered the boat, and Nebi led the way. I stayed alert; I knew there were bandits in the less populated areas. Of course I could handle myself, but quite honestly I didn't want the bother, it was far too hot. All I wanted to do was locate the missing mausoleum, find the clue and / or clues within it, then head back to Alexandria for some lumpy beer and a bunch of grapes.

Of course, that didn't happen. I eventually called it a day and headed back home. Somewhat to my annoyance, Nebi had deserted me, but it wasn't hard to find someone going in my direction, and I returned to Alexandria in time to get a jug of claggy beer before bedtime.

Very much to my surprise, Cat Malone – or a cat that looked very much like her – had been waiting for me on the bank and now followed me back to the apartment. Ventrian had gone, and someone had a left a gift of bread and dried fish, which Cat Malone and I shared. I put coverings on the bed and she curled up in the crook of my knees and fell asleep.

The next day followed the same pattern, and the next and the next. I'd hire a guide, sail away down the Nile, search – and find nothing. It was frustrating, the feeling that I was *so close* to the answer – and yet still so far away. So many times I thought I was on the right track only to be disappointed and head home empty-handed yet again. My face hurt from being in the sun so much, and I was getting seriously fed up. Not to mention, my eyelash-and-smile currency seemed to be undergoing something akin to Henry VIII's Great Debasement: word seemed to have got around that I was expecting rather a lot for rather a little, and the locals appeared less than enthusiastic about transporting me and acting as guides. But the Nile simply teemed with boats, so I always found someone in the end.

On the fifth day, I waved off Cat Malone and set off as usual. Today my tour guide was Shenti, who conversed by shouting the length of the boat as he steered us down the Nile. He told me about his young daughter who had just started walking – 'I have to tie her leg to the mast so she does not fall overboard!' he explained. 'She keeps falling over and hurting herself – like you!' Well, yes, I may not have been entirely elegant in the way I climbed into the boat, but I thought that uncalled for. Still, I didn't want to alienate my latest escort so I said nothing, just laid back and tried to enjoy the ride, listening to story after story about Shenti's daughter.

By the time we arrived, I felt like I'd known little Imi and her mother Mereret for years. I don't, of course, know what it's like to grow up with a family like that. Oh, I don't dwell on it. It is what it is. But my childhood was spent with the Order of the Silence, being raised to kill, rather than messing about on boats, and yes – I did envy Imi just a very tiny bit.

Shenti and I began walking, him still chatting away merrily as we made our way to the area outside the city walls where he suspected the tomb may be. The hours passed, and still we searched.

And then – then … could it be? Could this be it at last?

The structure was promising, to say the least. A mausoleum fit for a queen? Perhaps. I needed to examine it more closely – I suspected we wouldn't know for sure until we got inside. Shenti was nervous, not wanting to bring the tomb-robber's curse upon him; he had, of course, Mereret and Imi waiting at home for him, and it would not be convenient to pass through the Duat just yet. While not going as far as to ridicule his beliefs regarding curses, I nevertheless attempted to reassure him. I might not have a wife and child back in Alexandria, but I wanted to get back to my cat, I told him.

'Ah, the cat,' he said. 'The cat that scratches you so badly! Perhaps the curse has already come upon you in the form of Bastet!'

The cat, I assured him, was no goddess, carried no curses, and had certainly never scratched me.

'Then what is it that has scratched you?' he asked. And he held out a hand and touched my cheek.

And suddenly I knew something was terribly wrong.

My face. There was something wrong with my face.

I ran my fingers over my cheeks. They stung – but it wasn't sunburn. It was something else. Something my mind had been shying away from, refusing to accept.

'A mirror!' I said. 'I need a mirror!'

I'd seen polished bronze discs for sale in the market, but as I hadn't bothered to get any kohl, I hadn't bothered to purchase one of those either. I regretted that now. I regretted it very much.

Shenti had no mirror. 'Water, then,' I tried. 'Still water.' He nodded, and pointed the way. I followed, imploring him to hurry. The fear was building inside me.

He led me to a still pool, and I knelt beside it and looked at my rippled reflection. Even distorted I could see what my conscious-ness had been trying to hide from me.

There were four deep scratches on my face.

I knew they weren't cat scratches. Someone's fingernails had raked down my cheek.

My fingernails.

I'd scratched myself, again and again, and I didn't remember doing it at all.

I realised that I'd been trying to get a message to myself.

I'd grown up with *them*, remember. I knew how they worked. Erasure of memory. Post-hypnotic suggestion, so you didn't even realise there were things you didn't remember. Perhaps only moments to leave some sign, to attempt, desperately, to communicate with your future self. Protecting one's face is automatic, lifting your hands to shield yourself comes naturally. Your hand raises – but instead of protecting, you dig in deep. The pain will alert you …

But they mess with your brain. They get it to hide the truth from itself.

Five days. Five times I'd sailed along the river. Could it be that five times I had actually found the tomb? And I realised, suddenly, the worst thing of all: five times I'd brought a guide – Shenti, Nebi, Oba, Djal, Seti. On the first four days, my guide had abandoned me to find my own way home.

But they hadn't abandoned me, had they? I had abandoned them. I had escaped, and they hadn't.

I turned away from the water and retched.

I'm no stranger to death, and I'd brought death to others before now – voluntarily or not. But the thought of little Imi, fatherless, and Mereret, waiting for a husband who never returned, whose fate she would never know …

Death follows me, I'd told Ventrian, and I hadn't been lying. But maybe I could outrun death, just this once.

'Back,' I said to Shenti when I'd pulled myself together. 'No further.'

'But, revered mistress, you wanted—'

'And now I want to go back. Back to Alexandria. Please, take me now. And I swear that when I can, I will give Imi so many gold bracelets and rings and necklaces that you will struggle to lift her!'

I didn't think I would forget what I had discovered here. I suspected that on previous days I had actually made it inside the tomb, and that is where it had happened. But I couldn't risk it. I couldn't risk bringing another Shenti here tomorrow, in all innocence leading yet another man to his death.

I hunted for something to write with, and found a blackened stick. Not the best tool, but better than nothing.

The Silence are distinctive-looking, having bulbous grey heads with dark, hollow eye sockets like a skull's. I drew little charcoal symbols – upside down pear-shapes with two black eyes – on my hands, my arms, my feet, anywhere I could fit one. They'd easily rub off, but it was the best I could do – they just had to last until I was able to create a more permanent reminder.

Shenti was wary of me the whole way back. I wondered what he'd tell Mereret and Imi about the crazy lady, and imagined it wouldn't be very flattering. But at least he'd lived to tell the tale.

I was back in Alexandria earlier than on previous days, for obvious reasons. Nevertheless, Cat Malone was sitting on the bank of the Nile, seemingly waiting for me, just as she had been on every day before. A meal of fish and fruit awaited us back in the apartment; she naturally preferring the first, while my tastes ran more to the latter.

But before I went back, I wanted to check something. There was something about the book, something that was at the back of my mind, something I'd read. An addition of Ventrian's perhaps? One subtle enough that it hadn't fully registered? I couldn't quite remember, I just felt now that I'd missed something significant. Of course, I couldn't remember where in the book it had been, and I skimmed through quite a few chapters before I got to the relevant one.

There it was. The mention of a character called 'Silent Joe'. I hadn't put that. No 'Silent Joe' in my book. And what was said about him: *Always on duty at the door, throws you out and don't say a word?* That was telling me about the Silence guarding the tomb. Why didn't I click earlier? It would have saved so much pain.

'I'm an idiot,' I said out loud. 'I am slow and stupid and utterly ashamed of myself.'

I turned back to the book.

'Don't be so hard on yourself. I mean, Silent Joe? Who woulda guessed?' Melody Malone sounded sarcastic.

'Sorry,' I muttered, feeling as if the book were telling me off.

'Looks like you better pay a bit more attention next time, maybe.' Melody was still on my case. It was funny, it felt a bit like I was …

'Am I having a conversation with a book?' I said.

'Finally caught on, have we? Yeah. We're partners now, right?'

I laughed at myself. The coincidence of a couple of lines – a couple of fairly generic lines, at that – and I'm behaving ridiculously. 'I'm just imagining it,' I said.

'No. You're not. You're not imagining it at all.'

'I refuse to have a conversation with a book!' I said aloud.

'Oh, we'll find a way around it,' said Book Melody.

Feeling doubly stupid now, I read on. Melody Malone had walked off into another scene, and said nothing more that could be interpreted as a message to myself in any way. This whole thing had been a ridiculous brain blip – oh, I still liked to bandy around the word 'psychopath' to describe myself, and my upbringing and training had cemented things in my psyche that would never be removed, but the run of dead guides had knocked me off balance. And while I never doubted I would succeed in the end and rescue my parents – Deff appeared to have overlooked the considerable hole in his plan for me to obtain an all-powerful object and hand it over to him, which was that at some point in this process *I would have an all-powerful object* – perhaps having the

threat to them hanging over me had caused an unusual, unchar-
acteristic, and frankly unwanted vulnerability.

'Right, sorted. Is this better?' said the cat.

The cat. Had Spoken. To me.

This was ridiculous. I looked at the cat. 'I'm not in the mood
for this,' I said.

'Oh,' said the cat. 'I was guessing you'd find it easier this way.
You said you wasn't enjoying talking to the book, right?'

'So you thought you'd talk to me via a cat instead?'

'Uh-huh.'

'Perhaps we should introduce ourselves. I'll start. I'm River
Song, and I'm a human being. Well, more or less. Bits of me are a
tad Time-Vortexy. Your turn.'

'OK. I'm Melody Malone, and I'm a private detective in Old
New York Town. Also, a cat. Well, more or less. There's part of me
that's a bit more artificial-intelligence-created-by-Ventrian-
using-the-Eye-of-Horus-Device-y.'

'Well, this is a turn-up for the books,' I said. 'Or turn-up for the
book, I should say. Couldn't you have popped up before now? I've
wasted enough time.'

'Not my fault. I had to wait until *you* started talking to *me*.
Look, Ventrian – he was an OK guy. But honestly? He was tying
himself up in knots. He's paranoid about anyone apart from you
getting access to the Eye of Horus thing so he puts in all these
complicated safeguards, which is fair enough. But we're talking
about someone who's getting weaker by the day, his head's not
functioning properly, he's trying to fight this all-powerful Device
that wants to take him over, and if that's not enough, he's working on his first novel.'

If you put it like that …

'So I can't expect anything useful from you? You can't tell me a
safe way into the tomb, for example?'

152

'No.'

'OK ... Can you tell me if I *need* to get into the tomb safely?'

'No.'

'No I don't, or no you can't?'

'No I can't.'

'There's nothing useful you can tell me at all?'

'You happen to be interested in how to make yourself look real large in front of anything threatening you or the etiquette of sniffing other cats' backsides?'

I smiled. I could feel the smile, the ends of my mouth pulling upwards into my cheeks. I pulled them up as far as they would go. I've never seen the smile myself, never bothered to practise it in the mirror, because I'd seen it reflected many times in the terror of the person or persons towards at whom I'd been directing it.

It didn't bother the cat one tiny jot. Oh, of course not. It was a cat. Also, it was a cat who was sort of me. So it knew my tricks.

I let my mouth relax back into a neutral expression. 'So what exactly is the point of you?'

The cat tried to shrug, but its anatomy wasn't entirely cooperative. 'Look, Ventrian couldn't give you any direct answers, I've explained that. So I can't point you in the right direction either. I know zilch.'

'So I ask again, what is the point of you?'

The cat leant on her side and scratched herself behind the ear. 'Life's better with an accomplice,' she said.

Oh. Oh yes. I'd said that to Ventrian once, although it seemed like a lifetime ago.

'Plus I'm a detective. That's gotta come in handy. I'll even give you a discount on fees, seeing as we's almost family.'

That made me laugh, genuinely. I could imagine Melody Malone saying that.

Well, she *had* just said it. What I meant was, I could imagine writing that for Melody Malone to say. Somehow this cat-AI hybrid really had taken on the personality of my fictional character.

'Do you accept payment in grey mullet?' I asked, remembering the meal that was waiting for us back at the apartment.

'Hot diggity, sure I do!' she said.

We returned to the apartment where I paid Cat Malone her fee in advance, then we talked through the situation together. I brought up the rhyme at the front of the book, the nonsensical *'Beware the Ides – now Caesar's gone, The Eye's the only Rubicon.'*

'Yeah, I ain't got no fancy history degrees,' said Cat Malone, 'but I done a lot of reading about the Cleopatra dame, so I know stuff about this guy Caesar too. Ides, right? You heard of the Ides of March?'

'Of course I've heard of the Ides of March,' I say. I wasn't about to be condescended to by a cat. 'The most famous example is the Ides of March in 44 BCE when Julius Caesar was assassinated.'

'And Rubicon?'

'The river between Italy and the province of Cisalpine Gaul, named for its red colour – red in Latin is *rubeus*, ya rube – caused by a bed of iron-rich clay. *Also* best known for its Julius Caesar connection: he refused to disband his army and crossed with it into Italy, breaking Roman law and inciting civil war. Look, this isn't helping.'

Malone purred and started washing herself. I waited impatiently. Eventually she finished, and said, 'You know Suetonius, right?'

'The historian? Not personally.'

'Geez, you time travellers take things so literally. Have you read him?'

'I have, yes. Not recently, though.'

'He's got this whole bit about a supernatural apparition popping up at the river. Could be a clue. Maybe Ventrian moseyed back a few years and left some answers there?'

I admit, I thought this was a bit far-fetched. Riddles tended to be a bit more, well, *riddly* than that. A bit more esoteric. Not just 'Here's a place, go visit'. But as Cat Malone had pointed out, Ventrian was pretty ill by the end.

'So I'd go to the Rubicon and – anything supernatural at the Ides of March?'

The cat stood up and stretched, arching her back, then sank back down again. 'Guess there was some soothsayer handing out cryptic riddles, if that counts.'

'Fair enough.'

Well, anything was better than sitting around, hoping to alight on an idea. At least I'd be doing something.

'I'd take you with me, but this only carries one,' I said, indicating the Vortex Manipulator.

'You gonna be back in time to feed me?' Cat Malone asked, adding an insistent little *mew* at the end.

'I have perfect time sense,' I told her. 'I'll be back before you know I've gone.' I grinned.

History awaited me – quite literally.

CHAPTER TWENTY-TWO

CISALPINE GAUL, 49 BCE

What comes to mind when you think about a trip to Northern Italy? Skiing in the Alps? Milan Fashion Week? Cheese and ham tasting in Parma? A trip through Venice by gondola? Any or all of these, of course.

A day out following Caesar and his chums around Cisalpine Gaul was not quite so picturesque, delicious or romantic.

First, Caesar had been to the theatre. Not so bad, you might think. But the show was no *Antony and Cleopatra* (or even *No Sex Please, We're British*); the audience threw things, and they didn't have usherettes handing out little tubs of ice cream in the interval. But I got through it.

Then he goes off to inspect a gladiatorial school. Now, that sounded rather more up my street, and I was prepared to cope with an afternoon watching some oiled gentlemen waving swords around. I might even have joined in. But it turned out the school hadn't actually been built yet, and Caesar's 'inspection' was merely checking some plans and a few solitary bricks. Gee, thanks, Julius.

At least the food was good at his next stop. I allowed the slaves to provide me with honey cakes while I was waiting to see what

Caesar would do next. And what did he do? He went to a bakery. A bakery! Come on, Caesar, you've just eaten, what do you need a bakery for? A few boxes of doughnuts for the troops, a dozen each of jelly, sprinkles, glazed and chocolate frosted?

As it turned out, no. I hadn't been hanging around outside for long when he comes back with a couple of mules and gets one of his soldiers to fix them up to a gig. Ah. Could this be it? Were we on our way at last? It seemed so.

Now, if Caesar and co. were secretly heading off to the Rubicon in the middle of the night, they were going to be on alert. Following them might not be the best move. As I knew where he was headed, getting ahead of them might be a better plan. I waited until the mule-drawn cart had moved away and went round to the back of the bakery. There was another mule in the stable yard, which I decided no one would mind me borrowing – I did scratch *Benigne!* on the wall with my sharpened nail file, though.

I set off by mule, and thanks to the coordinates provided by my Vortex Manipulator, I was able to ride all the way down to the Rubicon and find the exact spot where Caesar was due to cross.

An Italian river by night. How wonderfully romantic. Or it would have been if I'd had someone to share it with – or if it hadn't been January and close to zero degrees. My Egyptian sleeveless linen tunic was not ideal, and I wrapped the mule's saddle-blanket around me as I waited.

And waited.

And waited.

Good grief, how long does it take for a man, a mule and an army to walk a few miles to a fairly unimpressive waterway?

I waited some more. Eventually the sun began to rise, and still no Caesar. I was seriously hoping I hadn't got the wrong day, I was eager to get back to Alexandria.

As dawn broke, I wandered down to the river. I'd known it was named for its red colour, and as the sun rose it looked like a river of blood. How appropriate – there was so much bloodshed ahead.

Further down the bank some shepherds were tending their sheep. I plucked some reeds and occupied myself with making a reed pipe, playing a few tunes to pass the time. The shepherds crowded around, clearly fans of 'Jailhouse Rock' and 'Bohemian Rhapsody'. I'd moved on to 'Vogue' (with the moves, obvs), when the soldiers finally appeared.

They looked at us as though they couldn't believe their eyes. Well, I am a bit of a vision first thing in the morning. I could see Caesar standing amid his men, and I gave him a little wave, before striking a pose. Right. Here we were. The crossing of the Rubicon – and a clue for me. The supernatural apparition would appear any time now.

'We may still draw back – but once we cross, we must fight,' Caesar announced.

I waited. Nothing happened. Caesar just stood there. Maybe a bit of inspirational music would help. I launched into 'When The Saints Go Marching In', trad. arranged R. Song. A few of Caesar's trumpeters (for what is an army without trumpeters?) came down to join in and we jammed a bit. But quite honestly I was getting tired of this. All you have to do is cross the damn river, it's not difficult. Yes, you're heading to civil war, but could you just get on with it so I can meet this apparition?

Fed up, I called up the text of Suetonius on my Vortex Manipulator to check what should be happening.

As Caesar stood thus in hesitation, an apparition of superhuman size and beauty was seen sitting on the river bank, playing upon a reed pipe. A party of shepherds gathered around to listen and, when some of Caesar's men, including some of the trumpeters, broke ranks to do the same, the apparition snatched a trumpet from one of them, ran down to the river, sounded a loud advance, and crossed over. Upon this, Caesar exclaimed, 'Let us accept this omen from the gods, and follow where they beckon, for vengeance on our enemies. The die is cast.'

Ah. Oops. Mind you, while I'm not complaining about the superhuman beauty part, I happen to know I'm exactly the same height as Caesar himself. Tall, yes. But Suetonius makes me sound like some sort of attractive giraffe!

Oh well, best get on with making history. I grabbed a trumpet from one of the men, gave a loud *halloo*, and ran across the bridge.

Now Caesar seemed to get the idea. 'The die is cast, let us follow!' he went, more or less as Suetonius would later report, and across they all came, some on the bridge, some wading through the shallow red water.

Not the first time I've had hundreds of men chasing me. And just like those times, I thought it best to remove myself from the scene. I melted into the trees as the army swarmed – better to remain a godly vision under these circumstances; I was getting no answers here.

I waited until the 13th Legion had gone on their way towards history, filling my time with a bit of research – more Suetonius, Plutarch, Dio. Then I reprogrammed my Vortex Manipulator and left.

CHAPTER TWENTY-THREE

ROME, 44 BCE

A few seconds for me, five years for Caesar. For him, so much time had passed, and so many things had happened.

Caesar had won the civil war and been made dictator of Rome – although never king, a title Romans abhorred above all others. He'd tried his best to overcome that hatred and adopt the crown, but the feelings ran too deep, and he had to pretend he never meant it, like a child protesting 'It was only a joke!' when their unacceptable behaviour has been exposed.

Of most interest to me, Caesar had supported Cleopatra in a war against her brother, after which they had made a baby together, helpfully given the name 'Caesarion' to make it extremely clear who his daddy was. Caesar had brought the queen to Rome and put her up in one of his houses – goodness, that meant she'd be around here somewhere!

How Caesar's wife felt about his activities I didn't know. What I did know (Suetonius again) was that she was soon to wake from her sleep, terrified because she had seen in her dreams a stabbed Caesar dying in her arms. I suppose it makes a change from finding yourself in an exam you didn't study for or losing your teeth.

Having discovered that I was myself the supernatural apparition Caesar had encountered at the Rubicon, I took myself directly to the correct time and place – I did not want to take on the role of soothsayer, jumping out at Caesar halfway down the Appian Way with a cloak thrown over my head croaking out 'Beware the Ides of March!'

Time travel is a strange beast. Caesar's death is a fixed point in time, no one can change it, but here I am, jumping up and down his time stream. I find it helps to look on the people you meet as cartoon characters – whoops, an anvil's fallen on them, oh here they are back again! Caesar means nothing to me personally. And yet I felt slightly squeamish, knowing his death was coming. But it's all part of the time-travel game.

Had Caesar changed since I saw him last? Yes, he looked older – by more than those five years. Did he know his time would soon be at an end? I suspected not. As a high-profile Roman and soldier, death was always around the corner. You'd take precautions, yes, but mainly you just kept going and assumed it wouldn't happen to you – after all, the ego of someone in his position, someone who was pretty much trying to become king of the world, would be frankly enormous. Not to mention Caesar was due to head off on a great campaign a few days after the Ides, his attention would be focused on that.

I watched man after man (and they were all men, of course) walk through the pleasure gardens of Pompey's theatre, on their way to the place where history records the assassination occurs.

I'm not a person who naturally blends in, but on occasion I can be discreet. I followed the senators through the theatre (offering up thanks to the Roman gods that I didn't have to sit through another play) and managed to slip into the meeting house where hundreds of senators crowded, many unknowing that they were part of history – and yet even the assassins would find it hard to believe their names would still be known and their motivations still discussed for millennia to come.

The murder was almost an anti-climax. Breath held, when will it come? Oh, there it is. A man pretends to ask Caesar a question, and stabs him instead. Caesar hits back with all he has to hand, his pen. More people join in. It was a stupid, scrappy, playground scuffle that would have been ridiculous if there hadn't been a man fighting for his life. There were no noble speeches, no 'Et tu, Brute?' – I couldn't even tell which one *was* Brutus, the supposed leader of the coup. A few grunts, and Caesar lay on the floor. And the noble conspirators, risking all for Rome? They all ran away.

There would be riots. There would be more deaths. The course of history was changed for ever. All from this feeble little scrap.

And I was no nearer to solving Ventrian's riddle. There was no sign that Ventrian had been at either of these incidents himself – I'd looked for him – or that there was a connection to my mission in any way at all. I'd got to witness two significant historical events, which I supposed would mean I'd always have something to talk about at dinner parties, but they hadn't taken me a step nearer to finding the Eye of Horus or Cleopatra's tomb.

Cleopatra's tomb …

Cleopatra! Could that be why I was here?

I ran through the streets, trying to find someone who wasn't rioting and could tell me where to find the Egyptian queen. The house – property of Caesar – was on the banks of the Tiber, and I made my way there, pushing through the crowds. The further I got from the senate house, the less it seemed people knew *why* they were fighting, just that fighting seemed to be the order of the day.

Of course, no one wanted to let me in. 'I have to see the queen. It's very important,' I insisted, but I can hardly blame their reaction, which was to say a very firm no. They didn't know me, and the city was burning. But saying I didn't blame them didn't mean I would let it go.

I thought about Cleopatra and everything I knew about her, and … oh yes. Ding! Lightbulb moment.

I went back to the forum and took advantage of the uproar to help myself to some goods, and found a slave to assist me (no, I don't approve. But this was very literally 'when in Rome').

If I tell you that what I bought was a rather nice woollen rug, you can probably work out what my plan was.

So, there I was, feeling like a sack of potatoes as I bumped along over the slave's shoulder, trying to simultaneously breathe, in order to stay alive, and not breathe, in order to not choke on the mixed scents of wool, rotten fish, myrrh and goat that laced this delightful carpet.

The bumping stopped, and I could hear my courier explaining his business. Then we started up again. We were going in. The ruse had worked. Get ready …

Suddenly I was falling, rolling … I lay there for a second, then scrambled to my feet.

A dozen swords were pointing at me. But I was where I needed to be.

'Hello, your majesty,' I said to Cleopatra. 'We really need to have a chat …'

Cleopatra. Her beauty, like Helen of Troy's, caused tragedy in its wake. That's what history says.

Except it wasn't really beauty. It took only a few moments in her presence to realise she had something much more alluring than mere good looks. She was *somebody*. She had charisma, she had personality, and I would soon learn that she had a fierce, burning intelligence.

I once impersonated Cleopatra – which is another story, and one I would not mention to the queen – and had darkened my hair to do so. Strangely, I need not have done so. She had reddish curls, much like mine, although elsewhere we were no match: she was a head shorter than I was and, strangely for an Egyptian queen of Greek descent, had a Roman nose.

'So you use my own tricks against me,' she said.

'I'd rather say that I learned from the best,' I replied. 'And I had to see you. I bring terrible news.'

'There have been rumours.' She looked away briefly. To hide the pain in her eyes? Had she loved Caesar? He was 55 and she was 25, but I'm hardly one to talk about the age difference in a relationship. But it was only a fleeting moment. She looked unmoved as she said, 'I would hear your news.'

I told her what I had witnessed.

There was no outbreak of tears, no outpouring of emotion. No panic about how her fate may be tied to Caesar's. She was there and then a queen; her back straight, her eyes steely.

'You must leave,' I told her. 'You and your child. As Caesar's son, he will be in danger too.'

'He is the child of Caesar, but of foreign birth,' she said. 'He has no rights, even though Caesar acknowledged him. However, if a child of Caesar were conceived here, on Roman soil, that is the child who would be in danger.' And she placed a hand on her belly, and I knew what she was telling me. 'Now, let me treat those bruises you have procured in my service. For you did not study your lesson closely enough: when I did as you tried today, I ensured I was set down carefully.'

As slaves rubbed my knees and elbows with healing salve, Cleopatra began to ask questions of me – questions *about* me. I decided to be a traveller from Ostia, and was elaborating on my journey when the queen held up a hand to stop me.

'All lies,' she said. 'Do you think I have survived seven years as queen without being able to tell a lie from truth? Although I admit you tell your lies fluently and well.' She looked curious, rather than cross. 'I am an incarnation of Isis, the mother goddess herself. Are you too of the gods? For what I see in front of me is not a traitor who lies for his own gain, or for fear of punishment, but one who weaves herself covering after covering of lies, as a hermit crab inhabits shell after shell.'

Well, I suppose my darling Doctor *has* been known to call me crabby ...

'I'm not a goddess,' I said. 'But you can trust me.'

And she nodded, and said, 'Strangely, I believe I can.'

The life of an ancient queen is fraught with danger, and I think Cleopatra could sense I had had experiences beyond those of most people. Her world was barbaric and she had to fit into it – but so was mine, and so had I. The 55 centuries between us couldn't disguise that in many ways we were kindred spirits.

Saying we became friends would not be entirely accurate. A woman in her position could not have friends. In what sphere would she find them? Friends could not be made of those of lower status, but her peers were either rivals or allies, often oscillating between the two – and if sometimes you had to court favour with a new ally by sending them an old friend's head in a box, well then, that was just how things were. Your main aim was to be the beheader rather than the beheadee. Family bonds did not exist. If you were of royal blood, you had to climb to the top over the bodies of your parents and siblings. Not wanting power didn't make you safe, it just meant you were easier to clear out of the way.

I should say that In Cleopatra's case, there was an exception to the family rule: her son, Caesarion, or to give him his full name, Ptolemy Philopator Philometor Caesar. I knew that in the future Cleopatra would make Caesarion her co-ruler of Egypt, hoping

166

for him to become sole ruler when she contemplated fleeing the country, so he could continue the Ptolemaic dynasty. A lot of her hopes and dreams lay on the child's shoulders. And aside from all that, she loved him – not as the incarnation of the mother goddess, just as a mother. I saw it with my own eyes.

Caesarion wasn't yet three years old, and I played with him – sparring with wooden swords, moving little figures around on a pretend battleground, tossing knucklebones – while his mother made plans to flee Rome. My pragmatic approach to time travel took a beating once more, knowing that the little boy who called me 'Wivver' wouldn't make it to his 18th birthday.

When it was time to leave, I carried the child until we reached the ship that would take him and his mother back to Egypt, to Alexandria.

It was time for me to return to Alexandria too. My method of transport might not be pleasant, but it was better than several weeks of sea sickness. (Plus there was a *smell*. Really. Cleopatra was a bit of a fragrance fan and liked people to smell her coming – she was always preceded by a wave of myrrh and spice, and she'd come up with this idea of sousing her ship's sails in the perfume too. I'm not saying the scent was bad, I rather liked it as a matter of fact, but I wasn't sure I could spend a thousand miles feeling like I was stuck inside a floating Danish pastry. Of course, I do have a respiratory bypass system – something else I inherited from my unusual parentage – but holding my breath for that long felt like a lot of work.)

'Come with me,' the queen had said. 'I will give you a position in my household.'

'No,' I said. 'My work isn't finished yet.'

'I could make you come with me,' she said. 'Or have you killed for your refusal.'

'Yes,' I said. 'You could.'

She smiled. 'Goodbye, River. May the gods guide you truly.'

'And you,' I said.

The ship departed. The sea voyage would be rough, but I knew Cleopatra was happy to be going home again.

As I watched her sail away, I wanted nothing more than to go home again too.

Trouble is, I don't really have a home. I just have places where I live.

CHAPTER TWENTY-FOUR

EGYPT, 30 BCE

I was back in the latest of my temporary 'homes': Alexandria 30 BCE, and I wasn't talking to my cat.

OK, if you want to be pedantic, Cat Malone hadn't actually ordered me to return to those parts of Caesar's past, she hadn't guaranteed I'd find answers there. Fair enough, I'd agreed with her reasoning and made the decision myself. But I was annoyed at finding myself no further forward and it's easier to take that out on a fictional character in the body of an animal than on oneself.

Not that the cat cared a jot how I felt about her, provided that fish still magically appeared in front of her at times of her choosing, so in the end I just shrugged and stopped the sulk.

We debated the rhyme once again. *Beware the Ides.* The Ides were a set day in a month, the 15th in months of 31 days, the 13th in all others. But 'beware', alongside the mention of Caesar – it had to mean that one particular famous example. What did we have to 'beware' of? What danger? I thought about having another look through Suetonius, see if he said anything –

Oh! I thought of the archaic language of the historian, all 'thus' and 'upon' and so forth.

'Maybe it isn't "beware" – it's "be-ware". Meaning, *be aware of*. Be informed about. What information do we know about the Ides of March?'

'March 15th said Cat Malone. 'Three-fifteen. Maybe it's the numbers. A safe combination?'

'A three-number combination would be fairly feeble.'

'Add the year, then,' said Cat Malone. 'Three-fifteen-forty-four.'

'Except we're not exactly surrounded by combination locks in Ancient Egypt,' I pointed out. 'It has to be something that Ventrian had access to that he thought I'd have access to as well.' And then it hits me. The book! I pulled it out of my bag. 'Ventrian marked out the pages on his papyrus! This is why! Page three, line 15, word 44? No. No line's long enough to have 44 words. Page three, paragraph 15 word 44? Not enough paragraphs on the page. Page 315? No, there isn't one.' I thumped the table. 'Damn!'

'Geez, don't blow your wig,' said the cat.

'Why on earth did I make you put on that ridiculous cod accent ... ' I began.

'Ooooh, cod,' said Cat Malone.

'Wait,' I snapped. 'Maybe that's it. Melody Malone – speaks like a detective in Old New York Town! Don't you see? You're using American dating conventions. But when I told Ventrian about the Ides of March, I would have said the 15th of March – so it's one-five-three, not three-one-five!' I turned to page 153. Counted down to word 44.

The word was 'ruby'. Well, that didn't exactly tell me anything I didn't already ...

But as my finger rested on the word, it came to life. Shapes soared out of the page, a maelstrom of diagrams, equations, instructions. I was caught up in them, a living component, the figures pulling themselves together through me, then swooping off elsewhere; a constellation of numbers as bright as any stars.

The Eye of Horus Device was capable of unravelling reality. This showed a way to make it unravel itself. I thought of Ventrian, lying on his death bed. He was capable of *this* and yet his life had become an Ouroboros, a snake eating its own tail, working only to undo the harm he had himself caused.

The complexity and ingenuity of the solution astounded me. I knew I could never hope to remember it. But once I had the Eye of Horus, I could apply it.

I knew all these elaborate measures were in place so the Device would only be found by someone set on destroying it – me. But how many more twists and turns were ahead? How many more blind alleys would I stumble down?

Talking cats, secret signals in books, diabolic riddles.

The Eye's the only Rubicon.

Maybe that meant there was only one river left to cross: finding the Eye itself.

This time, I had to get into the tomb.

'Come on, Malone,' I said. 'We've got a Silent to sort out.'

CHAPTER TWENTY-FIVE

EGYPT, 30 BCE

'You cannot kill me,' said the Silent. 'You cannot pass me.'

I kept staring at it. It was using hypnosis to implant that idea in my head, but as long as I stayed alert in its presence, I was safe. And I'd come prepared.

I'd brought no gun with me into the past, no laser pistol or photon blaster. But the Ancient World was full of weapons, and we were mere months past the Battle of Alexandria. This monster couldn't hurt me as long as I kept my distance, there was no electricity for it to draw on here.

I looked the Silent in the eye, raised my bow, swivelled quickly to one side and shot an arrow straight at the wall.

'What the – ?'

The cat looked up at me and shook its head. 'You can't see them, but there are now four arrows stuck in the wall,' it said in my voice. 'I did try to tell you. It hypnotised you the first time you got in and you're not seeing or hearing anything else while you have a weapon pointed at it. Now back away carefully, and we'll go through it one more time.'

I retreated, not breaking eye contact until I was out of the corridor and backing up the stone steps. I sat down at the entrance, and looked at my quiver. 'I hope I get it first time,' I said. 'How stupid of me to only bring two arrows.'

'*Did* you only bring two arrows?' said Cat Malone.

I indicated them. 'One, two.'

The cat sighed. 'For the fourth time, at the bottom of these steps is a corridor. In the corridor is a Silent. You are suffering from induced amnesia and post-hypnotic suggestion, which means that every time you step into that corridor, you forget you've done it before, and every time you leave you forget you've done it again.'

I grimaced, but I didn't doubt that the cat was telling the truth. I was brought up around these things, I knew what they could do. Not being able to trust your own brain is hard; not being able to trust your senses is hard. That's why the Silence are so terrifying.

I sat deep in thought for a few moments. Then it came to me. How had I missed such an obvious solution? 'Of course!' I said. 'I can use the Vortex Manipulator. Tiny hops can be tricky, but if I – what?' That was to Cat Malone who was emitting a strange growly purr that seemed to be her version of laughter.

'"Tiny hops can be tricky, but if I can figure out the spatial coordinates to four decimal places",' she said, exactly as I would have said it.

The words 'How did you know what I was going to say?' started crossing my mind, but I'm not stupid, I realised the answer before I'd said any of it out loud. 'I've said that before?' I asked.

'Look at your left thigh,' Cat Malone told me. I lifted my tunic. A red patch. 'That's the bruise you got the first time the deflection field threw you out and you landed on that rock over there.' Her whiskers indicated the rock in question. 'You only tried it twice before you started to listen to me, or you'd probably be hobbling by now.'

Damn. 'I can't use the VM, I can't shoot the Silent. So I need a better plan this time,' I said.

'Ooh, let me think, that must be ... one, two, three ... the fourth time you've said that!' said Cat Malone. I don't mind her jeering a bit when I'm writing her, but it was a bit much when she started being sarcastic *to me*.

'Well, do you have any ideas?' I asked her.

'Actually, I do,' she said. 'And I've told it to you every single time. You just forget it as soon as you get inside that thing's orbit.'

I was thinking. 'You're saying that it's not coming up with an idea that's the problem, it's remembering it.'

'That is the case.'

'So I need to come up with an idea of how I can not-forget an idea.'

The cat purred. 'Well, this is new, at least. Maybe we're getting somewhere at last!'

'Does it affect you?'

'The Silent? No.'

'Why not?'

'What is there to affect? I'm a fictional character who lives in a book and is currently using a cat as a portal to your world. Good luck in hypnotising that!'

'Then that's something we can use. What else?'

'You have faster reactions than average.'

'How do you figure that out?'

The cat made an unhappy yowling sound. 'There's a pile of bodies on the floor, but you're not one of them.'

All that time in Stormcage had served me well after all. Dodging through its defences again and again had honed my reflexes.

Oh! Maybe there was the germ of an idea there ...

The first Stormcage defence, the disorientation. You had to turn off everything your senses were telling you and just charge through. Could that work here?

175

'As soon as I enter that corridor I see the Silent and forget everything that's gone before,' I said, working it out as I went. 'I can't see my true surroundings. I can't even hear you. But what if I cut out the Silent? What if I just charge through, eyes shut?'

'It would kill you. Every one of those bodies had its neck broken.'

'Then you need to be my eyes and ears,' I told her.

The cat sat on my shoulder, her claws digging in. I ignored the pain – it was part of the plan. With eyes closed and fingers in my ears, I took step after step downwards.

Two quick claw pinches. That meant two more steps to go. I didn't want to stumble at the bottom. One quick claw pinch. One more step and I was down. Now both sets of claws dug in hard. That meant the Silent had opened its mouth and was about to speak.

I pushed my fingers in harder, stopping my ears as best as I could while yelling out 'La la la can't hear you!' to better block out the sound. I strive for dignity always.

Left claws dug in. I veered left. Right claws dug in. I veered right. Both sets – I went forward. Both in deep – I stopped. I obeyed the cat's directions instantly.

A double deep dig. I ran.

Suddenly she pressed her right claws in even harder.

I tried to change course and stumbled over something on the ground. My hands reflexively went to break my fall. I was touching something cold. Something with hands...

'It's behind you!' Cat Malone shrieked. But my fingers had found something smooth and metallic. I grabbed it, ripped it from the dead hands that held it, turned and plunged upwards...

There was a hiss and a burning splatter of acid blood.

'Get up and run!' the cat commanded, digging her claws in hard to underscore the message.

I did.

'One more step … Stop!'

I stopped, and opened my eyes. I was at the very end of the corridor. Behind me I saw the Silent, curled up on the floor.

'I don't think it's dead,' said Cat Malone. 'Just injured. But I don't think it's strong enough to affect you right now.'

I looked past the creature. There were arrows sticking out of the walls: I counted four, just as Cat Malone had said. Then there were the bodies. At this distance I couldn't recognise them individually, but I knew who they were. Who they had been. Nebi. Oba. Djal. Seti. My first four guides, whose reflexes weren't as sharp as mine. My only comfort was knowing that Shenti wasn't among them.

But what was done was done. I looked ahead instead.

When Howard Carter peered inside Tutankhamun's tomb, the first things he saw were gilt couches, ritual beds carved in the shapes of animals that were to help the king to ascend to his rightful place in the afterlife. If I remembered correctly, there had been three couches: a cow, a leopard, and a hippo. Here there were four: all stylised but easily recognisable as a jackal, a falcon, a baboon and a crocodile, representations of gods or sacred animals. I was slightly surprised to find them at a burial of this period, but Cleopatra had won the hearts of many people by adopting Egyptian ways despite being of Greek lineage.

There were other items in the room. Linen wall hangings decorated the chamber. Weapons, food, clothing, all were piled up along the edges. I went to have a closer look.

The second my foot touched the floor, the floor turned black.

Scorpions! A sea of scorpions, swarming towards me. Crawling on top of each other, wave after wave, faster than an incoming tide.

I scrambled backwards, not quite in time. A single scorpion touched the toe of my sandal. By the time I'd lifted my foot off the floor, ten more were clinging on. I whipped off the shoe and thrashed it on the wall until all the arachnids had fallen away. I recognised them as pretty much the deadliest type of scorpion on the planet. Oh, of *course* they were.

All that had barely taken two seconds.

There was a further doorway ahead of us, at the opposite side of the room, but I had to cross the floor to reach it. Crossing the room would take more than two seconds.

But there was a solution. The holy sofa things! Yes, they were a fair distance from where I stood, but I had faith in my abilities. You're looking at the Leadworth School Hopscotch Champion 2003.

Cat Malone gripped my shoulder again as I prepared to jump. I stopped. 'Could you please try not to actually draw blood?' I said. 'There are already more holes in my shoulder than in a Swiss cheese.'

'And how exactly do you expect me to stay anchored without sticking my claws in?'

'Can't you just jump by yourself?' I said. 'You're a cat now. Cats can jump much further than humans.'

She gave a feline sniff. 'Very well.' She crouched, wiggling her backside until she was ready to spring. Then she propelled herself through the air, landing on the falcon-headed couch.

The couch gave way beneath her.

With a yowl, Cat Malone leaped, grabbing on to a wall covering with her claws and hanging there as the couch tumbled down into a huge black pit below, its existence hidden by reed mats.

'Are you all right?' I cried.

'This ain't gonna take my weight!' she shrieked.

I didn't know how to get to her! But she was right – already her claws were ripping through the linen, soon she'd be deposited on the floor. I didn't know if scorpion venom could harm fictional characters, but it could most certainly harm a cat. I'd got used to having the cat about, both the original, simple feline and the mouthy Melody-alike.

It went without saying that the scorpion venom could harm me. I did not want those things swarming over me, like the nanobots in Stormcage ...

Oh. How stupid I'd been!

The first obstacle: the Silent who disorientates you until you can't trust your brain or your instincts.

The second obstacle: a multitude of small creatures that overwhelm you ...

These weren't traps set by the Egyptians to foil grave robbers! These were traps set by Ventrian, using the Eye of Horus Device!

He had to protect it – but he needed me to find it. He'd put clues in my book, he'd created an obstacle course based on the Stormcage defences I'd told him about!

So how did that help? I ran over in my head all the things I'd told him. He'd found the idea of my self-inflating crocodile stepping stones hilarious ...

'Help!' Cat Malone slipped down another few inches. I didn't stop to think, I jumped for the crocodile couch, my breath held ...

It did not give way.

I leaned over, making a bridge from bed to wall with my body. Cat Malone twisted and landed on me, pulling half a wall covering with her. With some effort, I righted myself again. One more jump and we'd be through.

But I needed to think ahead now. What came next in Stormcage? The laser maze, of course. Funnily enough, I didn't have my specially crafted mirrors on me right now. But would there be lasers? Ventrian had thought the Device would be safest somewhere low-tech as there'd be nothing for it to co-opt for its purposes. That hadn't quite worked out. Somehow it had brought a Silent to Ancient Egypt, for one thing!

Or maybe not! Yes, that was it – I knew the Silence had been on Earth since the Stone Age. All the Eye had to do was bring one here! The scorpions were native to the desert – a locally sourced hazard; visit Egypt for all your horror needs!

I leaned over to a pile of weapons and picked up a boomerang. I'd seen people using them to kill birds along the Nile and I'd had a few goes – not to kill anything, just to see how it was done. I knew I could throw it straight and true.

'Get ready to duck, just in case,' I told Cat Malone, as I drew back my arm.

And – throw! It soared out of my hand, across the rest of the room, through the door, through the next room – and a whole host of spears flew out of the walls. A trap, triggered by movement. It might be primitive, but a metal spearhead would hurt just as much as a laser beam.

I threw another boomerang, and another. Every time, more spears whipped across the room. Like the laser maze, they came from all directions and at every angle. I had to find a way of deflecting them.

There was a shield up against the wall, and it looked like a good one. If I timed it right and went fast enough, I thought I could get through. I leaned over and picked it up. Yes, it was a good one. Strong, dense … and heavy.

Very heavy. The sort of heaviness that would really hinder someone if they were, for example, trying to jump from a crocodile-headed bed over a field of scorpions.

Could I throw it? Yes, but not far enough. If it landed on the floor, it would be overrun with scorpions in moments. Still, that might be my best hope.

I grabbed the linen that had come across with Cat Malone, and tore it into strips, which I used to tie round my legs and ankles, mummy-style, then I did the same to my hands. It wouldn't stop the scorpions stinging me, but it was at least a slight barrier.

Cat Malone went first, landing in the doorway easily. Then I tossed the shield. It fell far short, and as I'd feared, the scorpions came scurrying out to examine it.

There was no way I could take a run-up, so I leapt from a standing start. I almost made it – but not quite. I'd barely landed and the scorpions were already on me.

'Hurry!' Cat Malone shrieked, as if I'd fallen short just for fun. I could feel all the tiny feet scuttling up me and I threw myself forward in a less than graceful half roll, landing where Malone waited. My bandaged hands managed to brush the arachnids from my bandaged legs and the sea of them retreated, like the turn of the tide.

'You know the worst thing about this?' said Cat Malone. 'You might have to do it all again on the way out.'

'*We* might have to do it all again,' I corrected. 'And let's hope we do get out!'

What came next? Sticking to the Stormcage parallels, it would be the marble game. Some sort of entrance through which I would have to time –

The pendulum blade swung out of nowhere. I dived forward as Cat Malone leapt too, both of us shrieking like cats whose tails had been trodden on. I didn't have time to pause for a second before another blade came down too. In fact I didn't have time even to think. There was no planning, no calculation of angles or speed of descent, just pure adrenalin-filled momentum combined with subconscious prayer. I don't usually let people see my vulnerable side, so I was relieved there was only a cat there to witness how close I was to sobbing when I reached the end of the run.

I looked down at the cat, who had performed some superhuman – no, that would be super*feline* – gymnastics to get through. She was looking woefully at the tip of her tail, which was missing the very ends of its fur. It had been close for both of us.

I took a deep breath and got ready to –

Cat Malone *screeched*.

Another blade sliced through the air, timed perfectly to whoosh down just as the tomb raider had started to relax, which I say from first-hand experience. I managed to dive out of the way, but if I'd had a tail, it would have been clipped too. Once again I had to reluctantly bless my upbringing. Oh, being brought up as an assassin screws you up, I won't deny it, but by god it hones your reflexes.

This time I looked carefully all around before I started breathing again. It looked like the coast was clear. Nevertheless, I felt wary as I made my way forward.

My hope was that this would be the final obstacle. In Stormcage, once past the deadly doors the labyrinthine corridors were all that lay between you and your cell. There the danger was dying of hunger / thirst / old age amid its twists and turns, rather than being sliced up or stung to death. I still had the linen strips tied round my hands, so I fastened the end of one at the entrance and unwound as I went.

The further I went, the lower the ceilings became. An unfamiliar sense of claustrophobia assailed me as I first bent my head, then my back, and finally had to crawl on hands and knees. More than once I turned a corner and found myself facing a dead end, and had to fight off a fear that I'd suddenly find the way blocked behind me, cutting off my retreat. The fictitious disaster that had befallen George Badger Senior's expedition, the sudden rock fall that barred entrance to the tomb, swam in my mind. Ridiculous to be haunted by the product of my own imagination, one that I'd dreamed up in seconds and had covered in a single line of writing, but there it was. I was no stranger to a tomb, but rarely had one felt quite so tomblike as this nightmare structure.

I crawled onward, unravelling the bandage-like strips behind me. Unfortunately, I ran out of linen before I ran out of paths to try.

The only options were proceed anyway or retreat. Ha! 'Retreat' isn't in my vocabulary.

Unfortunately 'RECKLESS' is written there in red, mile-high capitals.

I forced myself down a dark alley, but when it forked ahead of me I paused, trying to decide what to do.

'Any ideas?' I asked Cat Malone, not expecting a helpful answer.

'Christmas,' said the cat.

'What?'

She snuffled slightly. 'It smells like Christmas. Mulled wine and incense.'

Oh. 'Cleopatra's perfume!' I said. 'Cinnamon, cardamom, myrrh – is that what you're smelling?'

Cat Malone went backwards and forwards a few times, sniffing the ground. 'Yes,' she said in the end.

I sniffed deeply myself. Yes, there was definitely a trace of spice in the air – although my nose wasn't capable of tracking it down. A cat's sense of smell is about 40 times stronger than a human's, however, so I had no reason to doubt Cat Malone's ability to smell us out a route.

Her nose stuck to the floor, she led the way. I tried not to think of my bones lying in this godforsaken spot, a place hidden for ever. Even the Doctor would never know what became of me.

We seemed to go on for miles – a not impossible construction for a people who had built the Pyramids and the Sphinx, but probably attributable to the power of Ventrian's Device. I began to fear that it had created an infinite maze to which there was no actual end. My only comfort was news from Cat Malone's nose – according to her, the scent was growing stronger.

I threw up a prayer of thanks to any deity that might be listening when we finally turned a corner and there was *space* ahead of us. Oh, the joys of being able to stand upright! The pleasure of throwing out my arms and spinning on the spot like a ballerina doll! I spent a good two minutes dancing around before realising quite how exhausted I was and collapsing on to a carved wooden chest.

Having recovered slightly, we pressed on. There were three chambers full of burial goods. One contained food for the deceased's journey through the underworld, and I decided Cleopatra's ghost wouldn't begrudge me a few dried fruits or a sip or two of wine. Cat Malone preferred some salted meat.

Finally we got to the main event. There in the chamber rested a sarcophagus, its death mask portraying a woman – there were enough similarities for me to assume it was Cleopatra, those red-coloured curls were uncommon in Egypt. There was an elaborate carving on the wall, too, that clearly depicted the Cleopatra I'd encountered, cradling a child that must be meant for Caesarion. Poor kid, with his life cut so cruelly short.

I knew from historical sources that there was a chance, if not a certainty, that Cleopatra had not been mummified – the process took many months and Octavian would have wanted her out of sight and out of mind as soon as possible. She may therefore have been simply interred, with Mark Antony's ashes by her side. For a moment I was tempted to remove the lid and solve the mystery, but I've seen the bodies of enough friends – oh, I know Cleopatra and I weren't friends as such, but I still found myself unwilling to see what death and time had done to the proud, powerful woman I'd briefly known.

Besides, there was something else in the room that caught my eye.

And the thing that caught my eye *was* an eye.

The Eye of Horus: the all-seeing eye, symbol of protection, sign of royalty. A carved and gilded image on the tomb wall, and in its centre, the pupil of the eye – a ruby. A ruby the size of a pigeon's egg.

The Eye of Horus ruby was my invention, of course. I'd had no reason whatsoever to assume the real tomb of Cleopatra held such a thing, therefore it was a reasonable assumption that this was no jewel. This was the thing I'd been searching for – the thing Ventrian had hidden for me, and no one else, to find.

The only thing that gave me pause was that from Ventrian's description I had expected it to have an enormous aura of power. There was … something … in the air, some emanation or vibration, enough that I was aware of an unearthly presence, just not as strong as one would expect of something that could tear the universe apart. Perhaps Ventrian had managed to dampen the emanations so attention wouldn't be drawn to this time and place.

The Eye's the only Rubicon.

The clue must surely relate to this moment. Did it mean that, like Caesar's river crossing, there was no way back, the action was irrevocable?

'I guess this is it,' I said to Cat Malone. 'This is why I'm here. "The Eye's the only Rubicon",' I murmured again. 'And this is the Eye.' I reached out a hand to the stone –

'Stop!' yelped the cat –

I touched the ruby –

Whirling, swirling through space, breath whipped from my body, turning inside out, stretched to the skies then twanged *back like an elastic band* –

Then a landing, the world coalescing around me into normality. I wasn't in the tomb any more, there was sunlight through the windows and the sound of water and birdsong and people …

I shook myself and staggered upright.

'River?' said a surprised – no, an *outraged* voice.

I hastily flung myself into a bow. 'Your majesty,' I said to the very definitely not dead Cleopatra.

CHAPTER TWENTY-SIX

EGYPT, 30 BCE

The queen looked older than when I last saw her, but no less strik-ing. Such are the blessings on women whose attraction comes from character rather than beauty. I didn't believe she had been raised from the dead, which meant touching the ruby had thrown me backwards in time. Cat Malone had not come with me.

We were in a room looking over the sea. Only Cleopatra and two other women – waiting women, whose names were Charmian and Iras – were present.

'You intrude on my solitude,' Cleopatra said coldly. It was as though she was unaware that I had materialised out of the air, and I assumed some slight hypnotic field had been in play. That was reinforced when she gave a small shake of her head, as if to assure herself she was seeing what she was seeing. She studied me for a few moments, then spoke again, more gently than before: 'Yes, it is you. Nowhere in all of Rome or Egypt have I met another whose hair is so like my own. Yet you have not changed, even after 14 years.'

I was momentarily surprised she knew to a moment when she had last seen me, but of course it was also the time when her lover had been murdered. That's the sort of date that sticks in your mind. And '14 years' told me I hadn't been flung back very far in time; I was still in 30BCE, just earlier.

'But it is,' I said. 'It is me.'

'I wondered then if there was something godly about you,' she said, 'and now I know it is so. I believe you to be a handmaiden of Anubis himself. For you came to me first on the day of Caesar's death, and now you come to me on mine.'

She gestured for me to sit beside her on her couch.

I knew many of the things that had happened to her since we were last together. I knew that she had not given birth to another child of Caesar's, but had gone on to have twins by her new lover, Mark Antony, then another son too, children who would be marched in chains through the streets of Rome after their parents' deaths, and only one of whom's fate would be known to history. I knew that Rome had declared war on her, and she and Antony had lost in battle against Octavian's troops, and lost badly. I knew that Antony had killed himself and that she was a prisoner of Octavian.

I knew that on a day in August, 30 BCE, about ten days after Antony's death, Cleopatra would die – most probably by poison, perhaps by her own hand – with her handmaidens dying along-side her. If legend was correct, an asp was smuggled in to her in a basket of figs, she caused it to bite her and died of its venom, leaving behind a note for Octavian.

'You are going to die, then?' I asked her.

'I am,' she replied. 'I will not be an exhibit in Octavian's triumph. I believe he will let my children live if I die, so die I will and must.'

Now, there are fixed points in time, as you know. Caesar's death we've already mentioned. You might think Cleopatra's comes under the same heading – it's a huge part of history, after all. The thing is, though, sometimes there's a difference between what happens and what we *think* has happened. Caesar was stabbed in public by many people who knew him. But Cleopatra died inside a locked and guarded room. What if she just disappeared? Escaped? Octavian might still announce her death, and who would know otherwise?

'I take it there are guards outside this room?'

'Many, and armed,' said Cleopatra's maid.

Well, that needn't cause too many problems. I could use my …

My thought trailed off into horror. I raised my wrist. No, I hadn't been mistaken.

I was no longer wearing my Vortex Manipulator.

For several moments, I stopped breathing. No, not my respiratory bypass system kicking in, just something close to … yes, I think it was actually *fear*.

I wondered how long Deff would wait for my return before killing my parents.

'Don't go dying yet,' I told Cleopatra. 'I need to think some things through.'

I got up and paced around the room. I was thinking back to the moment I touched the ruby. I remembered Cat Malone calling out 'Stop!' – oh, if only I'd been able to react in time! The cat had worked out, somehow, that the jewel was a trap, another of Ventrian's defensive flourishes, not the Eye of Horus at all. I realised that had I not already been acquainted with Cleopatra, things wouldn't have gone well for me. She might have been a prisoner, but there were a lot of armed guards around.

I remembered the world starting to spin. Yes, as I replayed it again and again in my head I had the impression of the Vortex Manipulator falling away from me, as if whatever swept me from the tomb had rejected it. It must be lying there still – or rather, as I had gone backwards in time, it *would be* lying there sometime in the future; about three weeks by my calculations. So all was not lost. I could still get it back.

But getting into the tomb a second time, especially without Cat Malone's help, would be unbelievably hard.

Except … Ventrian's defences wouldn't yet be in place! From my conversations with the locals when I first arrived, I knew that Ventrian didn't set up his tomb traps until Cleopatra's body had been placed inside. This was my window, my way to get in! Then I just had to wait for myself to arrive again.

But I also knew that the tomb *was* guarded even before that, because it was filled with riches. Guarded heavily. Just because they weren't tortuous or alien didn't mean the obstacles to getting inside weren't deadly.

And talking of which … 'Are you guarded?' I asked.

Cleopatra nodded. 'The doors are locked. Once a day food is brought to us, once a day our leavings – of all kinds – are removed.'

'And when do they bring food?'

'It will be soon.' She smiled sadly. 'But today as well as bringing food, they will be bringing my fate.'

'Asp in the figs?' I asked.

Her eyes nearly popped out of her head. 'I have indeed arranged for a viper to be brought in secretly to me, one that can kill swiftly.'

I waved a hand, dismissing my mind-reading power. Of course I magically knew about her *felo de se* plans – I was a handmaid of Osiris, after all.

Guards, guards, everywhere. And I had no Vortex Manipulator, no hallucinogenic lipstick, I'd even lost my sharpened nail file somewhere in Cisalpine Gaul.

There was very little time to come up with a plan before the man from Asps R Us arrived. While I sat and thought, Cleopatra began to talk. Unsurprisingly, one thing uppermost in her mind was the fate of her son, Caesarion.

I was only half-listening, my mind occupied with potential schemes. Then a word caught my ear. 'What was that?' I asked.

'I said that Caesarion was to go to the seaport of Berenice,' she said. 'He is to go to Ethiopia, then onwards to India.'

Berenice. It's the title of an Edgar Allan Poe story, the one about the girl who's buried alive. (Not that that narrows it down, Poe was always writing about people being buried alive.)

Oh!

People being buried ... alive!

I was being allowed a do-over! From here, this place and this point in time, there was a way I could get back into the tomb! And perhaps I could achieve even more than that ...

I went and knelt down at Cleopatra's feet. 'Your majesty,' I said. 'You have been a queen all your life, and now you are ready to die. But answer me this truthfully. Would you be prepared to live instead? Not as a prisoner paraded in chains by Octavian – but not as a queen either. Just as a free woman. I can't promise it would be a life of riches, but you might find that freedom is better than any treasure.'

It took her a long time to answer me. A million thoughts, a thousand different scenarios, must have passed through her mind. In the end, though, she answered me: 'Yes.' Nothing else was needed.

I explained my plan to the three women. I knew it sounded bizarre, and wasn't without risk. But they seemed to have decided to trust me.

I was hiding underneath the couch as the door opened (an extra inhabitant might just have aroused the tiniest bit of suspicion). In was brought food and drink – including the promised basket of figs. Cleopatra had written her letter and handed it over, to be taken to Octavian.

'Why are you veiled, my lady?' a guard enquired.

'You dare to question me?' replied the queen. 'I am the goddess Isis. You know of the veil of Isis? No mortal may lift it.' Another tidbit from ancient literature, Plutarch this time. That visit to Rome had been useful after all – I'd learned of Cleopatra's identification with the goddess *and* caught up on my reading. And I was also now acutely aware of the power of curses in the Ancient world. That, with my own unique biology, added up to a near perfect plan.

As soon as the door had shut again, I came out and we staged our scene.

Neither Charmian nor Iras had a respiratory bypass system, obviously. But I was able to teach them some Venusian breathing techniques that would achieve a similar effect, even if only for a few minutes.

When the door was opened again, to collect the dishes, this was the sight that met all eyes: two handmaidens lying on the floor, and a woman prostrate across the couch, clothed in rich garments and jewels, red-gold curls hanging down, a heavy veil obscuring her face that no mortal could dare to lift, doused in strong perfume. *Obviously*, it was Cleopatra's body. Who could suspect an impostor?

Guards rushed in, checking for signs of life. There were none.

I heard the ladies-in-waiting being carried out. Dead bodies need no guards; if they kept up my Venusian techniques, they would be able to escape as soon as they were alone.

The body of 'Cleopatra' was taken too. The guards did not lock the room behind them. So the real Cleopatra, hidden beneath the couch, would soon be able to make her escape.

Cleopatra had requested in her letter to Octavian for her body not to be embalmed, but instead taken immediately to the tomb already prepared, where it would rest for ever alongside the ashes on Antony.

This was where my plan became only *nearly* perfect.

Conscious and aware, but unable to move, I hoped desperately that her wishes would be carried out. I really didn't want my brains to be pulled out through my nose while I was still alive. It would be awfully inconvenient.

People fussed all around; each new person increased the risk of discovery. Would someone notice Cleopatra had gained height? Would someone defy the gods and raise the veil?

But finally came a time of quiet. Finally I felt it was safe to come alive.

I opened my eyes – to total darkness.

I started to breathe again – but the air was thin and musty.

I tried to push back the veil. There was barely room for my arms to move.

I was back inside Cleopatra's tomb, just as I'd wanted to be.

But I was trapped inside her coffin.

CHAPTER TWENTY-SEVEN

EGYPT, 30 BCE

My limbs were stiff and weak from pretending to be a corpse. But eventually I regained enough strength to push aside the coffin lid. The air of the tomb was muggy, but heaven in comparison to the sarcophagal stink.

I was filled with triumph. Against all odds, my plan had succeeded! I *ruled*!

That euphoria lasted for, ooh, ten minutes?

And then I got a bit bored.

I like action.

Not just 'action movie' type action, narrow escapes and high kicks and karate chops. Sharing a quiet, still, endless night under the stars with one you loved – that counted too. Moments when you are fully *being*.

Hanging around in a tomb for weeks does not count.

I had harboured the tiniest secret hope that somehow I would get to communicate with Ventrian and cut out this whole sorry mess, paradoxes be damned. If the way to access the Eye of Horus Device was in this tomb, and I was in this tomb, surely our paths must cross?

This was not the case. When I 'awoke', things were already as I would find them weeks later. The Eye of Horus was carved on the wall, the deceptive ruby at its centre (I stayed very clear of it), the traps and protections were in place. Oh, how tempting it was to leave myself a message. DON'T TOUCH THE RUBY, IDIOT WOMAN, for example. But despite my defiant words, I knew I couldn't really risk a paradox.

The grave goods ensured I didn't go hungry or thirsty, that was something at least. And I got in a lot of reading – for example, the *Complete Works of Edgar Allan Poe*, which turned out to be a very slim volume when you removed all the 'buried alive' stories (way too soon).

I had no external way of telling whether it was day or night, but my innate time sense kept me centred and enabled me to keep track of the passing days. Finally I knew the day had come.

I didn't want to spend longer in the sarcophagus than I had to. It wasn't just the buried alive thing, they don't have any of those satin-lined padded affairs that vampires go in for back in Ancient Egypt so it really does your back in, and I'm not getting any younger, you know. Well, actually that's not entirely true, I had a little fun with my DNA when I regenerated, but the point stands. That sarcophagus could really do with a memory-foam mattress.

I was just having a snack of dried meat – reminding myself to leave enough for the cat to chomp on – when I heard myself kicking off my Sunday shoes in an anteroom. OK, we're on!

I climbed inside the sarcophagus and with some difficulty pulled the lid into place above me. The temptation to tell myself not to touch that ruby was immense, but ripping all of time and space apart was probably something to avoid. Once entombed, I couldn't hear what was happening outside, so I again had to rely on my time sense to know when it was safe to emerge. I'm not denying I would *love* to see my face if I jumped out of a coffin in front of myself, but again, ripping all of time and space apart, bad idea.

At last I judged it was time to rise from the dead. As I started to ease aside the sarcophagus lid, I heard a familiar voice calling, 'River! River! Where you gone?'

Well, I couldn't prank my actual self, but this was almost as good. 'I'm here …' I drawled in my best zombie impression, and Cat Malone screeched and was out of the door before I'd even finished speaking.

She trotted back in a few moments later, mumbling something about cat reflexes and not actually being scared. I rubbed her under the chin to apologise, then with great relief retrieved the Vortex Manipulator from the floor, where it lay alongside my bundle containing *The Ruby's Curse*, and fastened it tightly around my wrist.

It didn't take long to tell Cat Malone what had happened to me, but I had one big question for her. 'Why did you try to stop me touching the ruby? Did you know what was going to happen?'

Her cat head shook from side to side. 'No. But I suddenly thought of the clue of the rhyme, and what it might mean. We'd solved the mention of the Ides – but not the Rubicon.'

'I guess it's just a reference to me – a famous River.'

'No,' said Malone when I told her that. 'That's a coincidence – well, I guess an extra layer, rather. See, I'm thinking it's a separate riddle in itself.'

'And you think you've solved it?' How did that work? How could someone I had created solve a mystery before I could?

'Say it aloud,' she told me. 'See if you spot it too.'

'The Eye's the only Rubicon,' I recited. 'That's the eye …' I pointed to the wall. 'The eye is the ruby.'

'Try again,' she said.

'The Eye's the only …' I trailed off. 'Not Rubicon. Ruby – con!'

Only the Cheshire Cat can grin, but Cat Malone gave it her best attempt.

'Oh, that's good!' I said. 'That fits! What a lovely piece of misdirection. Of course, the ruby doesn't help at all, it's just the product of a paranoid delusional mind. We're right back where we started with no idea how to get the Eye of Horus.'

'But even with the con ruby, Ventrian made sure there was a way straight back here for you,' said Cat Malone. 'The real deal *has* to be here somewhere ...'

I slumped down on the sarcophagus. The carving of Cleopatra with baby Caesarion seemed to look down pityingly upon me. I wondered where the real queen was now. Had she safely left Egypt? I remembered that although Caesarion had been supposed dead, no one had ever seen his body. Perhaps I'd choose to believe that Cleopatra found her son and they headed off to an inconspicuous, but safe, life together ...

Cleopatra's son, Caesarion.

Cleopatra – the embodiment of Isis, the mother goddess.

Isis – the mother of *Horus*.

Horus – the *son of Isis*.

I didn't stop to think it through, I didn't want to talk myself out of the conclusion. I leaped up and put my hand on the baby's carved eye ...

CHAPTER TWENTY-EIGHT

SOMEWHERE OVER THE ATLANTIC OCEAN, AD 1939

I opened my eyes. I was staring straight up at a slightly curved surface barely a foot above me. My first thought was that I was back in a sarcophagus. My second thought was that at least it was a very *comfortable* sarcophagus. Someone had got my memo about memory-foam.

A knocking sound. Someone at a door? Yes. That's what had woken me. At which point I realised I must have been asleep. I was in a bed … no, a bunk. That's why I was so high up. It was a comfortable if narrow bunk, and I was no longer wearing linen but something sleek and silky – scarlet satin pyjamas.

A voice called out, 'Come on in!' My voice. No, *not* my voice. I hadn't spoken.

A door opened. 'Breakfast, madam.' A man in a suit stood there. Servant? Steward?

'Oh thank the good lord above. I'm hungrier than a dozen horses.' I was looking down. A pair of legs swung out of the lower bunk, sheathed in scarlet satin just like mine were. A head of red-gold curls poked out too, then a woman stood up to take the tray from the steward.

She turned to look at me. 'Toast?' said Melody Malone.

We both perched on the bottom bunk and ate toast. Every time I raised my hand to take a bite, she did too. It was disconcerting, perhaps more so because it wasn't like looking in a mirror as we were both right-handed.

I knew now where I was. I was on a flying boat, somewhere over the Atlantic Ocean.

Well, that's where I *appeared* to be. Where I actually was, was inside my own book, *The Ruby's Curse*.

But, you're perhaps thinking, you talked to Melody Malone via a cat in the real world so this isn't very different.

Yes it is! Because that was merely weird, whereas this is impossible.

I could not physically be in an actual book, of course. So where was this? Some strange little pocket universe? An offshoot of the Land of Fiction? That was my best guess. How I was here was a mystery, but a more pressing question was:

'Why am I here?' I said – to myself, but out loud.

'Cos I asked you, stupid!' She shrugged. 'Kinda weird I didn't think of asking you before. My sister being the bigshot bone-digger and all – shoulda had you come in on this ages ago. You just –' she looked a bit puzzled – 'just kinda slipped my mind for a minute.'

'Well, I'm here now,' I said, deciding I'd best not unravel the entire causal nexus. If I went all-out to convince her that I *wasn't* her sister, who knew what might happen?

I just wished I hadn't given her that ridiculous cod gangster accent. It had seemed a good idea at the time.

'Do you remember being in my world?' I asked her.

She frowned, raising a silver cloche to reveal a dish of kippers below. 'What sorta idiot orders fish for breakfast? What on earth was I thinking?' she said, picking up one of the flat fish and beginning to gnaw on it, before seeming to realise what she was doing and putting it down again. 'Ugh. I don't know what the hell's wrong with me this morning.'

I guessed that meant she didn't remember – consciously, at least.

'Tell me who else is here,' I said.

'Well, there's Harry, of course. I told you about him. Real hunk of beef, he is. Mm-mm.' She shot a look at me. 'Got a bit happy when he heard I had a twin, Harry did.'

Oh, I don't think so, Harry. 'Who else?' I said.

'Calvin Cuttling. You heard of him? Rich as Rockefeller, they say. Got his secretary with him, chick called Jones. Looks like someone's wafting kippers under her nose the whole time and she can't bear the stink.' Melody waved a kipper herself to demonstrate, taking a couple of bites out of it before catching herself and putting it down on the plate again. 'Then there's the Peterson-Lee dame.'

I frowned. Mrs Peterson-Lee? Had she been in on the flying boat denouement in my plan? I hadn't got that far before I'd had to flee Stormcage. Where had I left her? Released by the cops for lack of evidence? But then Ventrian had changed things a bit. I remember he'd had the ruby disappear again, and then …

And then …?

'Melody, what are you doing?'

She looked down and seemed surprised to see she'd poured the entire jug of cream into her saucer. 'Sorry,' she said. She looked as puzzled as I did. 'I was doing it for … Hey, I don't have a cat, do I?'

'Not as far as I know,' I said – but I realised I wasn't sure. I was getting a headache. I *never* get headaches. Maybe it was the altitude. I guess it was affecting my sister too; I'd never seen her do weird things like that before, and (obviously) I'd known her her whole life.

'Sorry. You want coffee?'

'I'll do it.' I picked up the coffeepot and filled my cup.

Melody put her head down and started to lap at her saucer. Then her head shot up, milk dripping off her chin, and she grimaced. She took out a handkerchief and wiped her mouth and chin. Neither of us said anything.

I pushed my cup away. I wasn't in the mood for black coffee, and the milk was a bit too ... *licked* for me.

'Is that everyone?' I asked, trying to ignore the elephant in the room of my sister's table manners. I would keep blaming the altitude.

'Well, Phil's here, of course. Like I'd go anywhere without the Kid!'

Phil. Of course, Phil 'the Kid', my sister's invaluable protégé slash dogsbody. I used to tease her about him, the little puppy dog that followed her everywhere and –

I shook my head, trying to clear it. No. I *didn't* know Phil. I hadn't even *created* Phil. I'd never teased Melody about him; I'd never even interacted with Melody pre-cat. I was River Song, and I was *real*. I had to remember that. I'd play along with this scenario, yes, but I mustn't become part of it.

'Let's get dressed, then we'll go and see everyone,' said Melody.

There was a wardrobe, hung with two sets of identical clothes. I splashed my face with cold water at the washstand, then changed into a navy-blue buttoned dress with sailor collar. I wasn't that surprised when I looked over to the other side of the room and saw Melody buttoning up exactly the same dress.

We left our cabin together and went to the lounge. As a flying boat, the craft was more like a cruise ship than an aeroplane and the lounge had comfortable armchairs in two rows, one either side of the room, facing each other.

Harry looked up and smiled when he saw me. Then he looked from me to Melody, and his eyes widened – as did his grin. He stood and gave us both a quick bow. 'Now I get it! I know why you smuggled your sister on board last night!' he said to me. 'You realised there's no way I could sleep knowing there were two such dolls nearby!'

I smiled back, although I was somewhat disappointed in Harry. He was superficially good-looking, as per the physical description in the book, but rather than being charming he actually came across as slightly smarmy. All surface. I obviously wasn't as good at creating characters as I'd thought. But I indicated my double and said, 'I think you're talking to Melody.'

'Let me introduce you to everyone,' Melody said, taking my arm and leading me away from the leering Harry. 'My sister, River. This is Mr Cuttling – Miss Jones – Mrs Peterson-Lee.'

I murmured all my 'pleased-to-meet-you's and sat down in an armchair facing Miss Jones. Melody sat next to me, facing Harry. Cuttling was reading a newspaper which had headlines including 'FRANCE ENDS PUBLIC EXECUTIONS' and 'CHURCHILL TO HITLER: IT'S NOT TOO LATE TO CHANGE COURSE'. Always handy to have a newspaper to subtly set the historical context.

'If you're twins – why do you have different accents?' Mrs Peterson-Lee (of Esher) asked me. Oh, good question.

'Split up at birth,' Melody said. 'I went to New York with Dad –'

'– and I was found in a handbag at London Waterloo,' I completed. 'We tracked each other down later on.'

Well, that invention did at least give us all something to talk about. Not that I felt like talking. I was getting another headache. Oh, you'd have got one too if you had to listen to these boring people. They were *very* dull, falling immediately into silence as soon as Melody or I turned our attention elsewhere. I still didn't understand what my sister saw in Harry. She usually had pretty good taste in men.

No no no.

Melody Malone is not my sister. She is my *character*.

So is Harry.

So are all of them. They stop talking when they're not part of the plot.

I mustn't forget who I am: I am River Song, I am *real*!

A woman's scream rent the air, followed by a shout of 'Miss Malone!' in a boy's voice.

Melody and I jumped up and ran towards the noise, the others slightly behind us.

'In here!' The shout had come from a youth who wore a jacket and trousers that were slightly too big for him and a newsboy cap on what looked like a shaved head. He was indicating the cabin Melody and I had left not that long before.

'Phil! What is it?' Melody demanded.

The youth stepped back to let us see for ourselves.

A maid in cap and apron was kneeling on the floor beside the steward who'd brought us breakfast. He was lying there, his mouth a rictus, foam spewing down his chin. It was clear he was dead and had died quickly and very probably painfully. Coffee spread out around him from a broken cup.

Both Mrs Peterson-Lee and Miss Jones looked like they were going to faint. Cuttling looked more annoyed than anything.

I picked up the coffeepot, still half full, and sniffed. 'Poison,' I said. I looked at Melody. 'Lucky you fancied milk this morning. This poor man must have had some of what we left.'

'You should have a food taster, Miss Malone,' said Phil. 'My mother and father both had one, and thought them invaluable.'

Funny household the kid must have grown up in, I thought, but all I said was, 'Why would someone want one of us dead? And is it one of us – or both of us?'

'I don't know,' Melody replied.

Harry and Cuttling lifted the body onto the lower bunk and covered it with a sheet. 'You'd better move to another cabin,' Harry told us. 'Hey, point us in the direction of an empty room,' he said to the maid, who had managed to stand up but was still hyperventilating.

'I ... I don't think there are any more,' she gasped.

Harry raised an eyebrow and looked at Melody and me. 'Guess you'd better move into mine,' he said. 'Both of you.'

Miss Jones gave an indignant squeak. Peterson-Lee looked outraged.

'I would move in with Cuttling, of course,' said Harry, all butter wouldn't melt.

'Oh, we'll worry about all that later,' said Melody. 'I think I could do with a drink. *Not* coffee,' she added.

Mrs Peterson-Lee went to lie down, to recover from the shock, but the rest of us trooped back to the lounge area, and another maid brought us an (unopened) bottle of brandy. I refused a glass. I had no idea if fictional alcohol could dull one's faculties but why risk it? Especially as the shock seemed to have brought me back to my senses; I was thinking more clearly now – and I needed to stay that way. This world was clearly able to exert some sort of control over me, pulling me into its narrative. I couldn't afford to lose myself like that again.

Ventrian had sent me here, I was certain of that. All his strange and cautious clues had led to this. And I guessed the tortuous route wasn't merely down to a tortured soul. This was his last, best and only shot at ridding creation of the Device for good, if the route to it was too obvious, the Device would know. It would grasp what was happening and seek to stop events. So now, having come so far along this harrowing route, I was more determined than ever to quite literally finish the tale. Ventrian's purpose had become my all-consuming goal: to find and destroy the Device; or rather, its avatar, the Eye of Horus.

So what was supposed to happen now?

Beware the Ides – now Caesar's gone
The Eye's the only Rubicon.

The rhyme had got me this far, but I had a feeling there was more meaning I needed to squeeze out of it.*

Were there further clues here, inside the book? Would I find instructions written on a wall somewhere? Did I need to go up to, say, Mrs Peterson-Lee and whisper something like, 'The blue duck flies west for the winter,' and she'd reach into her handbag and pass over a sheaf of secret documents?

No. None of that really fitted. I had to assume that if I were in a 'book', what I had to do was connected with the book in some way. We were, after all, close to the end of the story, which was presumably significant. What had happened in Ventrian's final few chapters?

I ... couldn't remember.

But I'd read them. I'd definitely read them. I couldn't remember the detail, but I could remember my own sensations. Ventrian had changed my ending – my intended ending, I should say – and I remembered feeling slightly superior that he hadn't figured out the clues I'd laid, then wondered if his solution was actually better than mine. Perhaps I should have made the murderer ...

Hold on – who *had* he made the murderer?

My brain couldn't go there. Not exactly as though there was a barrier in my mind – more that, well, that the information just wasn't there to access.

---

* Spoiler – I was right. Just popping back to say I explain it all on page [250]; see if you can get there before I do. Just don't skip ahead. I might be in a book now, but that doesn't mean you can cheat.

Try again. All the characters were on the flying boat, heading to Egypt, and then ...

Nothing.

I reached out and poured myself a brandy, and topped up Melody's glass too. I could do with a drink, after –

Stop! I was getting pulled back into the fiction. I pushed my glass away.

Try as hard as I could, I could not recall a single detail past this point in the narrative.

Because it hadn't happened yet? Perhaps that was it.

No one had said a word while I was thinking. They weren't frozen statues, they sipped drinks, they smiled occasionally, the women tidied their hair, the men smoothed their moustaches. But they were waiting for something. They were waiting for the plot to move on.

Perhaps that was the solution.

'Why are you here?' I asked Melody.

'Seriously?'

'Oh yes.'

'To find Wallace's murderer and get back the ruby.'

'So just another day at the office, then.' But that had told me what I was working towards. I had to move on with the plot, but no one said *which* plot. Maybe my original ending was still valid! When I'd worked out the story, I'd made the murderer –

The murderer had been –

Melody had discovered the murderer was –

No. I couldn't remember my solution either. Both Ventrian's ending and mine had gone.

But there was no need to panic. If my mind couldn't go forward, it would have to look backwards and solve the mystery that way. I'd placed plenty of clues along the way ...

Which had also vanished from my brain.

I still felt sure I was right: the reason I was here would be revealed at the story's end. But I couldn't cheat. I couldn't turn to the last page. I couldn't skip a chapter. I had to experience it, the same as any other character.

I had to hold my nose and dive in. I would *be* a character. Would I retain some awareness of my own reality? All I could do is hope.

'Melody,' I said. 'I need you to tell me everything. Every single thing that's happened to you – from page one onwards.'

CHAPTER TWENTY-NINE

SOMEWHERE OVER THE ATLANTIC OCEAN, AD 1939

Me and my sister. We get along – more or less. Trouble is, we're too much alike. Not just on the outside, either. There's one thing that's always got both of us going, ever since we were toddlers trying to figure out where Mom and Pop had hidden the Christmas presents, and that's a mystery. As we grew up, we embraced it in different ways. I went the Private Eye route. I'd considered applying to Pinkerton's; they're ahead of their time, there, they've had a Female Detective Department for quite a few years now. But I like my independence. Don't say I've not come close to regretting it a few times – you can't eat independence and it don't pay the rent either – but in the main it's been good.

River, she went in another direction. Archaeology, that's her thing. I might have become an *Inc.* but she's got a lot more letters after her name. 'Professor Song' is how she gets introduced these days (yeah, we have different surnames. I adopted a new one for professional reasons. Bad enough being a female PI, can you imagine what it's like when you're called Melody Song on top of that? Might as well be called Ms Tuney McTuneface). Yeah, I'm proud of her, and I think it's mutual, but we don't one hundred per cent get each other's calling. I'm here looking at what's going on in the here and now, trying to make a difference to everyday folks; she's over there trying to solve mysteries from hundreds of years ago and yeah, I get it's pretty interesting finding where Troy was and all that jazz, but is it really making life better for anyone now? Can't really see it. But it's meat and drink to River, and like I say, I'm proud of her.

All this stuff about Cleopatra's tomb – well, I get why that's more of a big deal, being full of rubies and gold and stuff. But I knew River would just flip for the history of it all, so I had to bring her along. In fact – not quite sure why I didn't call her in earlier. Still, she's here now, so it's all good. We work pretty well together, bouncing ideas and so forth. Harry and me, we'd got a bit of a rhythm going, but that can't replace the rapport you get with someone that's pretty much literally your other half. Way to split that egg, Mom!

Talking of Harry – I was getting vibes off River that she wasn't into him, but what I was getting from Harry was the exact opposite. Well, nuh-uh. That's a big no.

Anyway, River and I are still coming to terms with the fact that someone's tried to kill us, and she wants to know everything that's been going on. 'Right from page one,' she says, which I found a bit of a weird way of putting it – but then she's the one with all the book learning, maybe that's how she thinks about things. Yeah, I had to study for my PI licence, but … well, let's say she's probably got every single volume of those encyclopedias and I reckon she's read them all too, *Aar* right the way through to *Zu*.

She drags me out into the corridor so we can talk privately. She wants to know everything, so right back to the beginning I go. I tell her the whole story. Wallace, the letter, the ruby. George Badger. The map, Harry, Wallace's murder. Peterson-Lee's arrest and release. The re-disappearance of the ruby. All the way up to right here and right now, somewhere above the Atlantic on a flying boat, on our way to Egypt and – we hope – the discovery of the century and the Angel Detective Agency Inc. becoming a household name.

The map and the letter excite her particularly. 'How do I get to see them?' she says. For a moment I want to demur – I hadn't cracked the cipher and I'd been trying for weeks, I just knew she thought she'd get it in two seconds flat, which was basically calling me stupid. Then I told myself I *was* being stupid. River and me – we're not like that. We don't do each other down, we build each other up. If she could solve it, it'd solve a hell of a lot of our problems too.

'Cuttling's got them,' I tell her, 'and he's guarding them real good. Crazy, cos Harry and me, we've seen them enough times – heck, I see them in my sleep sometimes. But when the ruby disappeared, he got it into his head that someone would swipe them too. Still, if anyone can talk him into getting them out again, it's you.' She can charm the birds out of the trees, my sister, and I have not met a man yet who can resist her when she puts her mind to something.

There might be an issue if Miss Jones has any say in the matter, though. Miss Jones don't know I've seen the way she looks at Harry – sheep's eyes is understating it. And if she looks at Harry like a sheep, she looks at me (and River too now) like a wolf. 'What big teeth you have, Grandma,' kind of thing.

Harry puts his head around the lounge door. 'Hey, you've been out here for an age!' he says. 'Whispering secrets in each other's ears?'

'Something like that,' I say. 'Hey Harry, do me a favour, OK?'

'Sure thing, doll.'

I can see River's about to jump on that 'doll', and I put a hand on her arm to warn her off. Yeah, I love my sister, but she can get a bit … psycho. Usually in a good cause, it's true, but she's never quite got the hang of discretion being the better part of valour. Shoot first, ask questions later, that's River. Also punch first, ask questions later; karate chop first, ask questions later, and put into an iron maiden and kick the door shut, ask questions later. Don't get on her bad side, is what I'm saying.

'Can you distract Miss Jones for a bit? Take her for a little walk, show her the flight deck, that kind of thing?'

He smiles. 'Why don't I take the pair of you for a little walk, show you the fight deck, that kind of thing?'

'This is business, not pleasure. We want Cuttling to get the map out, and we can do without Miss Jones putting a spanner in the works.'

We joke around for a few minutes, but in the end Harry agrees to get her out of the way. Miss Jones looks surprised at the invitation, but very, very pleased. Cat that got the cream.

Hey, I could go for a saucer of cream myself right now. What? Scrub that. No idea where that came from.

River and I bookend Cuttling who's still making his way down the brandy bottle. I top up his glass and River makes her move.

It's fun to see River get to work, and she's got a big advantage here anyway – besides her obvious ones – because she can speak his language a lot better than I can. He's a collector, and she's dug up more artefacts than a squirrel has nuts.

Soon they're on to such *fascinating* topics as what might be found at Sutton Hoo (some place in England where the Vikings might've been) and the discovery of 30,000 clay tablets at Persepolis (yawn). But she knows her stuff, my sister – turns out Persepolis was burned to the ground by Alexander the Great, that takes us to Alexander founding the city of Alexandria, and that takes us to (yes, you've got it) Cleopatra. And by this time they're thick as thieves and Cuttling is so desperate to show her the map and letter he's practically begging. She graciously agrees to the favour of inspecting them. Phil and I exchange amused glances, we both appreciate the skill on display here.

The papers are locked in a case that's locked in a cupboard that's locked in Cuttling's cabin, with an extra padlock on top that Cuttling alone has a key for. I'd have said that was a bit over the top when there were only six of us plus crew on the flight, but now we know for sure there's a murderer on board, I'm thinking it's fair enough.

Soon the documents are spread out in front of us, giving me major flashbacks to the hours Harry and I spent staring at them. But we're all disappointed. Yeah, River's interested all right – especially in the hieroglyphs, which she describes as 'pidgin Egyptian' – she can't crack the code and don't get anywhere near to solving the mystery. She looks real cross with herself. 'Hey, don't sweat it,' I say. 'Harry's probably right – once we get there, it'll all fall into place.'

'It'd better do,' says Cuttling. 'Cleopatra's bones are coming home with me or you're all gonna be very sorry …' Phil's just pouring Cuttling yet another drink. When Cuttling utters his threat, Phil's hand suddenly wobbles. River's lightning reaction scoops up the documents just in time to stop them being splattered with brandy. 'Idiot boy!' barks Cuttling. 'Watch what you're doing, can't you? These things are priceless!'

Phil don't look embarrassed or ashamed, he looks furious. 'Let's go get you cleaned up,' I say hastily, and hurry him out of the lounge, leaving River behind to clear up the mess.

'That man is an ill-bred ignoramus,' Phil says, and I ain't saying I disagree with that.

'You're not usually clumsy like that, though,' I say. 'Look, he's just making empty threats—'

But Phil's not listening. 'The disrespect,' he says. 'Does he not know he speaks of a goddess? He speaks of her bones as if she were no more than a dog!'

'To guys like Cuttling,' I say, 'people only exist as a means to an end. And that's real people, folks he sees day to day and talks to, like you and me. Someone like Cleopatra? He knows all about her, wants her possessions, all that stuff. But he don't have the smarts to think for a minute that she was someone who lived and loved and had hopes and dreams and all that. Her bones don't mean any more to him than her *hat*. They're just another thing for him to put on a shelf and gloat over, because no other collector's going to get anything to rival them. Yeah, it's wrong – but he's a crackpot. Heck, if he'd been in New York at the time, he'd be top of the suspect list for Wallace's murder.'

That distracts Phil at least, which is what I'd intended. We start to go over the evidence yet again – maybe this time we'll find some flaw in Cuttling's alibi. We know there's a murderer on board, after all …

Then River appears. Her eyes are shining. That's the look I see in the mirror when I think I'm about to solve a case.

'You've done it!' I exclaim. 'You've cracked the code!'

She shakes her head, but she sure as heck still looks pleased with herself. 'We need to find somewhere private,' she says. 'Somewhere we can talk. Our cabin?'

'There's a corpse in there,' I remind her.

She shrugs. 'I'm sure it won't mind. But I suppose that does make it a tiny bit crowded. Any other ideas?'

'If Harry was around, I guess he'd let us use his cabin,' I say. 'But he's still off tomcatting with Miss Jones, poor egg.'

She looks quizzically at me. 'Do you really like him?' she says.

'Sure,' I say. She's seen Harry, right? What sorta question is that?

Phil has a bunk in the staff area (which he ain't happy about one bit – the Kid's got some funny ideas about stuff being 'below his dignity') and he suggests we go there. No arguments from either of us, so off we go. 'OK,' I say to River, once the door is shut behind us, 'what's got you all hot under the collar, then?'

She perches herself on the edge of Phil's bunk, but don't answer directly. Instead she says, 'Tell me again what happened in George Badger's hotel room.'

I oblige, right up to its unpleasant climax.

'He took a revolver out of the dresser drawer and shot himself through the head,' she echoes. 'And later you realised that Badger Senior's letter had been on the dresser, so you went back for it.'

'Uh-huh.'

'Tell me what happened to the letter after that. Exactly. Every detail.'

I shut my eyes, marshalling my facts, then say, 'Harry picked it up off the dresser. He folded it - it already had fold lines, I guess it'd come in an envelope originally - and put it in his pocket.'

'And when did you next see it?'

'Well, we got pretty distracted by the whole murder thing,' I say. 'But we looked at it later that night. We couldn't get any meaning from it, but back then we assumed it was because we didn't have the map. Yeah, we'd both seen the map, but we sure hadn't committed it to memory. We put the letter in my office safe, and that's where it stayed, apart from when we was working on the thing, all the way until we handed it over to Cuttling.'

'Right. So, the letter Cuttling just showed us - notice any difference between it and the one you were studying back at your office?'

I frown. I look at Phil, and he's frowning too. What is River getting at?

'You reckon Cuttling's pulling a fast one?' I ask. 'Why would he do that? This is his expedition.'

My sister shrugs. 'I don't know why,' she says. She turns to Phil. 'When you spilled the drink, Mr Cuttling was quick to grab those papers. He didn't want them getting messed up. Imagine getting something on such an important document ... '

She stares into my eyes as she says it, like she's trying to get an idea from her head into mine.

And I suddenly get it. Call myself a detective? If there's an imbecile on board, it ain't Calvin Cuttling, that imbecile is Melody Malone.

'There was blood on the letter!' I say. 'Maybe only a few drops, but it was there. Gee, I'm a fool. It was one of the reasons I didn't move anything from Badger's room the first time – the cops might have noticed the gap in the spatter pattern on the dresser and gone down the wrong route, didn't want them getting some idea it was murder instead of suicide.'

'So Harry picked up the soiled letter and put it in his pocket. What about the next time you saw it?'

I almost answer straight away, a reflex. But I need to be sure. I shut my eyes again, go through it all step by step. Can I trust my memory? I finally decide I can. 'The next time I saw it – it was clean. Yeah. I'm sure. Not a drop of blood.'

'Someone stole it from Harry and replaced it with a copy?' asks Phil.

River and I look at each other for a moment, but although Phil's idea ain't impossible, we both know it ain't the correct solution.

'No,' I say, my heart feeling heavy. '*Harry* replaced it with a copy.'

'There could be an innocent explanation,' River suggests.

'Sure there could,' I say.

'But why would he do that?' asks Phil.

I don't know. But one thing I *do* know for sure – Harry could not have murdered Horace P. Wallace. In that, at least, he is one hundred per cent innocent. Heck, I even mentioned it at the time. His alibi is watertight – because his alibi is one Melody Malone.

I go through it in my head again. We leave Wallace's office together. Wallace is alive, no question. There wasn't no trickery, nothing like that. Does Harry go back for any reason? No, he does not. Could he maybe have left a booby trap of some kind? I couldn't see how. We go off to the Liberty Crown, we get the letter, we return to the club, we find the body. And no, it was no fake body, no trick. I've seen dead before, and that was dead.

'I want to have a look in his cabin,' I say eventually.

'Harry's?' asks River.

I nod. 'Yeah, I guess it's a long shot, but maybe we'll find some sort of clue that'll tell us what he's up to.'

I'm feeling like the biggest chump known to mankind. There's me getting the trembles whenever Harry's around, and he's been playing me like a fool. Ain't my heart that's broke so much as my pride.

Well, maybe my heart's got a bit dented.

I'm trying not to show any of this. A gal's got her reputation to think about. But River gives me a look, and I know she's feeling sore on my behalf. Ain't hiding anything from my sister.

'Yes, I think it's a good idea to search his cabin,' she says.

'It will be locked,' Phil points out. 'Do we, then, break down the door?'

'I can probably pick the lock,' River says. See, she'd have made a swell gumshoe.

But I shake my head. 'We don't want to make him all suspicious. We've got a real good excuse – we're moving our things to his cabin! It was his idea, no way he can carp about it. Phil, go find the maid who found the body and ask her for the key. She was there when Harry offered his cabin to us, so she knows it's a legit request. River and I will go grab our stuff and meet you there.'

Phil heads off, and River and I go to our cabin. My thoughts are churning with maybes and whys and hows as I put my wash things in a sponge bag then start to take my clothes out of the wardrobe. River does the same, and we've just finished when Phil arrives with the key.

He lets us into Harry's cabin. It's identical to ours, except it don't come with a cadaver; nice touch. 'Phil, go on watch,' I say. 'Let us know if Harry's coming. I'll make a search of the room. River, pack up Harry's stuff and hang up our clothes, that sort of thing. We need to look like we're doing what we say we're doing, you get me?'

They both nod. Phil goes and loiters outside the door and I begin my standard search: left to right from floor to ceiling, moving through the room methodically, checking every possible hiding place. River begins to carry Harry's clothes from wardrobe to bunk as I go on to the wash-stand. Remembering Harry's skills I make one hundred per cent certain there ain't nothing you could stash a paper in – even that face cream trick could work if you folded the letter up very small and wrapped it in something waterproof. But there ain't nothing to be found at all, not nowhere in the whole room.

Well, I guess it was an outside chance, after all. But hey! Maybe all ain't lost. River's going through Harry's clothes, and suddenly there's an 'Aha' from her.

I join her. She's pulled a sheaf of letters from an inside jacket pocket and is riffling through them. 'Something from his bank – envelope addressed to a men's outfitters … '

'Nothing else?'

'Not a thing.'

I hold out a hand – it ain't that I don't trust her, just I like to make sure of things myself, you know? But Phil starts whistling outside the door, the sign that Harry's on his way, so River shoves the letters back into the jacket pocket and a few seconds later we're leaving Harry's cabin arm in arm, not a care in the world, me calling out to Phil that he can move Harry's things now, and acting all, 'Oh, hey there, Harry!' surprised to see him.

'You are such a darling, giving us your cabin!' says River in her most eyelash-fluttering way, putting a hand on his arm and thereby letting the eternal wrath of Miss Jones fall upon her.

'Phil here's going to take your belongings to Cuttling's cabin,' I put in. 'That's right, yeah?'

'Oh, sure, sure,' he says, but here's the thing, he does not look happy about it. He's trying to, real hard – but he ain't succeeding. Which is maybe because we have invaded his privacy, or maybe because there really is something to find. It's like he's trying to hold off shouting at us, trying really hard. You can see the effort when he smiles, takes the bundle of clothing and the sponge bag from River, and says he'll see to it himself and come meet us back in the lounge in a few minutes.

Outside the cabin, Miss Jones trots up and joins us. I ask if she had a nice time touring the flying boat, and she assures us it was 'perfectly pleasant, thank you', with only a slight undertone of wanting us dead.

The sound of a gong rings out. Lunchtime is here. 'Watch out,' River whispers to me. 'Remember the coffee.'

'That can't have been Harry … ' I say, but I guess I'm really trying to kid myself. Maybe he's not the straight-up swell guy I'd thought he was, but a killer? A killer who tried to kill *me*?

'Keep an eye on everyone,' she says. 'People are going to be careful about food and drink if there's a poisoner about – but the poisoner doesn't need to be. See if anyone seems less prudent than the rest.'

When we get to the lounge we find it transformed into a dining salon. As there's only a few of us passengers we're all seated at one big table, don't matter what the etiquette manuals say, although Cuttling sits at the head of the table and Miss Jones, being as she's only a secretary, is right at the far end. Phil ain't here, he has to eat with the crew – not my decision, but I'm not footing the bill so I don't get any say in it. Mrs Peterson-Lee is up and about again and joins us, although she don't eat much. Her 'nerves' are still playing up, she says. I mean, yeah. Cleopatra was really known for her nerves.

Waiters skate from place to place dealing out the slop. River and me are on high alert, but no one else seems to be worrying about arsenic burgers or cyanide soup. Turns out we underestimated their sangfroid. No clues to be had here.

'Imagine poor old Charles Lindbergh back on the *Spirit of St Louis*,' says Cuttling as he chows down, completely unconcerned that there might be strychnine in the starters. 'I don't imagine he had turtle soup and filet of sole Amandine.'

Lindbergh was the guy who made the first non-stop flight across the Atlantic in the twenties. 'I guess he'll just have to put up with being in the history books,' I murmur.

Miss Jones sends me an evil look. 'Of course, Mr Cuttling will be in the history books too,' she says. 'As the discoverer of Cleopatra's tomb.'

'I sure will,' he agrees with a self-satisfied smirk.

'Interesting the people who end up in the history books,' River puts in. 'Caligula, Attila the Hun, Vlad the Impaler ... '

I flash her a look. Sheesh, sis, maybe wait until I get paid before winding up the boss, OK?

After peach pie and coffee (River and I steer clear of the coffee, no one else does), Cuttling asks for his bunk to be made up so he can get in a nap. The rest of us are asked to return to our cabins for maybe a half-hour while the dining saloon gets turned back into a lounge.

River and I go back to what had been Harry's cabin. I'm thinking maybe I'll search it again just for something to do, but I'm pretty darn sure I didn't miss anything last time. Either Harry is clean – or he's clever. I say as much, and River nods.

'We've been concentrating on what he did,' she says, as we sit side by side on the edge of a bunk. 'We haven't discussed why. Why go to all the bother of forging and substituting the letter?'

'So he can sell it twice?' I suggest.

'What, so two millionaires can make two separate secret trips to Egypt? That doesn't feel right. What's been the consequence of having a fake letter?'

'No one's solved the cipher!' You know what? I'd been thinking I was real dumb – it had been getting me down. Turns out it wasn't my fault after all! Big relief.

'Why would Harry have you sit around for weeks, staring at the thing, when he knew there was no chance of you solving it – and then suddenly come up with this idea of Cuttling flying you all over?'

The answer hits me like a fist. 'He solved it. He got the real letter and he goddamned solved it! Then all he needed was the transport. We're just ... window dressing.'

222

She nods. '*Disposable* window dressing.'

'So you think it *was* Harry who poisoned the coffee?' I still don't wanna believe it.

'Possibly. But I don't know why he'd want to tip his hand this early.' She sighed. 'We don't have even the tiniest proof of any of this. We really need to find that letter. Think! Where could it be?'

River suddenly gasps out loud. 'Edgar Allan Poe!' she says.

'You think the letter's been buried alive?' I say.

'He didn't just write about premature burials,' she says. 'He did detective stories too …'

And I get it. '"The Purloined Letter"! The blackmailer hides a stolen letter in plain sight: reversed, readdressed and put in a letter rack!'

'Of course! Why would anyone carry a stamped, addressed envelope in their pocket on a transatlantic trip? They could easily have popped it into a post box on the way.'

'Well, he might've just forgotten about it,' I say, trying to be fair. 'Oh, who am I kidding. River?'

'Yes?' she says.

'I need to know for sure, one way or another. We gotta get hold of that letter. Please.'

River nods, but looks serious. 'Melody, if he realises we suspect him, we don't know what he'll do. I know you don't want to think he's behind the poisoned coffee, but we've got to be careful.'

'The thing is, though, he could have killed me a dozen times in New York! Heck, he could've just left me behind! Why's he suddenly turning to murder now?'

She shrugs. 'Murder in New York would be investigated. You might know too much to be left behind. What if he plans that no one but himself will make it to Cleopatra's tomb? We know he needed Cuttling's money and contacts to set up the expedition, but if you heard that Cuttling and co. had mysteriously perished along the way, you'd have kicked up a fuss.'

I ain't so sure I would – sometimes a fuss-free life is more important than justice – but I like that my sister puts me on some sort of righteous pedestal. 'Let's just find the letter, then we can start speculating. Trouble is, Harry's things are in Cuttling's cabin now,' I say. 'And Cuttling's in there. We'll have to wait.'

'No. No waiting. We'll just have to persuade someone else to let us in,' she says. Oh, I know that look. That's a look that says she wants to have some fun. 'I wish I had my lipstick, that would save a lot of trouble,' she adds.

I open my purse. 'I can lend you one – "Sinful Scarlet" suit you?'

She takes it, but frowns. 'I think it has to be my lipstick. It's a special one.'

'Special how?'

'I'm … not … quite … sure.' She looks confused for a moment, then regains her composure. She undoes a few buttons – one, two … oh, we're going for the full three, are we? This must be serious – and takes a deep breath. 'Come on, let's get it over with.'

Rat-a-tat-tat. A low, subtle knock on Cuttling's door.

For a moment, he doesn't respond. Then a sleepy, rather hostile, 'Whatdya want?'

'It's River Song, Mr Cuttling. I'm so sorry to trouble you, but I'm in desperate need of a man – a man's help, that is.' (As if she's ever needed a man's help in her life! As if she's ever needed *anyone*'s help in her life!)

I hang around near the door, listening to River turning it up real high – he's her target and she's pointing her torpedoes right at him, if you know what I mean. Not many minutes in and he's agreeing to go back to our cabin – she's manufactured some sorta archaeological crisis that she needs advice on, and the details are in there. He's eating it up.

Soon as they're out, I slip in and go straight to the wardrobes. The first one is locked, and I hope it's Cuttling's or I'll have to waste time picking the lock (not just my sister who can do that). No way do I want to be caught by Harry, but more importantly River's relying on me to interrupt her little heart to heart with the millionaire, soon as. Don't mean she can't handle herself, but we might want to keep him on the hook for later.

Lucky for me the second wardrobe opens easily, and I recognise the clothing as Harry's. Don't take me more than a second to find the envelope, but the hope I had that I could maybe see the map through the envelope is dashed. No, it's gotta be opened. I'd have to do it quick as I can – if it is an innocent letter to his tailor, Harry probably won't notice it's missing; trouble is, if it's a priceless map then I'm reckoning he's gonna check in on it every now and then.

I don't want to fold the envelope to fit it in my very small purse, so I tuck it into my stocking top and exit the cabin cautiously. Once in the corridor I throw off the cautious stance and mosey on down to the lounge, now restored to its former state and hosting Harry, Miss Jones and Phil. 'Hey, Kid, I could use a hand,' I call over to my assistant.

'What's up?' asks Harry. 'Anything I can do?'

I don't think so, Mr Durkin. I do a vague wavy gesture that's supposed to convey the lack of importance of my request. 'Thanks, sweetie, but I'm good. I'm looking over some notes and I just *cannot* read Phil's shorthand.' I see Phil open his mouth to say he don't know shorthand, but a sharp look stops him, and he just gets up and comes over to join me. 'Ain't gonna be long,' I call to Harry and Miss Jones. 'Why don't you two have a game of Gin Rummy or something.' I give them a breezy little wave. 'Toodles!'

Phil follows me down the corridor.

'We can't go in my cabin because River's there,' I tell him. 'You reckon yours'll be free?'

He shakes his head. 'Every time I have attempted to enter there has already been at least one occupant,' he says. 'While the retinue is not large, the servants appear to have many periods where they do not work. It is inefficient.'

Yeah, well we'll just have to complain to the aviation authorities when we get home again. 'Guess we'll go in the old cabin,' I say. 'The corpse one.' Phil nods. Ain't nothing that fazes the Kid. 'Right, this is what I need you to do,' I tell him. 'Go to the galley and get some hot water – and by hot, I mean it's gotta be boiling. Maybe say I want to make a tisane like I'm Hercule Poirot or something. And find me a paperknife. Quick as you can, OK?'

He nods and hurries off. I let myself into the corpse cabin and whip out the envelope. Was the cipher letter inside? I wish I'd never seen the thing. I'd been happy with the stash of greenbacks Wallace had given me; why the heck did I let Harry drag me in for more? That sure hadn't been my best move.

Maybe it hadn't been his best move either. Remember what some poet said about a woman scorned?

Phil don't take long, but I'm pacing the room by the time he gets back. He puts a jug of steaming water on the washstand, and I hold the envelope over it, hoping the steam won't disperse before I'm done. Slowly, real, real slowly, the seal begins to weaken.

'Did you get a paperknife?' I ask the Kid. For answer he whips out a knife that, yeah, would definitely slit through paper, but would also slit through many other things, for example human flesh. 'Couldn't get anything any bigger?' I comment, meaning it ironically, but he just shrugs and says it was lying around in the galley and would serve its purpose. Guess that's fair enough. I wriggle the blade underneath the envelope flap and it glides along, smooth as butter.

The moment of reckoning. I ease out the envelope's contents. I know from the look and feel of the paper even before I unfold it, but I unfold it anyway.

It's the letter. The letter from George Badger Senior to his wife, carried all the way from Egypt to England alongside a certain famous ruby. There on one corner are flecks of blood – minute but unmistakable – from that poor kid George Junior. That 'curse' sure hit the Badger family hard – real spooky to think George Junior's sister had gone over the side of a boat only a couple of days before he gave himself lead poisoning. Even more spooky to think that Peterson-Lee and Harry had been there at the time.

I can't recall the hieroglyphs on the fake letter in exact detail, but I can tell they're different on this one. For a moment I think about making a quick copy of the letter – my ego wants to prove I can figure out the cipher – but then I think of River stuck in a cabin with Cuttling and decide to have mercy. I better get this back in Harry's pocket as soon as I can.

I put the letter back in the envelope and push down the flap, hoping it's still tacky enough to hold. It isn't. 'I need something sticky!' I say.

Phil produces a bag of toffees from his pocket. Considering the state of his teeth (you'd think he'd been chewing on rocks) sugar is something he should steer well clear of, and no way are they ideal for my purpose, but I guess it's better than nothing. It should, at least, keep the envelope closed well enough so Harry don't notice it's been opened the first time he checks his pocket.

I'm concentrating on practical matters only, because I don't want to think about how Harry has betrayed me, now it's been confirmed for sure. It's not a broken heart, nothing along those lines; yeah, so maybe my loins had angled themselves fairly strongly in his direction, but my head hadn't followed. Well … not all the way. But you know how I was real cross with myself for not solving that code? That ain't nothing to how furious I am with myself for being taken in by a smooth grifter. Call myself a detective? I couldn't detect a chisel right under my nose.

I slip the envelope back in my stocking top, and peer into the corridor. To my horror, I see Harry heading my way. I duck back into the cabin and pass the envelope to Phil. 'I'll distract him. You take this back. Then you gotta rescue River – and me!' I describe the jacket he needs to find, then Phil and I saunter into the corridor, all casual.

'Where're you off to, sweetheart?' I ask Harry. Gotta make him think I'm still hot for him.

'Just need something from my cabin, sugar,' he says. I remind him that Cuttling had gone for a nap. 'Hey, I won't disturb the old goat,' he says. 'Quick in and out.' He frowns, seeing where I've come from. 'Why'd you go in there? They moved the corpse now?'

I shake my head, then lean in and whisper confidentially, 'I got this feeling River's busy in our cabin.' Best not say with who, seeing as I've just talked about Cuttling being in his own digs.

He raises an eyebrow. 'Hey, that don't sound like a bad idea to me. You wanna get busy too, Malone?'

I know I mustn't let him see Phil entering Cuttling's cabin, so I've gotta go along with it. I put a hand on his arm. We lock eyes as I take hold of Harry's jacket and pull him into the room. The grin's creeping right up his face now, and I make sure to mirror it.

Making out with a murderer? I've done worse. And I'm still hoping he's not the killer. Oh, he's got something dodgy going on, no question. But he didn't murder Wallace – I was one hundred per cent certain about that. So there was still a chance he didn't poison the coffee.

'I've been waiting for this,' Harry says, kicking the door closed behind him.

'Me too,' I lie. I drape one arm over each of his shoulders, still keeping eye contact. His smile shows smug satisfaction, a man getting no more than his dues. He opens my top button. Then …

'Miss Melody! Miss River!'

I turn away at Phil's shout. Harry, annoyed, tries to pull me back, but I shake myself free and head back into the corridor. River emerges from our cabin, not a hair out of place, with a slightly dishevelled and clearly irritated Cuttling trailing behind. Mrs Peterson-Lee pops her blue-rinsed head out too.

'What is it, Phil?' I say, putting a bit of alarm into my voice.

'There – there is a mongoose loose in the kitchen!' Phil says.

Everyone stops and stares at him.

'A … mongoose?' says Peterson-Lee. 'Isn't that something Kipling made up?'

'They're very common in Egypt,' River puts in. 'They keep down the snakes, you know.'

'But what is one doing on a *plane*?'

Phil sticks his chin up in the air, eyes flashing. 'You are calling me a liar?' he says to Peterson-Lee.

'No, no!' says River, putting on a real good act of concern. 'A mongoose! We'd better go and investigate at once, Melody!'

Harry snorts and has another go at pulling me back into the cabin, but I pretend not to notice and tug my arm out of his grasp. River and I follow Phil down into the crew area while the others look after us with a 'like, what?' expression on their faces. The minute we're out of sight, I burst out laughing.

'A mongoose, Phil? A *mongoose*? Really?'

His eyes start flashing again. 'A mongoose can become most violent if cornered. One would be extremely disruptive on board this ship.'

Well, that was true enough. And Phil had done what I'd told him to all right – even if it was one of the dumbest distractions I'd ever heard of.

River ain't surprised at all that I found the real letter in Harry's pocket. But it don't make our course of action any clearer. Phil's in favour of a pre-emptive strike – killing the lot of them just in case. I'm thinking that's maybe a bit extreme, but can't deny I'm worried about what might be in store for us. I still can't get my head around Harry. Killer or not? I'm not gonna be happy until I know for sure. That's the other problem with Phil's plan – not only would we end up on Death Row, it'd leave a heck of a lot of questions unanswered.

We decide to keep playing it cool. We're due to land in the early hours – if we can keep safe till then, the sensible course of action is to give Harry the slip, then maybe persuade the captain of this ship to take us straight back home. Trouble is, that's leaving other folk in danger. But there ain't no way to warn them without tipping our hand.

'We'll just have to solve the mystery before we land,' says my sister. Gee, why didn't I think of that?

Because we're gonna be landing soon, they're laying on an early supper, and we're still jawing when the dinner gong goes 'dong' again. Phil goes off to do his own thing, while River and I head back to the lounge-cum-dining room.

Thank the good lord above, this will be our last meal together on the airship.

Mrs Peterson-Lee looks up as River and I sit down. 'Did you catch it?' she asks.

I'm wondering if she's talking about some sort of disease, but River gets there first. 'Oh, the mongoose? Yes, that's all dealt with. Don't worry.'

'*How* did you catch it?' the woman asks. 'Was it difficult?'

Geez, leave it already, lady.

River and I exchange glances. 'Er … yeah,' I say, buying time. 'It wasn't too hard. Um … River here got a box and … '
Help me out here, sister!

River brings up her hand from under the table. Looks like she's drawn two eyes on the back of it with the lipstick I'd given her, and she starts weaving it about, her fingers pointed like she's playing with a sock puppet that ain't

231

wearing a sock no more. 'Well, as soon as it saw what it thought was a snake it came running. I lured it into the box and shut the lid. Problem solved!'

'But what was a mongoose doing on a flying boat?' demands Cuttling. 'I paid a lot of good money chartering this flight, and no one said anything to me about livestock on board.'

I'm cursing Phil – not the full-scale Eye of Horus curse, just a little one. But River rises to the occasion again. 'Well, it turns out that mongooses aren't allowed in America,' she says. She tells me later this is actually true, don't ask me how she knows about it. 'The captain was repatriating it. But it got out of the luggage bay somehow. Never mind, it's all right now. Bread roll, anyone?'

Gotta say, she's pretty quick, my sister. Maybe she should think about writing fiction.

Finally satisfied, everyone begins to eat.

'Don't reckon Lindbergh had Grenadin de veau on the *Spirit of St Louis*!' says Cuttling as the entrée is presented, because if you're a millionaire you can make the same funnies over and over again and people are still gonna laugh.

'Oh, Mr Cuttling, you're so droll!' says Mrs Peterson-Lee, and he preens himself like a parrot.

I politely agree with Cuttling that as transport goes, this is pretty damn luxurious.

'Although it's more like a ship than an aeroplane,' says Mrs Peterson-Lee. 'I suppose that's why they call it a flying boat.'

Well, yeah, that and the whole thing about it landing on water, of course.

'It's a darn sight nicer than the *Caesarion*,' Harry says. 'Well, third class, anyways.'

Cuttling frowns. 'The *Caesarion*? Wasn't that the ship you crossed on?' he says to Miss Jones.

Mrs Peterson-Lee looks at her. 'Really? You mean three of us were on the same ship? How strange!'

'She was at the auction for me,' says Cuttling. 'Got an interest in jewels, came highly recommended. Perfect person to send.'

At least the change of subject stopped Cuttling goggling at my sister like she was an especially appetising Grenadin de veau. Thankfully, Harry had steered clear of the love-struck teenager thing, but he was sending a good few dirty looks my way, and I'm meaning that in the sense of 'down and dirty' before you ask. The full glower type of dirty look was also coming in my direction, though, for good measure, and it was coming hard and wolfish from Miss Jones. '*What big teeth you have, Grandma,*' I thought again.

And suddenly all these thoughts are springing up in my brain, ricocheting off each other like bagatelle balls.

What big teeth you have ...

Spirit of St Louis ...

'So you docked in New York?' I say to Miss Jones. 'You get a chance to sightsee before heading back to Chicago?'

Cuttling laughs and answers for her. 'She lives in the place! I got people all round the States. Dolores here's been one of my New York agents for years now. Got top reports from everyone. Knows her jewels. Best person to send.'

Well, what d'you know. I'm thinking that's a piece of information I could've done with earlier.

I put down my knife and fork. My mind's racing so fast I ain't got any energy left for eating.

Then I carefully and deliberately wipe any concern off my face and look straight into Harry's eyes, letting him know that I am his and only his and all his.

'I guess we all need an early night tonight,' I say. 'What time is it we're due to land? Four a.m.?'

I'm addressing everyone but I'm still looking at Harry. He knows what sort of 'early night' I have in mind. 'Quarter after four, or thereabouts,' he says. 'So yeah. An early night seems a real good idea.'

The meal drags on, as does the tedious evening's conversation. River and I are the first to leave. 'Midnight, old cabin,' I whisper to Harry as we say our goodnights. He virtually licks his lips.

'Come on, then, what was all that about?' River asks when we're back in our cabin. 'Don't tell me you're really planning a happy night with Harry.'

'It's all part of the plan,' I say.

So of course she asks, 'What plan?'

I throw myself back on the lower bunk, hands behind my head. 'Oh, thing is, I've solved the mystery,' I say. 'I know who murdered Wallace.'

'And are you planning to tell me who it was?'

'Sure, sis!'

I pause for dramatic effect, letting the events replay themselves in my head. Harry and I leaving Wallace with the map in his office at the back of the Pink Tiger club. The singer crooning away – the same canary who'd later be the one and only witness to Mrs Peterson-Lee going into Wallace's office. I remember her singing 'Meet Me In St Louis, Louis'. I remember thinking of her as 'all teeth and curls' – but those curls were a wig.

I look River in the eye, and I smile. 'It was Miss Jones. She murdered him.'

'What? That dismal little woman?'

'Didn't you hear? She was *in New York* when it happened! I'd assumed – we'd all assumed – she came from Chicago with Cuttling. No! She was auditioning to be a singer at Wallace's club – and soon as the coast's clear, she sticks a knife in his back.'

'But if she took the ruby – and the map too – how did they end up in Susan Peterson-Lee's hotel suite?'

'Oh, come on,' I say. So I'm the detective, but she doesn't have to *embarrass* me.

She gets it. 'Harry.'

'Mm-hmm. Harry. Maybe they met on the boat, maybe he knew her before then – whatever, they were a team. He'd know how to get her the gig at the Pink Tiger, straight off the boat. She slips the stuff to him and he hid them while he was allegedly searching for them – then, hey, surprise! He finds them again, neatly incriminating a woman who his partner in crime has already pointed the finger at. If Susan hadn't had that alibi, she could be on Death Row right now.' I sigh. 'Which is why, even if Miss Jones was the one who did the deed, Harry's just as guilty.'

The trouble is, although I'm now certain Miss Jones is the killer, I still ain't got a scrap of evidence. No proof she was the nightclub singer. No proof she stabbed Wallace. No proof she poisoned our coffee – yeah, I'm sure that was her too. I don't reckon that bit was part of Harry's plan, it was a little bit of freelancing because she hated me. I've seen the way she looked at me – which is why I'd goaded her at the dining table by making such an obvious play for her man.

Oh yeah, I'd made a date with Harry all right. But I didn't think Miss Jones would let that happen, and that's where I'd get my evidence.

*

I was listening out for the others to make their way to bed.

'Goodnight, Malone!' Harry calls as he passes our cabin.

'Goodnight!' I call back.

'Goodnight, River!'

'Goodnight!'

Then follows clunk after clunk as the cabin doors are shut noisily behind everyone.

I ready myself for bed. Well, for 'bed'. Black chiffon negligée with a scarlet silk kimono, so it's clear as can be I ain't got no concealed weapons. A dab of *Femme du Temps* here, here and here, remembering Coco Chanel's advice to apply perfume where you wanted to be kissed – or at least where you wanted people to think you wanted to be kissed.

I lay back on my bunk and wait for the clock to creep to midnight.

Two minutes before the hour, I hear a cabin door open.

I open my door too. Yes, it's Harry. He hasn't bothered changing into nightclothes, but he's wearing a smarter shirt and jacket than earlier. Fine by me. The more buttons there are to undo, the longer I can draw this out.

But his eyes are greedy, and I know as we enter the old cabin that drawing things out is not what he has in mind. Sorry, Harry, we're going by my timetable, not yours.

I slip my arms under his jacket and check for weapons under the guise of a caress. He's clean. It's safe for me to step back.

He looks like he wants to return the favour, but I take a step back and put a finger on his lips. 'Slow down, sailor! We're not coming in to land yet.'

He steers me backwards, then growls in disappointment and disgust when he sees the lower bunk is still occupied. 'They haven't got that *thing* out of here yet?' he says. 'I thought they were going to.'

I shrug. 'I guess they forgot. But hey, dead men tell no tales. You ain't gonna let it put you off? A big brave man like you?'

No, seems nothing's going to put him off. I'm hoping I don't have to drag this out for too long before Miss Jones makes her move.

I'm hoping she *does* make a move.

Thank the good lord above, I hear a door opening – slowly, carefully, but unmistakably. I can turn things up a gear. I cup his head in my hands and lean in for a kiss. He don't seem to mind one bit.

The door opens behind Harry. For a moment he's too busy to notice, but as Miss Jones shuts and bolts the door he spins around.

She's pointing a bean-shooter at us.

Harry's eyes pop out of his head. 'Sweetheart, honey –'

'Don't you honey me,' she says. Weird thing is, she's suddenly gone all British. Guess her accent was as phony as mine is.

Harry holds out his hands, palm up, like he's approaching a wild animal (maybe a mongoose) and trying to show he's not a threat. 'Just keeping her sweet, honey, we agreed ... You're my girl, you know I am.'

'Then you won't mind if I get rid of her right now,' says Miss Jones.

The gun barrel is pointed straight at my heart. Her finger tightens on the trigger.

And River bursts out from under the sheet, where she's been doing her best corpse impression. She grabs the Jones dame by the knees and pulls her down. The gun goes off as she falls – and Harry falls too. Blood is already soaking through his shirt; he looks so surprised. And then his expression just fades into blankness.

Miss Jones lets out a wail. She lifts the gun again, waving it between us.

River's looking all weird. Blinking and shaking her head. She's staring down at her wrist. The weird bracelet thing she wears there is all hanging off in bits. She curses.

'Maybe it's not really broken,' she says. 'Maybe it's not real.'

It looks both real and really broken to me, but funny thing, it's not the thing most on my mind, what with the gun pointing at us and all.

'Oh, well, at least we did it,' she says. 'We found the murderer.' Well, I guess as twins we get to share everything. I used to borrow her hair ribbons when we were kids, so now she shares the credit for solving a homicide. Fair enough.

'It doesn't matter, I'm going to kill both of you!' Miss Jones says. 'You lured Harry here to murder him, and I didn't turn up in time to save him, but I still got you both. You're going to rot in hell, you twisted twins.'

'Come on, you gotta tell us your evil plan first,' I say. 'That's how this is supposed to work.'

'What?'

'Just the bare bones,' I say.

River and I start to fire questions at her, and she's so flustered she actually answers a few. (You'll find out later.) But it ain't long before she pulls herself together again – and she's still pointing the gun at us. Right now, it's aimed right at River.

But River's not looking at Miss Jones, she's looking over her shoulder. 'No, don't!' she cries out, and again, it ain't Miss Jones she's talking to.

'Do you really think I'm that stupid?' says Miss Jones. Then she looks down at her chest, maybe to see why it's suddenly hurting – but sad to say, the knife didn't make it all the way through, so I'm guessing she died still not knowing. She crumples, revealing behind her Phil, standing in the wardrobe. He's holding that super-sharp 'paperknife' he'd borrowed from the galley.

I'd known River was hiding in the cabin, of course – I mean, it was my idea. She'd been in place long before the others went to bed, so there'd be no doors creaking to warn anyone someone was on the move, and being identical in voice as well as face, I'd called out a few additional goodnights – in my original accent. Sounded just like there was two of us in our cabin. But Phil – nope, him I hadn't known about.

'That your idea?' I say to my sister, and she nods.

'He's not the type of kid to hold back when someone's in danger,' she says.

I smile at him. 'Thanks, Kid.' I would have ruffled his hair, but he never takes that cap off. Oh, and he don't have no hair. But apart from that.

Phil gives me a little bow. Yeah, he's a funny kid all round. But we suit each other.

Someone's banging on the door. 'What's going on in there!' demands Cuttling's voice.

River unbolts the cabin door and opens it, to reveal Cuttling (in a pair of mustard and brown striped pyjamas) and Mrs Peterson-Lee (in what would be a simple white nightdress if she hadn't added to it a gold-coloured belt and a gold collar that resembled nothing so much as an Egyptian Usekh and – oh, right. She was being Cleopatra. If Cleopatra had been a 60-year-old white woman with cliff-ledge bosoms who pranced around in a nightie, that is).

Wearily, I suggest going elsewhere to explain. I mean, we're just swimming in blood here.

Susan Peterson-Lee is hyperventilating and fluttering her hands wildly, her eyes rolling into her head as though she's about to faint – or maybe wants to give the impression of someone about to faint. 'Come on, Susan,' I say. 'I reckon Cleopatra saw a lot worse. She bumped off a whole heap of folks, didn't she?'

'Assassination is a necessary tool of princes,' put in Phil. 'The alternative is to be killed oneself.'

'A good point by my young and slightly bloodthirsty assistant,' I say. 'Miss Jones was trying to plug my sister and me, see? Come on, let's go to the lounge and tip a few. I could sure do with a brandy, and I guess you could too, Mrs P-L.'

But Mrs Peterson-Lee is still looking down at Miss Jones. The secretary's severe hairstyle is lying about a foot from her body – it turns out it wasn't only her night-club curls that was a wig. Her real hair is revealed: a jet-black bob that has a hint of the Ancient Egyptian about it.

'I know her,' says Mrs Peterson-Lee. 'I've seen her somewhere before, I know I have.' And then her eyes widen in recognition. 'But it can't be! She's dead!'

'Who is?' I demand.

'Why, I saw her at the auction! That's George Badger's daughter! That's Ruby Badger!'

We make the move to the lounge. Phil pours glasses of brandy for everyone, himself included, although he wrinkles his nose at the taste. I down mine and hold out my glass for a refill, before I start on the story.

River and Phil chime in here and there, and Cuttling and Mrs Peterson-Lee jump in with questions, and between us, with the information Miss Jones – sorry, Ruby Badger slash Durkin – gifted to us before she died, we work out what happened.

As Wallace's agent in Egypt, Harry acquires the map, that much was true. What he didn't spill was how much he wanted to find that tomb. He had a go while he was out there, but no luck. He needed a proper expedition. Trouble is, that sort of thing costs money. He wanted Wallace to fund a huge expedition, but Wallace says no, not without a definite location. So Harry starts sticking his fingers in the till. He's eyeing up Wallace's sweet, sweet New York empire, and he's decided to transfer a substantial cut of the profits into his own pocket and fund the thing himself.

January 1939, poor old Mrs Badger kicks it. Ruby inherits the Eye of Horus ruby, along with her father's letter to her mother. She don't know nothing about the map, she just wants cash. Lots and lots of cash. So, off to Bothesy's she goes, and they say, 'Oh yeah, we'll get you a boatload of cash for that, just you wait and see.'

Peterson-Lee wants the ruby. Cuttling wants the ruby. Cuttling sends over his New York agent, one Dolores Jones. Wallace has already got an agent in England, Floyd. They all go begging to Ruby, wanting to negotiate a private sale. No way, is her answer. It's going to auction and they can take their chances alongside of everyone else.

Now Harry, he happens to be in England, so he swings by to see Floyd. And Floyd, who's still trying to put pressure on Ruby, suddenly finds himself with a real pip at his disposal, and he decides to set him on the girlie in question. That Ruby would fall for Harry – not the biggest shock. That Harry would fall for Ruby – well, that was maybe less on the cards, although how much of it was her personal attraction and how much all the folding green that she'd get for that sparkling red, who knows.

Here's the auction. Present: Ruby, Harry, Floyd, Susan Peterson-Lee, Dolores Jones, George Badger Junior. Junior kicks up a fuss but the hammer falls anyway and Horace P. Wallace has a shiny new toy, Floyd's got it.

Harry and Ruby celebrate. She – and therefore by extension they – are up a cool million or so. But then, for the first time, Harry sees what she's been selling. He sees the letter. He recognises the 'hieroglyphs' immediately, and he wants that letter. He wants it real bad. It could be the key to finding that tomb, and he's not handing that chance over to anyone.

Ruby tries to withdraw the lot, but the sale's gone through; that wire transfer's already on its way from Horace P. in good ol' NY. She asks for the letter back – Floyd says no way. It's part and parcel of the lot. The pair of them are sore as a boil.

But all ain't lost. Badger sent hundreds of letters to his wife, Ruby says, they can work out the cipher with those. Back they go to the Badgers' house and search it top to bottom. Not a letter in sight. Not a single one. Looks like Mrs Badger burned the lot of them before she croaked. So that letter that got sold to Wallace? It's the sole survivor.

Back to Floyd. He says the stone ain't got there yet, but they ain't getting it anyhow. It's going back on the *Caesarion* with Marvin Motson. So what do Harry and Ruby do? They book a couple of passages on the ship themselves, maybe intending a bit of persuasion, maybe intending a bit of burglary, maybe just cos they liked playing deck quoits and fancied the trip. Other folks who had the same idea: one, Susan Peterson-Lee and two, Dolores Jones. While they're waiting, Harry and Ruby spring for a special licence and become Mr and Mrs H. Durkin. I'm guessing Harry wanted to make sure he had hands on her money, if nothing else.

They report to the RMS *Caesarion*, ready to make friendly with Motson. Trouble is, Floyd had fed everyone a yarn. Marvin Motson had already made his getaway the day before on the *Tithonia*. Main coincidence was that Badger Jr, running away from his troubles, had also ended up on the *Tithonia*, not knowing to start with that his pop's letter (not to mention the ruby) was a couple of berths along.

Now Harry, he's pretty sore. Why? you might ask. All he's gotta do is talk to Wallace, get him to set up the expedition at last. Big problem: from a few things Floyd let drop, it looks like Wallace is about to wise up that Harry's been glomming on to his profits. Just in case Floyd passes on any gen to the boss, plus to pay him back for sending them in the wrong direction, Harry arranges for Floyd to get rubbed out.

They set off on the *Caesarion* anyways, they've already sprung for the tickets and it can be their honeymoon. And like all young lovers, they spend the time plotting a few murders. First off, they find Cuttling don't know Miss Jones all that well. They spot an opportunity right there, and she gets tipped overboard. Except hey, they tell everyone it's Ruby. What a tragedy. Ruby Durkin née Badger is now Miss Dolores Jones, and Harry pretends he don't know her at all.

While I'm running all over New York dealing with Ruby's baby brother, their ship gets in. Ruby, in a blonde wig, does her canary turn at the Pink Tiger – Harry had told her who to ask for, was pretty sure she'd be put in place where he needed her to be. He sees Wallace – and while he's there, Wallace takes a call from Peterson-Lee, handily making herself a suspect, something Harry's gonna grab with both hands.

Here's where I come in. See, I think Harry really took a shine to me. But what he took a shine to even more was the chance of a better alibi. He feeds his moll the dope about Peterson-Lee then he comes fetch me. Hey look, Wallace is alive and well! Then the pair of us drift off, with Harry calling out to let Ruby know the coast's clear. She does the deed and gets the stuff – passing it over to Harry while crying on his shoulder. We head off to find Peterson-Lee and 'find' the goods on her. Geez, I was such a patsy. It's embarrassing.

Of course, Harry has already swapped the real letter for the fake – so no one can crack the cipher except themselves. The real one they work on in private until they figured it out, at which point 'Dolores' lures in Cuttling so they could get their expedition funded for free and gratis.

What they had planned once we all arrived in Egypt – well, we ain't no mind readers, but wouldn't be a wild guess that another 'native revolt' might have 'coincidentally' happened.

But here's the thing: if it hadn't been for Ruby going full-on cuckoo with jealousy and bringing on that murder part of their programme ahead of schedule, maybe we'd have fallen for it. Yeah, River and I can handle ourselves good, but – and this is my sister's words, not mine – 'it's always best to try to avoid a potential bloodbath unless you're *really* bored.'

Plus, you know what? Yeah, she tried to bump me off and all, but I'm maybe feeling a bit sorry for Mrs Durkin.

Because I saw the way Harry looked at me, and he didn't never look at her that way. She was just a walking, talking pile of dough, and I'm kinda getting the suspicion that she weren't any too likely to get back from that expedition any more than the rest of us.

Seems like Ruby was pretty well cursed after all.

Incidentally, Cuttling looked down in the dumps for maybe three seconds when he learned that his new Girl Friday killed his old Girl Friday. His attention, which should have been squarely on the swell story I was telling, kept being directed at old Susan Peterson-Lee in her Cleopatra get-up. I'm guessing the collector was planning to add a new Egyptian *objet d'art* to his collection. I don't get it – a number who was happy as a clam playing along with River earlier in the day tuning in now to the phony pharaoh? Ain't no accounting for taste.

When they ain't going all moony at each other, Cuttling's and Mrs Peterson-Lee's faces cycle between shocked, horrified, relieved and angry as I'm piecing together the story. After I finish the tale it all goes quiet, just for a moment. Then Cuttling says, 'So this whole thing is a sham. The ruby's gone, and we don't have a chance of finding the tomb without the real letter.'

'But the real letter's here,' says River. 'Harry had it in his pocket. Melody found it earlier.'

Cuttling turns to me. 'Then hand it over, damn you! That thing's mine by rights!'

So much for 'please' and 'thank you' and 'well done for helping us not be murdered'. But I do suddenly remember something. 'It's in Harry's jacket!'

'So go fetch it!'

'It's in Harry's jacket *that he was wearing* when Ruby plugged him. I felt it when I … felt him.'

Cuttling's up and out of the door almost before I've finished speaking. We all follow him to the cabin where Harry and Mrs Harry still lie on the floor in a puddle of the red stuff. Mrs Peterson-Lee is once more overcome by the sight so Cuttling attends to her (very closely) and gestures to me to do the deed instead.

I reach into Harry's inside jacket pocket and attempt to pull out what's there. All that emerges are soaked fragments. The bullet had gone right through the pocket. The scorched remains of his correspondence are soaked in about a gallon of blood, no way we can read even a single hieroglyph.

Now Susan's sobbing even harder. So near to finding the tomb – and yet so far. 'Don't cry, kitten,' says Cuttling. 'Heck, we'll still go and look for it anyway. Maybe make it a honeymoon …?'

Well, Susan Peterson-Lee ain't no Cleopatra, and Calvin Cuttling ain't no Julius Caesar or Mark Antony. Unless they do find Cleopatra's tomb I'm guessing they'll never end up in the history books. But maybe they'll get through their lives without being assassinated or otherwise driven to death, and I guess they might think that's a win overall.

The story's all rounded off when a steward pops in to dole out the wake-up calls prior to landing, and is all surprised to see everyone up and about already. He's even more surprised to see all the corpses and blood. But Cuttling plutocratically starts handing out wads of folding stuff to 'compensate the crew for their trouble', and I got a feeling that things might get straightened out without anything as undesirable as major police investigations or arrests. Gee, what it is to have money!

*

We wave our farewells to Mr and Mrs Cuttling-to-be. The flying boat has to be refuelled and scrubbed down a bit before it can make a return trip. (River passed on some tips about how to get blood out of furnishings – a paste of water and salt is quite good, she says. It's not the first time she's had to deal with it. They don't enquire further.)

'So Cuttling and Susan are heading into the desert without the faintest idea where they're going,' River comments. I nod. 'We found the murderers and solved the mystery.' I nod again. 'So *why*,' River demands, sounding real unhappy, 'have we not yet come to "The End"?'

'What?' I ask. Not the most erudite response, but it gets the point across.

She don't answer, just furrows her brow and sits there, chin on hand, for a few moments. Then suddenly her face clears. 'Oh, of course! The ruby! We haven't recovered the ruby. That's what we need to do. No loose ends. We find the ruby, then we can draw a line under the whole thing.'

'Wait for someone else to drop dead, then search their pockets,' I suggest, not entirely seriously.

She raises an eyebrow. 'The curse?'

Of course, I still don't believe in curses. But pretty much everyone who touched it is dead. Well, except for me. I tell River that.

To my surprise, she seems to be giving it serious consideration. 'You never claimed or wanted to own it,' she says. 'Everyone else did. So you escaped.'

'Is this like Mrs Peterson-Lee's baloney about being its "true owner"?' I say. 'You mean the ruby's real choosy about who it hangs around with?'

And a huge grin spreads across River's face. 'I don't blame it,' she says. 'I don't blame it at all. And I know now who has it.'

CHAPTER THIRTY

EGYPT, AD 1939

As soon as we'd identified the murderers, my head started to clear again. It felt like my job was done.

Except it wasn't. Not by a long way. And the reason I knew that was because I was still there. Stuck in the 'book'.

It was very strange being fictional. I had free will, yes, but there was a gnawing feeling forever in my head insisting that things were going on that I couldn't quite see or hear or touch – but which had power over me. It was like living in a world of conspiracy theories. If someone had told me that the Earth is flat, or that the moon is an egg, or that vaccines aren't good for you, I had the most horrible suspicion that I might have listened to them.

I very much wanted to get out of this place now. And I suddenly knew how.

'Phil?' I called. 'Phil, can you come here?'

The boy joined us. Melody was looking really confused now. 'Phil?' she said to me. 'Are you saying that Phil's got the ruby? No. No way. I trust him with my life.'

'I think that's the point,' I told her. 'I think he's got your life in his hands. *All* our lives in his hands.' I hold out a hand to Phil, who's said nothing throughout this, just watched us and listened to us with a patient, slightly superior expression on his face. 'I didn't write you, Phil. But you were put in this story for a reason.'

He continued to look patient, waiting for me to work it out.

'You didn't fit in this world. You did your best, but the mask slipped too many times, especially when you had dialogue. Then there was the way you reacted when Cuttling spoke about Cleopatra. Your shaven head and – if you'll excuse me mentioning them – the teeth ground short by Egyptian bread.

'Ventrian even changed the name of a boat in the book to give me a whacking great clue, in case I hadn't solved the riddle yet. "*Now Caesar's gone*" – your name means "Little Caesar", it was talking about you, not your father. It was telling me you'd gone, but it was all a part of the "ruby con". You'd gone from your world, and ended up here.'

I smiled. The joy of someone being alive when you'd been told they were dead! So many rumours – so many explanations of exactly what way the boy was lured to his death by Octavian, exactly what method of murder had been used. There were no witnesses, no body, no burial place, but the whole world agreed that he was dead. Yet here he was – a real person inside a book, just as I was.

I turned to Melody. 'I'd like to introduce you to Phil – or more specifically Ptolemy *Phil*opator *Phil*ometor Caesar. More commonly known as Caesarion. And I'd like to say – Phil? Maybe now's a good time to take off your hat.'

Phil smiled. 'Hello again – "*Wivver*".' And for the first time since I'd come into this strange world he raised his hand to his head and carefully pulled off his 1930s-style newsboy cap.

And there it was. The ruby.

Oh, I don't mean he just had a jewel sitting on top of his head. It was shining, spinning, radiant, bathing everyone in its glow – and then it was something else, something still radiant but full of every colour and was all shapes and no shape at once, and I could feel the light inside my head, it was ... it was *tickling* my brain (and yes, I know how ludicrous that sounds, but it's the closest I can get to the sensation).

I couldn't really think clearly. I focused on one thing and one thing alone: this was what I'd been searching for. This is what I'd come back to the past for. It was deadly dangerous and unutterably beautiful but most importantly it was the end of my quest.

I reached out a hand. I couldn't tell if I were touching something or not, but I closed my fist to take hold of – whatever was there. At last, I held it. The Device was mine. The Eye of Horus. Not some ridiculous jewel, but pure *power*.

I closed my eyes, but I could still see *it*. Not a light burned into my retinas, the actual thing itself was still there, still making no sense. If what I was starting to feel was even a thousandth of what Ventrian had felt when he discovered his 'Device', then the fact that he'd resisted it at all was superhuman.

Surely this meant we had got to the last page of Melody's story? Surely we'd finally come to 'The End'? Perhaps it was because there was still a ruby-like halo surrounding us but I found another image invading my head: Judy Garland clicking her ruby slippers together and saying, 'There's no place like home.' *The Wizard of Oz* film would be released soon, back in 1939 – but was that my home? It was where my family was, but ... Stormcage? Definitely not. The TARDIS? It was where I felt most at home, but more in the sense of someone returning to a comfortable place where they'd once felt happy. If I thought, 'There's no place like home,' I had no idea where the ruby slippers would take me. Not for the first time, I thought: *I don't have a home. I just have places where I live.*

But those words joined with the jewel and spun and sparkled in my head, and I began to spin too. Oh, I flew so high! I was part of the universe but the universe was also part of me and it was *mine*, to do with what I would. All the things I could do! All the things I could change! I was empress of the universe, and I would be a benevolent god.

And the universe would pay me tribute.

I reached out with my mind, and I touched another mind. I knew its feel, but I did not know its shape.

It was my home.

My home was not a place, but a person.

The other mind – *her* other mind? Goodness, *that* was new, but I guess surprises keep a marriage from getting stale – spoke inside my head. 'Aw, River, love, not like this. This is not how it's meant to be, you know that.'

CHAPTER THIRTY-ONE

EGYPT, 30 BCE

The Doctor's touch, so familiar and yet unfamiliar, cooled me, calmed me. I pushed the feelings down, out from my head, out from my heart, down and down until it floated out of me, surrounding me like a miasma until it dispersed completely. Once she knew I was safe, she let my mind go. I took a deep breath, and suddenly I was grounded again, my feet on solid earth.

I opened my eyes. I was in Cleopatra's burial chamber, my hand still on the relief of 'Horus' – touching Caesarion's eye, could Ventrian have made the clue any clearer?

I looked down at my wrist. The Vortex Manipulator was still broken. I suppose I'm going to get to know Ancient Egypt really well. My hand dropped to my side. I heard a voice say, 'Where the hell are we?'

It sounded like my voice. But I hadn't spoken.

I turned around. Standing behind me was Melody Malone.

Melody Malone doesn't like to show weakness. I know that, it's how I created her. So I knew things must be pretty bad by the degree of shock that was showing on her face.

Caesarion was there too, crumpled on the floor. I hurriedly checked him – he was still breathing. The shock of the transition had knocked him out, that was all.

The cat came running up to us. I didn't know how long she'd been here all alone; I hoped it hadn't been long. I reached out for her – and she ignored me completely, throwing herself at Melody, weaving in and out of her ankles until Melody picked her up, then purred in great, but entirely feline, contentment. I guess they did have a special sort of bond. The cat wound herself around Melody's neck and stayed there, as though she were Mrs Peterson-Lee's fox-fur stole.

Melody reached out and traced her finger around a wall painting of the jackal-headed god Anubis, god of death and the afterlife, then drew back her hand and looked at it. She ran fingers down her own cheek, then through her hair, and looked at her hand again. Her fingernails were painted scarlet, and she examined each one individually. 'Everything feels … ' She trailed off, then after a few seconds added, 'I don't know the right words for it. Was that all a dream? Have I been asleep?'

'No,' I said. 'Not exactly … '

She was breathing heavily. 'I can … Are these smells? I can't believe that's a question I'm asking. I know what a "smell" is! I can't tell you how this is different. But it is. It's different and it's the same, and – colours! I've never seen colours like this before.' She studied her painted nails again. 'Red. Red is my colour. Scarlet. But this isn't red. It's more than red. More vivid. Deeper.'

'How are you here, Melody?' I whispered under my breath.

I didn't mean her to hear, but she did. Perhaps sounds were clearer to her now, as well as colours. 'Maybe if someone tells me where "here" is, I can try to answer that!' she said. Her voice wasn't loud, she was holding it back, but somehow it still felt like she shouted. She began to look around, taking in the carvings, the wall paintings, the sarcophagus with its gilded death mask. I tried to explain, but she just started to giggle. 'Right,' she said. 'So, the short answer to my question is, where I actually am is Hart Island Lunatic Asylum.'

Giggle? Melody didn't *giggle*. She was a tough cookie with a heart of gold, a straight shooter and heartbreaker, who beat the men at their own game.

I tried to explain further. It sounded utterly ridiculous to my ears. How would you feel if someone dragged you out of the only world you'd ever known, the only world you knew existed, and told you that you weren't real? That you'd been *created*? That your every action, every thought – every breath, every tiny whim – was down to someone else?

I reached out a hand and touched her arm. 'Hands off, sister,' she said, and she was no longer my funny twin. At least she wasn't giggling any more. She was hard and angry.

She was also absolutely solid. I don't think I'd quite believed it up to that point. A projection, a phantasm, an illusion – perhaps. A real person – as real as me – nope.

'I suppose I'm not as good a writer as I thought I was,' I said, trying to lighten the mood with a joke. 'If this is the first time you've really experienced colours or odours or textures, I suppose I can't have described them very well.' But truly, how could those things be described accurately? They all relied on a shared set of references, a knowledge and experience of sensations. How do you describe red? It's impossible. I had only been able to experience those sensations in the book world because I expected them, because I knew what 'red' was so, when I looked at something red, my brain knew what it was supposed to see. Melody had no frame of reference. Melody was a two-dimensional character who had suddenly become three-dimensional without ever having known there *was* a third dimension. She didn't even remember being a cat.

And perhaps that's part of being a fictional character. The author can make you do anything, feel anything, believe anything – and you won't know it's odd or wrong or even impossible unless the author makes you come to that realisation. I'd felt for a few brief minutes when I touched the Eye of Horus Device that I was a god. I hadn't realised I already *was* a god – to Melody and the rest of my list of characters at least.

I guess Melody had just become an atheist.

My bundle of possessions was still on the floor of the chamber. I picked it up and pulled out the book.

The Ruby's Curse: A Melody Malone Mystery.

Melody looked at it. Then looked away. It was just too big a thing for her to take in. She turned her back on me, and I didn't know what to do.

I wondered what would happen to her when the Eye of Horus Device was destroyed. Would she just find herself back in the book, with the characters 'River' and 'Phil' having gone off somewhere – or having never been there at all? Would she remember any of this? Would it feel to her like death?

I needed to get it over with. Rip off the plaster.

I turned to the relevant page in the book. Or thought I did.

The word 'ruby' wasn't there.

Page 153, word 44. I counted again. Again, no. The 44th word was the less than inspiring 'in'.

I hurriedly looked at all the pages around it, maybe I'd slipped up somehow.

Nothing.

I pressed random words, waiting for that explosion of equations that would let us deal with the Eye of Horus. The paper remained stubbornly solid.

I turned to page 153 again.

... at him. 'Thanks, Kid.' I would have ruffled his hair, but he never takes that cap off. Oh, and he don't have any hair. But apart from that.

Phil gives me a funny little bow. Yeah, he's a funny kid all round. But we suit each other.

Someone's banging on the door. 'What's going on in there!' demands Cuttling's voice.

River unbolts the cabin door and opens it, to reveal Cuttling (in a pair of mustard and brown striped pyjamas) and Mrs Peterson-Lee (in what would be a simple white nightdress if she hadn't added to it a gold-coloured belt and a gold collar that resembled nothing so much as an Egyptian Usekh and – oh, right. She was being Cleopatra. If Cleopatra had been a 60-year-old white woman with cliff-ledge bosoms who pranced around in a nightie, that is).

Wearily, I suggest going elsewhere to explain. I mean, we're just swimming in blood here.

Susan Peterson-Lee is hyperventilating and fluttering her hands wildly, her eyes rolling into her head as though she's about to faint – or maybe wants to give the impression of someone about to faint. 'Come on, Susan,' I say. 'I reckon Cleopatra saw a lot worse. She bumped off a whole heap of folks, didn't she?'

'Assassination is a necessary tool of princes,' put in Phil. 'The alternative is to be killed oneself.'

Oh my god.

This was not what Ventrian had written. There had definitely been no character called 'River' in Ventrian's rewrite – I think I would have noticed.

It bore no relation to anything I'd written either.

But what it described was very familiar – because I'd lived through it.

There was only one conclusion I could come to. What had taken place while I was in the 'book' had overwritten the content of the original, and wiped out the portal to Ventrian's research.

I no longer had access to the information I needed to destroy the Eye of Horus.

I went through the book and found every instance of the word 'ruby'. I knew it was pointless, but desperation was building inside me. Was there any way I could remember the spiralling equations and formulae I'd seen just once? Could I go back in time to before the book was changed? Solution after hopeless solution was shot down.

Although – did it really matter? Why would one want to destroy such a powerful object? In the right hands, it could be a boon for the entire universe!

Destroying Deff would be only the start. Once I had shredded his body, atom by painful atom, I would disperse them into the void, make him never have existed at all.

I would reorder the stars. The sun would rise and fall on my command. I would give my mother a necklace made of moons and my father –

Melody slapped me.

I shook my head, coming out of the trance.

'You brought me here, you're damn well staying here with me!' she said.

'I was going to use my infinite power to make my mum a necklace of moons,' I said dreamily. 'I think I was only going to get Dad to shave off his moustache, though.'

I could still feel the Eye of Horus in my head. It was shaping itself around me, making an outline that it would fill to the brim with itself.

'Can't you feel it?' I said.

'Feel what?'

There was a groan from the floor. Caesarion sat up.

'Phil!' Melody cried, and rushed to him, helping him to his feet. 'Or – not Phil.' She threw a wary glance at me. 'She called you – Caesarion?'

The boy, still slightly dazed, nodded. 'Gaius Julius Caesar, greatest man of Rome, was my father. Cleopatra the Seventh, pharaoh of Egypt, is my mother. She sent me away because Octavian, my father's heir in Rome, saw me as a great threat to him as being of my father's blood as well as of the blood of many kings. My life was in grave danger. But as I reached the port of Berenice, a god visited me in the form of a beggar man.'

Ventrian, I thought. With all that he'd been through, it wasn't surprising he looked like a 'beggar man' to the young king of Egypt.

'It was not yet time for me to journey through the under-world, the man said, but I must hide there, as it was a place no living man could reach,' Caesarion continued. 'Yet if one should come who divined my true identity, I must reveal myself to them, and give to them the jewel he left in my keeping, and I would return again to my mother's land. This, then, is my mother's land?'

He looked around. I was still half-dazed myself, or I'd have realised earlier what he must be thinking. 'This is not my moth-er's land – this is my mother's tomb!' He was trying to act with the dignity befitting a king; in the place he had come from he was considered a man, but however his society viewed him, inside he was still a 17-year-old boy standing by his mother's coffin. He threw himself onto the sarcophagus. 'I have returned too late, and she is gone!'

'It's all right!' I said hurriedly. 'She's not in there. She's not dead!'

He raised his tear-filled eyes. He didn't believe me.

'Look!' I said. I gestured for Melody to help him up, then I took hold of the sarcophagus lid. 'I'll show you. The coffin's empty.'

Strangely, the lid was stuck tight. I'd say it was immovable – if you didn't have the power of all things. Lucky me. I pushed the lid aside with my mind.

The three of us looked inside the coffin.

'Oh!' I said.

The coffin … was *not* empty.

I looked down on the grisly, twisted thing staring up at me – a glimpse into hell itself.

And I smiled.

There it lay in the coffin: proof of what was to come. Another signpost, directing me. Showing me what must be done.

I had infinite power at my command, and before I destroyed that power, clearly I would use it.

I turned to Caesarion. 'I will reunite you with your mother,' I said. 'Your other siblings too, if they desire it. I will hide you all from history.'

He bowed his head. 'I accept the judgement of the gods,' he said.

All I had to do was wish it, and he was gone. It was so *easy*!

'Malone,' I said. 'No, not you – I mean *Cat* Malone.' The cat turned her eyes to me. There was, deep inside, I thought, a slight remembrance of what had been. I thought she could understand me. I picked up my bundle from the floor and filled it with Cleopatra's jewels – carnelians, emeralds, turquoises, red jasper, all in golden settings. (I did *not* include any rubies.) I tied the bag around Cat Malone. 'Back in Alexandria, you will find a young girl called Imi,' I said. 'Please take these to her. Please keep her safe from harm.'

And with a flick of my mind, the cat, too, was sent to a new life.

Just Melody and me, now.

'You're sure as heck not sending me back into some book,' she said.

'I don't know what to do,' I said. 'I don't know how you're here. I don't know how you can exist.'

We looked at each other. There was pain in her eyes. I don't know what she saw in mine.

'Just because we don't know how, doesn't mean it's wrong,' she said. 'If you were me, wouldn't you want to carry on living?'

Of course I would. And there was no reason to send Melody Malone away. I had the Eye of Horus! I had power over all things!

Melody grabbed my wrist. 'Look at me!'

'What?'

'I don't have a mirror. But look into my eyes.'

I did.

In her eyes, I saw my own. They were redder than any ruby, a shining red like the eyes of the sacred crocodiles of the Nile at night.

'It's taking you over.'

'I can handle it,' I told her. 'Hey – how would you like to see New York – for real?'

And just like that, I took us there.

Chapter Thirty-Two

New York, ad 1939

In my office, the closet door was open. Deff was pointing an energy weapon at me. A look of pure bewilderment crossed his face, and I realised he'd just seen Ventrian and myself disappear – and here I was again, popping into existence, but with the diadem of an Egyptian queen on my head and the look of an avenging angel in my eye.

Oh, honey, if you didn't want to meet an avenging angel, you should never have come to the Angel Detective Agency.

No, that's not me. That's …

Am I me?

'Boo!'

Deff jumped, startled, and I burst out laughing. No, *Melody Malone* burst out laughing. I couldn't tell where I ended and she began …

He looked from her to me and back again, and she gave him a little wave. 'Hello,' she said. 'You know, you look a lot better than last time I saw you.'

I held up the Eye of Horus, still in its guise of a ruby. 'This is what you wanted, isn't it? Now call off your attack dog and let my parents alone.' Deff opened his mouth, but I didn't let him speak. 'You do realise that's me doing you a *big* favour. I could unwind your DNA so not only do you cease to exist, but every ancestor is undone too, back to the beginning of time.'

Without lowering his plasma pistol (did he *really* think he still had any authority in this situation?), he activated the communicator on his non-Raxacoricofallapatorian wrist and stammered out an order. The syntax was strangled, but I was satisfied he'd done as I requested. Bless him, perhaps he even had some idea he was going to get out of this alive.

'Don't worry, I'm not going to kill you,' I said. 'Cross my heart and hope to die.'

'Stick Cleopatra's needle in my eye,' Melody added with a chuckle.

'In my Eye *of Horus*,' I said, like it was the best joke ever. Melody's eyes were glowing red now too. I could feel us becoming one with each other, one with the Eye, and I loved it.

Deff had started whimpering and begging. 'I slave you for all time! You have no death of me, and I servile endlessly! I much obliged to magnanimous Señorita.'

Oh honey, I thought. *I don't need a slave. I just want to have fun!*

I could play with him all day. Hey, perhaps I would play with him for a century or two – before I sent him to his final destination.

No. I was already bored. We flicked my hand and Deff was gone. I remembered what we'd found when we opened Cleopatra's sarcophagus. He probably hadn't been trapped in there *that* long – if I sent him back to just after I'd exited the coffin myself, assuming the book episode happened in real time, it would only have been a few days. But it had been long enough for those Slitheen talons to be reduced to nothing from clawing at the lid. It had been long enough for him to be covered in blood from his efforts at escape. It had been long enough for him to nearly run out of air and only just be clinging to life.

But we had been magnanimous Señoritas. I'd promised not to kill him, and I'd kept that promise.

With the lid off, he could start to breathe again. There was food in the tomb, and drink, and even the possibility of escape through the labyrinth and the scorpions and the Silent and so on – or so he would think. Of course, I'd made sure it was actually impossible. Nasty? Oh no. This was a better fate than Deff had meted out to many.

Oh, I almost forgot. I needed to make sure that coffin lid was on *tight*. I sent a wisp of my mind back and fixed that.

And while it was there, I sent a little message. Just a short one. 'Dear Deff. You really shouldn't have threatened my mum and dad. Love River.'

And now there was just me and myself.

'We're going to have such fun,' I told me. 'I'm so glad I manifested you.'

'Me too,' I said. 'I needed me to owe your life. I knew once you were here me could never let go.'

I was one and three. Me and Melody and the Eye.

'No!' I forced the idea into my head. 'I won't *let* you! I will *destroy* you!'

'Oh, you are silly,' I said. 'One person can't destroy me. You already know that. You accept me – or you die, and I go on to someone else.'

'But I'm. Not. One. Person,' I said. 'You. Made. Me. Two. And you don't understand either of me ...'

I looked at Melody. Our hands reached out to each other. We embraced. And we *pushed* ...

Neither of us could tell when we were me or when we were me.

But we knew when we were *not* me. We knew what we had to fight.

And as we fought, we became ourselves again – yet two selves that still felt part of one whole. I could feel Melody's euphoria at the sensations she was experiencing, her desperation to retain this life she'd never known. I sensed her discovery of the part of me that belonged to the Doctor alone. I knew when she found my father, who razed armies to find me. I felt her heart explode when she understood the force that was my mother.

She, who thought she'd found love with the paper-thin Harry, finally experienced what that word really meant.

She found how someone could cherish the whole universe, and how our lives, as precious as they were to ourselves, could do nothing but serve a love that big.

The battle raged on. I attacked, but the Eye pushed back. My life was being torn away, shredded. Time unwound. Each push propelled me further away, deeper into the void from which return is impossible.

But I would *not* let go of that love.

And it made me so powerful. Almost powerful enough to win.

But as Ventrian had warned me, so long ago, no one person could ever destroy the Eye.

My last drop was spent.

And Melody surged forward. I felt that power in her too. A paper person, who had found an impossible exaltation.

Her strength flowed into me, but momentum carried her onwards. It was as though we were on a cliff edge, and she threw herself over, a force that could not be denied, carrying the *presence* before her.

The Eye was gone.

And so was Melody Malone.

And there I stood, alone in my office. Bereft – yet whole.

Melody had wanted to live. I'd felt it. But she was a tough cookie from Old New York Town, and in her book, the bad guys never won.

EPILOGUE

NEW YORK, AD 1939

I went to tea with Mum and Dad, and told them … some of this.

My mother, as is a mother's wont, understood the parts that I *hadn't* told her. Not the zip-zap adventure parts; the parts that remained deep inside me.

If there were an incarnation of motherness on Earth, it would not be Cleopatra. It would be *my* mother.

But then, perhaps everyone thinks that about their own mother.

No. It just turns out I'm the luckiest person in the universe. And I wish I deserved her.

I'd have to content myself with knowing that because I carry her love inside me, with that of my father, with that of my husband – well, that's how the universe was saved.

Ventrian's equations might have worked, I don't know. Which is better, love or sums? *That's* a question for a long winter's night.

Talking of drawn-out suffering, Woolton pie wasn't on the menu, thank goodness, but I endured father's carrot jam. 'I'll send you food parcels from the future when rationing starts,' I told them.

'No,' said Amy, although she knew I was joking. 'We're ready to take our place here, and whatever comes with it. About Melody Malone ... '

'Yes?' I said.

'We talked about me taking over, didn't we. I think perhaps I should start now. You won't be able to write about her any more. She's too real to you.'

Once again, the maternal sixth sense was demonstrated.

She picked up the tattered bound proofs that had made a round trip of several thousand miles and several thousand years too. 'I'd better read your new ending,' she said. 'I'm sure it's better than Ventrian's.' But she added, 'Poor man,' because she's a nice person. She opened *The Ruby's Curse*. Then she frowned. '"Chapter One: Stormcage, AD 5147"?' she read. 'You've put yourself in the book?'

I snatched it from her. It was true! *I* was in the book! Everything I'd done – everything I'd thought. It was all there, weaving in and out of Melody's story, as if I were narrating my own life for an unknown reader. One last trick from the Eye of Horus. Well. Perhaps it was doing me a favour, in a way. Because I'd wanted to share those deep-inside feelings with my mum, but couldn't imagine it happening.

'This can't be published,' I said, after I'd read through a few chapters. It wasn't because it delved so deeply into my head; I'm not shy, you've probably gathered that. Thing was, it outed Mum and Dad as time travellers. That could cause problems not only now, but for their younger selves, too.

'Oh, don't worry about that,' Amy laughed, after I'd explained. 'How about this. I'll lock it up somewhere, leave instructions for it to be published a few years after the Angels took us. That was 2012 – I'll make it a decade or so after that. "RIVER SONG in THE RUBY'S CURSE: A MELODY MALONE MYSTERY." Great sensation: *The incredible truth about Melody Malone*. That'd be nice.'

I could see she was set on it. 'All right,' I said at last.

She was still looking through the book. 'Yeah. I'll get it typed up properly. We'll leave Melody's signature on the postscript, though. That's a nice touch.'

'What postscript?' I said.

She handed the book to me.

I turned to the last page.

And read this:

Postscript

New York, AD 1939

Come through the doors of the Angel Detective Agency Inc., Floor 33, RCA Building, Manhattan, and maybe you're expecting just another private eye. I've got the trench coat. I've got the fedora. I've got the hip flask. I've got a .357 Magnum in my drawer and a .380 ACP in my boot.

And I've got a Song in my heart.

Harry's gone and my faithful dogsbody Phil's moved on to better things. But that's just the way it is. Things change, and I'm fine with that. I've got enough cabbage to pay my rent and the sun is shining, and I don't regret a thing.

Thanks for everything, sister. See you in the next book – and maybe I could get a bit more action, then, huh? Maybe even the Doctor could pay a visit?

Hey, don't worry. I'm just kidding. It's all good with me.

Give my love to the universe.

Ever yours,

No –

Ever *you*,

ACKNOWLEDGMENTS

I must thank Steven Moffat for birthing such a complex character as River Song (Crazy Love), and allowing her to have play dates with so many Doctors, including the likes of Matt Smith, David Tennant, Peter Capaldi, all the way back to Tom Baker and my Big Finish friends!

Thank you to my other mother and father, Amy and Rory, otherwise known as Karen Gillan and Arthur Darvill. If it had not been for that fateful night on the Tardis, this story could never have happened!

I'm thankful for the deep joy during lockdown in being able to collaborate with my new friends Jac and Steve who provided wonderful editorial assistance; Albert, Joanna, Morgana and Síofra at Penguin Random House; and the divine Grant and Gordon at Curtis Brown, all of whom stopped my home from ever feeling like Stormcage and kept me sane.

Of course, a massive shout out to all Whovians globally and their insatiable appetite for time travelling adventure. May you always be hungry for more! To my personal favourites, The Kinglets (hmmm, I wonder why?) – Stay the gorgeously fierce, proud, confident women that you are!

And finally, to my husband Jonathan and dog Wolfie – I love you for keeping me as happy as I am ever going to be.